PROJECT A

H.S. THOMPSON

Table of Contents

PROLOGUE

Monday, October 18, 2060

Jan smiled at the handsome, middle-aged man as she handed him a demitasse of double shot espresso, its fragrant steam wafting from the dark liquid. With his left hand, he brushed back an unruly blond lock and accepted the cup and saucer from her.

"Thank you," he said in the rich, baritone voice familiar to billions of people around the world.

She barely squeaked out a "You're welcome." Even in the jaded streets of L.A., where famous stars and celebrities were common sightings, the multi-bazillionaire businessman with the renowned, megawatt smile was in a class all his own. But today he wasn't smiling.

He returned to the window table where James, a regular older patron with thick glasses, fidgeted with a pen and sipped his usual latte.

Jan finished serving the next customer and then hurried back to the kitchen. Laila removed the blueberry muffins from the food synthesizer.

"Laila," Jan said breathlessly. "Guess who's here?"

The older, dark-skinned girl with cornrow braids smiled indulgently at her younger friend. "Who is it?"

"No, guess," the teen insisted, squealing as quietly as she could while jumping with excitement, her blonde curls bouncing up and down. She didn't want their boss, Ahmed, to overhear from the main part of the café.

Placing the muffins onto a display tray, Laila named several well-known actors and politicians. Jan impatiently shook her head at each one.

"You'll never guess," Jan said, tugging on her friend's arm as they headed toward the front part of the coffee shop. "Go see, but don't let Ahmed catch you looking." He was a demanding boss and didn't like idle hands.

Laila turned to pick up the loaded muffin tray she would insert into the display case on the front counter. She saw the owner, Ahmed Haddad, chatting and laughing heartily with one of the customers at his table. Sliding the tray in, she scanned the customers and recognized a few regulars before she saw the man Jan was so excited about. He sat facing the counter in an intense conversation with James. Outwardly calm, Laila headed back into the kitchen with her heart pounding.

"Oh, my God!" Laila also squealed in a hushed voice. "It's really him? You talked to him?"

"Oh, yes! Can you believe he's here—at our café!"

The older girl laughed with excitement. "Guess he needs his caffeine fix, too, just like us regular mortals."

"Double shot espresso," Jan mimicked the customer. "Straight up, no cream." She would remember his order if he ever came in again. She remembered everybody's order.

The bells jingled as the front door opened.

"Back to work," Jan said, pivoting to go back out front.

"Lucky," Laila said, sighing. "You get all the fun."

"Yeah, what a day! First the awesome fight and now this!" Jan tossed back as she turned to look at her friend with a bright smile. She swooped around the wall separating the kitchen and the front counter, disappearing from view.

Laila shook her head and smiled. Now, what shall I make next? Ah, baklava! Loading the necessary ingredients, she programmed the food synthesizer. Since it would take a few minutes for the food to be printed, she decided to sneak out the back for a quick puff.

Leaning against the outside wall of the café, she looked up and down the alley. Then she extracted the small cylinder from her pocket and inserted a red-rimmed cartridge, indicating it was spiced with a stimulant. After taking a deep inhale, she felt the fatigue draining out as the drug entered her bloodstream.

She smiled as she thought about her new boyfriend. He also liked to try new spices, especially while they were in bed together; they made him more—creative. She took one last drag and had one foot inside the back door when an intense blast of hot air and noise slammed her back into the wall of the adjacent building. Crumpled in a heap, she vaguely noted that her head, back and ears hurt before everything faded to black.

CHAPTER 1

Monday Afternoon

Even through the respirator, the overwhelming acridity of ash and the unmistakable, pungent odor of charred flesh stung his nostrils. Detective Gabriel Furst walked with dread toward the floating gurney that contained the remains of Ahmed Haddad, owner of the Rialto Café, which was now a black hole in the ground. He stared down at the charred and barely recognizable head and torso of his good friend. Forensic Science Division techs hadn't found the rest of him yet.

Under the helmet and protective suit, Gabriel's eyes watered. He last saw Ahmed months ago—at Adeline's fifth birthday party, just before the LAPD's move to Beck Tower a few blocks away. Waves of nausea swept over him, and he swallowed hard several times to keep his lunch down. He'd seen burned and dismembered bodies in his seventeen years with the LAPD, but this was different. This was a good friend—someone like a brother. Taking several deep breaths, he steadied himself with his hand against the floating gurney. He refused to vomit in front of his brand new partner—especially given who her dad was.

His nausea abating somewhat, Gabriel pressed a button under the stretcher, and the lid of the floating gurney quietly slid shut. Placing a gloved hand on the closed stretcher, he said quietly, his throat tight, "*Maa alsalama ya*, Ahmed. Goodbye, my friend. I promise I'll find out who did this and make them pay."

"Positive ID on the café owner?" a woman asked from behind, her voice muffled by the respirator used to filter out ash and other particulates. Detective Irene Bolton was just promoted from the West L.A. Station to join Homicide Special at the famed Robbery-Homicide Division of the Los Angeles Police Department. She was rumored to be a Plat—a Platinum, a genetically-enhanced human—tall, beautiful, intelligent and athletic. He didn't care whether she was or not; he was more concerned with whether her dad sent her to spy on him.

Sliding his fogged visor up, he took a deep breath and then turned around. "Yeah, Ahmed Haddad, his wife Aahad and daughter Adeline." He indicated the two stretchers on either side of Ahmed. "They were in the small apartment above the café during the blast. No family to notify. They were the last in their families. Their relatives all died in the Middle East Holocaust eight years ago."

With his wrist computer, he confirmed their identities to the digital labels on the stretchers. The lids of the other two gurneys slid closed. Then all three lifted higher off the ground and headed toward the Medical Examiner's large van, neatly stacking themselves on top of the other enclosures with identified remains.

The incident commander from Central Division approached and told them that the 3-D laser reconstruction scan was complete. He transferred it onto the detectives' wrist computers, more commonly known as "communicators," or "comms," though they had multiple other functions. Most civilians also wore comms. But those for law enforcement were bulkier, could access more databases and included other specialized features.

They were joined by fellow Robbery-Homicide detectives, Artie "Suit" Fitzsimmons and Dan "Smiley" Johnsen, also in white personal protective suits with "LAPD" emblazoned on the back, helmets with visors, and respirators. Fitzsimmons was the designated lead on this case.

"Bolton, Mav," Fitz, a slightly rotund, balding man in his early fifties, acknowledged them, using Gabriel's LAPD nickname "Maverick.'" "Sorry, we're late—had to go exchange the fuel cell cartridge. Do we have IDs on the vics yet?"

His throat still aching, Gabriel nodded to Irene.

"A few. Besides Detective O'Malley, here's what we've got so far," Irene said, using her Human Digital Interface to quickly instruct her comms to transfer the data to her colleagues. In her mid-twenties, she was one of the few officers in the LAPD who grew up with the HDI brain implant and deftly used it to interact with any digital device.

"Rick O'Malley was undercover for Gang and Narcotics," Irene said.

"Somebody blow his cover?" Fitz asked.

"Don't know yet," Gabriel said in a hoarse voice, the lump still in his throat. Luckily, the respirator made his voice sound rough anyway. "The Captain say how we got the case?"

Fitz nodded. "Counterterrorism and Major Crimes are still busy with all the bombs at the Cal-Trans stations today. Since O'Malley was found, it became our case."

Facing Fitz and Johnsen, Gabriel continued, "There were fourteen people total in the café and two in the apartment upstairs. Three survivors—all of them sent to University Hospital. Two of them baristas in the café, Jan Winter and Laila Harvey. The other was a customer named—" he said, looking at his comms, "—James Patton. He was in the back using the john, which was protected by the reinforced wall Ahmed installed after The Big One."

"That guy, Patton, got a record?" Fitz asked.

"No, his chip read that he works at Titan," Gabriel said, referring to the Radiofrequency Identification chips implanted into everyone legally in the United States.

"Titan? Titan Robotics?"

Gabriel nodded. "Yeah, some big shot there. He was lifted to University Hospital before we got here. They're ruling out a concussion since he hit his head in the explosion."

Fitz asked, "What about Ahmed? Was he here? Did he make it?"

Gabriel shook his head solemnly. "They found his body—what's left of him—over there." He pointed to the street along the side of the café. "Aahad and Adeline, too."

"Aww, shit!" Fitz sighed. He used to be a regular at the café as well before the LAPD headquarters was relocated. All were quiet for a moment.

"Anything on O'Malley?" Smiley asked.

"He works—worked—in Gang and Narcotics for five years and was presently undercover in a Central American gang," Irene replied.

"So he may have been the target?" Fitz asked.

Gabriel shrugged. "Don't know. The chips inside a couple of the vics were too damaged to scan, but the others were ID'd. No one else sent up an obvious red flag." He paused. "Could be a hate crime, too, but no one's taken credit or posted anything on social media yet."

Chapter 1

Fitz nodded. "Mav, you and Bolton go collect the footage from the video cams around this area while we check out what's left of the café."

"OK," Gabriel said.

Fitz and Smiley headed toward the bombed-out café, and Gabriel could hear Fitz muttering as the duraglass crunched under his shoes, "Damn, I just got these shoes."

"Told you to wear tac boots like everyone else instead of that overpriced designer shit," his partner replied.

"Yeah, so I can be just another LAPD drone."

A year ago, LAPD mandated full tactical, camouflage uniforms for all divisions. Shoes became the only article of clothing to distinguish the detectives any more. Before that travesty, Fitz was known as the best-dressed detective in all of LAPD, hence his nickname "Suit." But even he reluctantly admitted that the waterproof and bulletproof properties of the black camos occasionally came in very handy, although they were not totally immune to hand blasters, which, thankfully—so far—only law enforcement carried.

Despite his grief, Gabriel smiled slightly at the exchange between the long-time partners. Polar opposites, the more serious Dan Johnsen— quiet, tall, thin and also in his early fifties, rarely smiling, hence his LAPD nickname "Smiley"—and the extroverted practical joker, Artie Fitzsimmons, somehow worked well together. While Fitz was in the middle of his fourth divorce, the steadfast Johnsen was still married to his high school sweetheart.

A dark-brown, particulate-filled pall still hung over a several block radius of the epicenter of the bombing, making the already cloudy, overcast day seem even dingier. His eyes starting to sting, Gabriel put his visor back on. The condensation had cleared.

He looked up and down the street and pointed to the bank across the street. "They should have a high-res camera," he said to Irene.

"Yeah," she said.

They found two cameras aimed at the front entrance from different angles.

"We'll need the recordings from both," Gabriel said.

"I'll get them."

"Make an extra copy for us."

She nodded and went into the bank to speak with the manager while

Gabriel left to check out other surrounding cameras.

Irene was exiting the bank when Gabriel came out of a drugstore down the street. He walked toward her and shook his head. "Their cameras were down since an electrical surge fried them a few days ago. It affected this whole sector."

"Luckily, the bank got theirs repaired this morning—ahead of schedule, if you can believe it."

"Who the hell gets things repaired early these days?" Gabriel's brows arched. He looked around for street cameras. "Grab the recordings from those street cameras," he said, pointing to the cameras at the intersection a block away on First and Spring Streets. "I'll get the ones over there." He pointed to the cameras in the other direction. "Hopefully the circuit breakers worked and were reset, and we have some video to look at."

"Yeah," Irene said, heading over to the corner of Spring and First.

Gabriel walked to the other end of the street. He removed the crystal data chips and copied them into other chips and then inserted a copy back into the camera. The original chips from the cameras would be submitted as evidence for the official record and legal proceedings. He kept the unofficial copies for the team's use. From experience, like most seasoned LAPD detectives, he learned it was much more efficient to have his own copies rather than wait for the Technical Investigation Unit to analyze it.

Gabriel saw his partner finish her lollipop just as he finished transferring his recordings. Guess those Borg implants do come in handy at times. But there's still no way in hell LAPD will ever put one into my noggin—no matter what the Chief of Police or Police Commission mandates.

They logged in all of the evidence bags with the data chips in their cases and inserted them into a large evidence container in the Forensic Science Division van, parked in front of the café. FSD would sort out which lab would analyze each piece of evidence.

Fitz and Smiley emerged from behind the café.

"Forensics thinks it was a high explosive, probably Semtex K. They found this metallic fragment which may have been part of the bomb." Fitz held up a transparent bag with a 2-inch long metal shard.

On one side, the sliver was completely charred with a slight orange tinge, characteristic of Semtex. The other side was silver-colored with a matte, cross-hatched texture and very sharp, curled edges where it had been ripped apart by the blast. Semtex K was the newest, eleventh-generation Semtex with an ingredient to make it gelatinous, easier to fill into tubes, and even more powerful.

"What do you think that was?" Irene asked.

"I don't know. Looks like it was small and curved," Fitz replied.

"Maybe part of a small cylinder?" Gabriel said, examining the small metal shard.

Fitz squinted. "FSD'll figure it out."

Several FSD techs milled about collecting evidence. The Robbery-Homicide detectives watched as one of the nearby techs used tongs to pull a black stick from under some rubble, holding it up for closer inspection. It was part of a left human forearm, burned down almost to the bone, the fingers charred and shriveled, with a partially melted lump at the wrist. The tech put the gruesome find into an evidence bag for the Medical Examiner's office. Gabriel called for the tech to bring his finding to the group. A blackened band encircled the wrist.

"O'Malley's," Gabriel stated. Even burnt, police comms were distinct from a civilian's. An ash-streaked gold band with a hexagonal emblem encircled the charred fourth finger.

"It looks like this'll take a while." Fitz sighed as he looked down at the shredded soles of the protective shoe covers. "Mav, you two go interview the survivors at the hospital."

Gabriel and Irene started making their way back to his Air Raptor, parked four blocks away from the center of the explosion, outside the crime scene perimeter. At the portable white dressing booth, placed just inside of the electronically-cordoned area, Gabriel removed his respirator and helmet. His short, dark hair with the occasional gray strand was dank with sweat. He took a deep breath and coughed. The air was still a little sooty, but pulling off the respirator helped ease his lingering nausea.

Irene shed her white suit and equipment, revealing her wavy, shoulder-length, blonde hair. She peeled off the transparent nitrilon that had been sprayed on over her hands and comms.

"God, I hate this stuff," she muttered, flicking her hands. "If they're going to suffocate us inside these things, why don't they at least give out hand towels?"

"Or better yet, a shower," Gabriel said, wiping his sweaty hands on his black camo pants after stripping the white protective suit from his lean, six-foot figure.

They headed toward the perimeter. A uniformed robo-officer guarded that section. Its red, laser eyes, set in a smooth gunmetal face, followed their progress. Acknowledging them in a synthetic voice, it deactivated the electrified field between two of the portable, electrified pylons surrounding the crime scene. Their departure was automatically recorded.

A large throng of reporters and curious spectators crowded just beyond the outer police cordon. They swarmed the detectives as soon as they stepped outside the inner barrier.

"Detective Furst, can you tell us what happened?" one reporter called out, holding up the arm with his comms to record any response.

Gabriel groaned inwardly that he had been identified and shook his head. He recognized the reporter, who covered the crime beat for the L.A. Times, an all on-line news service.

"Who did it?" a female reporter shouted.

"Who are the victims?" the L.A. Times reporter asked. "Why is RHD involved? Is one of the victims famous? Is it a cop?"

Arriving at the Air Raptor, Gabriel reminded himself of Chief Renata Lopez's edict to be more open and friendly to the public and reluctantly turned to face them. "One of the victims is a police officer, but we can't release his name until his next-of-kin has been notified. I'm sorry, but I won't be able to make any comments beyond that at this time. This is still very early in the investigation. Someone will come out to update you later," he replied, trying not to show his impatience. Damn the Chief's ambition to be the next mayor!

"Was this a terrorist incident? Is it a hate crime? The owner was a Muslim, wasn't he?" somebody else asked.

"Does it have anything to do with the Cal-Trans bombings earlier today?" the female reporter yelled out.

Gabriel waved them off as he and Irene got into the car.

After shutting the door and powering up the Raptor, he muttered with a grimace, "God, I hate reporters." Gabriel pressed the button on the steering wheel to activate the bottom thrusters, lifting them up off the ground. He peered down at the reporters scrambling to escape the vortex of dust and air with amused satisfaction.

CHAPTER 2

Monday Evening

As the Raptor rapidly climbed and accelerated to the usual cruising speed of 100 MPH, Gabriel noted with amusement Irene gripping her armrests and bracing her feet against the floorboard. He turned the car west toward the ocean and University Hospital, joining the heavy L.A. rush hour traffic.

"I heard you like to drive on manual. Why not use the autopilot like everybody else?" Irene asked, her voice tight and her fingers maintaining their death-grip.

Gabriel grinned. "I prefer driving on manual. One of the few times I was on autopilot, I ended up in the hospital for a week, but I've never had an accident driving myself. The only automated thing I ever use in here is the GPS, and that's frequently on the fritz. Speaking of which . . ." Gabriel voice-activated the navigation screen, which displayed several, horizontal white lines of static over the barely recognizable street map in the background. He tapped his knuckles on the unit, which responded feebly with fewer lines of static. "See? Good thing we know exactly where we're going, and I always carry my trusty street map."

He pulled out a yellowing, spiral-bound book—"bound" being an optimistic and historic description—with "2019 Los Angeles and Orange Counties" barely legible on the front. Despite several layers of clear plastic laminate, the cover was almost completely worn down from decades of use. Several pages were loose or partially ripped out with barely discernible print.

"How old is that thing? And what is that made out of? Is that paper?"

she asked in an incredulous tone.

"Yes, these were used many years ago before everyone had GPS, and that was the very last print edition. It was my dad's." He didn't add that it was the only thing of his dad's that had ever been of any use to him.

"Your dad was on the job, wasn't he?"

"Yeah, killed in the line of duty."

"When was that?"

"End of watch December 18, 2029. I was eight."

"I heard he was good cop."

Gabriel glanced at his partner and shrugged. "Probably better than he was at being a father—to me anyway."

"What do you mean?"

He stared straight ahead and was silent.

She looked down at the street map and then thumbed through the worn pages. The airlanes were marked in by hand after the last official printing, long before The Big One, the 7.9 tremblor that destroyed much of Southern California ten years ago in 2050. She held the atlas up, turned it sideways and tilted her head. "How the heck did people ever use these things? Give me a working GPS any day—or, of course, my HDI."

Gabriel grinned. Although their initial reactions were similar to Irene's, most of his previous partners eventually learned how to use the relic. However, none of them had a Human Digital Interface or optical implants. He conceded that her system was probably much faster and more efficient, assuming a working OmniNet and satellite system, which were not always a given. From long experience, he never assumed things always went as planned. "You know, they used paper books for many, many centuries."

She snorted. "Yeah, and now we've got a tree shortage. You can carry around a lot more information on our comms, and it's much lighter. That's called progress."

He gave a skeptical grunt.

As they headed toward University Hospital, the temperamental GPS decided to work for part of the way and then fritzed out again. The autopilot function on the older cars, like his Raptor, did not work without a functioning GPS.

"Why don't you just get your GPS fixed?" his partner asked, not unreasonably.

Chapter 2

"Service'll probably junk it. And I'm rather attached to this baby." He patted the dashboard with affection. "This was my old partner's vehicle since before I started at RHD, and he passed it down to me."

Gabriel glanced at her. Irene's silent facial expression seemed to indicate she'd agree with Service about retiring the old Raptor.

They flew by multiple quantum dot screens that completely covered the sides of various high-rise buildings and constantly broadcasted news and commercials. Even through the thick, shielded duraglass windows, he still heard the booming announcements.

"... Congress passed a bill today ensuring the safety and security of all Americans by authorizing the monitoring of all communications between Asia and Australia, where Islamic terrorists are suspected to ..."

"... the newest addition to our Romance line of spices—Impassioned Green. Give the green light to your fantasies ..."

"... why use VR Glass when you can have your own Sim World Studio at home for only 3 million dollars plus FREE installation ..."

"... your new life awaits you on Mars Colony, the chance to begin again in a golden land of opportunity and adventure! The Sixth Mars Xpedition will be launching in nine months. Reserve your spot today! ..."

Gabriel missed the days when there wasn't the constant, noisy barrage of "news" or commercials.

"So, you were friends with the owner of the Rialto?" Irene asked.

Gabriel nodded. "Yeah, I used to go there often before our offices moved to Beck Tower. Ahmed taught me everything I know about the history and making of coffee. He probably could've taught at the U." He paused, a lump forming in his throat again. He blinked his tears away.

Irene glanced over at him.

After a few moments, his voice hoarse, he continued. "He was a huge fan of old movies, too. You saw the picture frames at the café? He used to have the original theatrical posters of a lot of great classics, like *Raiders of the Lost Ark*, *Star Wars*, *Citizen Kane*, *Wizard of Oz*, *The Avengers*, and *The Godfather*. He had a huge collection all over the walls and in his apartment upstairs."

He remembered the last time he saw Ahmed, Aahad and little Adeline—only a few months ago—but too long. He'd been so busy since the move to Beck Tower, but that's no excuse ... and now it was too late.

"*Ammo* Gabriel!" Adeline had shrieked with joy and laughter as she opened her birthday present, a new American Girl doll, which looked just like her—with olive skin, large, dark eyes and braided, dark hair down her back. "Thank you! I love it!" She threw her arms around his neck and planted a wet kiss on his cheek.

"Happy Birthday, *Saghir*, Little One!" He gave her a bear hug.

"I'm not a baby anymore! I'm five!" the little girl insisted, clutching her new doll and stomping one foot.

"OK. Do I have to call you Adeline now?"

"Yes, because I'm a big girl now!"

"Gabriel, you are spoiling her," Aahad admonished, laughing, handing him a plate of baklava. She brushed off some crumbs off the sleeve of her bright blue shift.

"I'm the one who's getting spoiled. Are these the real thing?" Gabriel grabbed the plate and shoved a piece into his mouth.

"Of course! You think I make that printed garbage for you?" She frowned at him, wrinkling her brow, hands on her hips.

"These must have taken forever to make!"

"For *akhouna*, our brother, it's no trouble."

"Hey, save some for me!" Ahmed laughed, reaching over to grab a piece off the plate.

"Those are for Gabriel. Yours are over there!" she said, playfully slapping her husband's thieving hand. "And I make tabbouleh—your favorite!" she said to their sole party guest.

"Ah, Aahad, if you weren't already married . . ."

"Hey, she's taken. Go find your own wife!" Ahmed laughed heartily, pulling her close and kissing her. Laughing, she wrapped her arms around his neck.

Gabriel snapped out of his reverie when he realized that Irene was talking to him. "Hmm?"

"Do you think this could've been a hate crime?" she asked.

"They had a few incidents before—mostly vandalism, nothing this serious. In fact, that's how we met—somebody tagged the café."

"You said they had no family left?"

"That's right. The rest of their families all died in the MEH."

The Middle East Holocaust in 2052 involved the nuclear annihilation

Chapter 2

13

of several states in the Middle East, the exact cause of which remained unknown. For some reason, Israel fired all its conventional and nuclear arsenal toward the surrounding enemy states, and they in turn had released all their weapons, ending in mutual annihilation. Many speculated that Israel must have thought it was facing an existential threat, but no one involved survived to tell what happened in those last few minutes. Hundreds of millions died, and the affected areas were still uninhabitable. The soot particles in the upper atmosphere reduced sunlight for a few years, creating widespread famine, killing billions more. Ironically, the nuclear winter that followed briefly offset the greenhouse effect.

"Did he have any terrorist ties?"

Gabriel bristled at the assumption, but he had to admit it was a reasonable question, given the circumstances. "No, he was the most America-loving guy I've ever met. They were Muslim but not at all radicals."

"Despite their entire families being destroyed in the MEH?"

"Yeah. Ahmed never blamed us for that. He said it was Middle East politics and hatred that had simmered for over a thousand years. They were waiting for the rest of their families to immigrate when it happened."

"I'm going to check the DNS file on him."

He shrugged. "You won't find anything."

Formed after The Day in 2049, the Department of National Security tracked all potentially problematic foreigners, especially those from certain countries or of certain religious persuasion. The men and women of LAPD and their compatriots throughout the country joked that "DNS" really stood for "Does Nothing Sufficiently," "Does No Shit," or "Dumb 'N Stupid."

He quietly flew while she used her HDI and comms to search the DNS database on Foreigners of Interest. If the DNS files were sealed, it meant there was an ongoing investigation. Only closed cases would be available to them.

Irene looked at him. "They vetted him in Lebanon and again here, watched him, and found nothing. No ties with religious extremists and no suspicious financial transactions."

Gabriel gave her an "I told you so" look and kept driving.

"I had to check."

He nodded.

Thanks to one-way, multi-level airlanes, they arrived at University Hospital Medical Center in under 10 minutes despite heavy traffic. As usual, parking around the hospital was impossible, so Gabriel set down the Raptor in a firelane along the curb just outside of the Emergency Room. "Hope there're no fires in the next hour."

The automated stanchion monitoring that space started flashing lights and sounding sirens. A loud, strident, robotic voice ordered him to move his vehicle until it finally recognized his police transponder code and deactivated.

"Well, that took long enough," Irene commented as they headed toward the Emergency Room entrance. "That thing is even more obsolete than your Raptor."

Gabriel scowled at her.

CHAPTER 3

Monday Evening

In the University Hospital Emergency Room, they saw the patrol officer who had accompanied one of the victims. He informed them that Jan Winter was in the Operating Room, and both Laila Harvey and James Patton were still in the ER. The clerk at the Nursing Station instructed them to wait for the doctor for an update while she notified her of their presence.

After a few minutes, a beautiful, young woman with bright, green eyes and a long, dark ponytail walked up to them. Her badge read "Katherine Miller, M.D."

"I'm Dr. Miller. I'm the senior resident in charge here today."

"I'm Detective Furst, and this is Detective Bolton." Gabriel showed her his badge. He caught a flicker of recognition in her eyes, but he was sure they'd never met. She was definitely memorable.

"I understand you want to speak with the patients from the café explosion?"

Gabriel nodded. "Yes, Laila Harvey, Jan Winter and James Patton. What are their conditions?"

"Miss Winter is in surgery right now. She has severe head trauma as well as other critical wounds to her chest and abdomen. She was unconscious when they brought her in. If she survives surgery, she'll be in Surgical ICU later. But she won't be doing any talking in the near future," Dr. Miller said.

"And the other two?" Irene asked.

"They're both doing well—just some minor blast injuries. Should be able to go home in the next few days, Dr. Patton probably tonight. We're doing some Micro Body Scans to make sure they didn't sustain any serious injuries not evident in our preliminary exams. Miss Harvey's should be complete in a few minutes. She has a little difficulty hearing at present due to the blast, but she's very lucky not to have been more seriously hurt."

"So, they'll be okay?" Gabriel asked.

Dr. Miller nodded. "You can wait over there by Room 1. When her scan is done, they'll bring her back in. Dr. Patton will be back in Room 5. The techs are just starting his scan."

"Dr. Patton?" Gabriel asked.

"Yes, he's a Ph. D."

"Ah." Gabriel nodded. "Thank you, Dr. Miller. Did they tell you anything about the incident?" Their eyes met. His pulse quickened.

"Not really, other than there was an explosion. Miss Harvey was still in shock, but she's recovering. I'd like her in the Observation Unit for a couple of days. Dr. Patton was a little agitated but physically doing well. He's asking about his boss, Gerald Carmichael. How's he doing? He wasn't brought here."

Gabriel replied, "Gerry Carmichael? He wasn't on our victim list." He started to check his comms.

Irene, who obviously used her Human Digital Interface to access her comms, quickly stated, "No, definitely not. He's also not among the unidentified bodies. Both are female."

"Hmmm. Well, I'm sure Dr. Patton will be relieved," Dr. Miller said.

"Thank you, Doctor."

Dr. Miller partly turned away to leave and then turned back to Gabriel. "Are you by any chance related to Officer Stephen Furst?"

"Yes, he was my father. How do you know of him?"

"My father was Daniel Miller. His first partner after his boot year was Stephen Furst. It's funny that you're the second person involved in this case who knew my dad."

"Who was the first?"

"Dr. Patton. I remember he used to come to our house when I was a kid. Small world, huh?"

Gabriel nodded.

"Well, nice to meet you."

"If you think of anything else, please give me a call," he said and transmitting his contact info to her comms.

She nodded, smiled and walked away to take care of her next patient.

"Daniel Miller? As in *Chief* Daniel Miller?" Irene asked.

Gabriel nodded. Daniel Miller had been Chief of the LAPD for five years, retired three years ago and passed away soon afterwards from cancer.

"Patton mentioned Gerry Carmichael—as in *the* Gerry Carmichael of Titan Robotics?" Irene asked. "He was there at the café but not in the blast?"

"Sounds like it. Let's check with Fitz."

Gerry Carmichael was a superstar among celebrities in Los Angeles, indeed in much of the civilized world. His company, Titan Robotics, built the majority of the robots running almost every household of means in the U.S. and other parts of the first world. His father Edgar Carmichael started the company decades ago and created a global empire with political and economic ties to many governments and major corporations. Upon his death, the very ambitious and handsome eldest son, Gerry, became CEO. By his early forties, he established a reputation for his business acumen as well as his epicurean lifestyle, including the finest wine, fastest cars, best gourmet foods and most beautiful women. He was on his third marriage, with an ex-supermodel whom he married when she was only sixteen. Gerry's younger twin brother Harold stayed in the background, overshadowed by his more outgoing, publicity-hungry and photogenic brother.

Irene completed her call. "Fitzsimmons said no one mentioned seeing Gerry Carmichael at the scene."

"Maybe he was meeting Patton. Maybe he's Patton's boss." Out of the corner of his eye, Gabriel saw some men in suits—feds? —but they had disappeared when he turned around.

Just then, a transport bot accompanied a young, black woman on an anti-gravity stretcher into Room 1. Though Gabriel was a regular at the café before the move to Beck Tower, he didn't recognize her.

Irene whispered to Gabriel, "Let me take this, okay?"

He nodded hesitantly. This was their first day together on the job. But detectives making it into Robbery-Homicide were among the best, and Irene was considered a rising superstar in the LAPD.

The young woman lay on the stretcher with her head tilted up. Looking around at the antiseptic walls of the examination room with wide eyes, she had several small gel bandages, blood and dirt on her honey-brown face and other exposed areas. Otherwise she appeared well for having survived an explosion.

"Laila Harvey?" Irene asked.

The young woman cupped her ears. "I'm sorry I can't hear very well," she said in a loud voice.

Irene said loudly and slowly, "I'm Detective Irene Bolton from LAPD. This is my partner, Detective Gabriel Furst. We would like to ask you some questions about what happened at the café."

"I really didn't see anything. I was in the back," Laila said.

"I understand." Irene put a hand on the stretcher.

What is it with witnesses always denying they saw anything? Gabriel mentally rolled his eyes.

"Did you come out front at any time in the hour or so before the explosion? We can't identify some of the bodies, so any help you could give us would be great."

She hesitated. "Um, well, maybe for a second."

"Did you see anybody?"

"There were a few people."

"Anybody you recognized?"

She nodded. She described some of the regular customers that were in the cafe that afternoon. "One guy always comes in alone—an old guy with glasses—oh, what's his name? It's James. But today, someone joined him."

"Did you recognize this other person?"

Laila nodded slowly. "That's why Jan called me out. It was Gerry Carmichael. Double shot espresso, straight up. No cream."

Irene tilted her head. "What's that?"

"That's what he ordered. Jan told me. She remembers everybody's orders."

"I see," Irene said.

"Is Jan OK?"

"She's still in surgery."

"Oh, I hope she's OK," Laila said.

"Back to Gerry Carmichael. Was that the first time you'd seen him there?"

She nodded again. "Did he get killed?"

"It doesn't appear so," Irene said.

Laila looked relieved.

Chapter 3

Irene asked, "Can you show me where everybody was sitting?"

"I'll try, but I only got a quick glimpse."

"That's OK. Do your best," Gabriel said, patting her gently on the shoulder.

Gabriel projected a 3-D diagram of the café from his comms. Laila showed them where the patrons she had seen were sitting. She added, "Earlier when I brought out some cookies, I think a preacher was here. He carried around a bible, but he was gone before I came out again."

"Where was he sitting?"

"On the side by the street in one of the booths—with James."

Irene projected a picture of Detective O'Malley with her comms. "Did you see this man there?"

Laila paused, clearly trying to remember, but shook her head. "There was a guy who was by the door, but he was facing the street, and I didn't see his face. Jan would know. She gets all the fun—like there was a huge fight earlier between a couple of guys that Ahmed broke up."

"Do you know who was involved?"

The young woman shook her head. "No, but Jan said one of them left. Did Ahmed make it?"

Irene shook her head. "No, I'm sorry."

"Oh." Her eyes welled with tears. "He was a tough boss but a good man. How about his wife and daughter?"

Gabriel shook his head.

The tears now streamed down her cheeks. He gave her arm a gentle squeeze and brought over a box of tissues.

"Thank you, Laila. We'll need more help with the two unidentified bodies. Do you think you can work with a police artist?" Irene asked.

Laila nodded slowly. "I'll try, but Jan'd be more helpful. She remembers everybody."

Gabriel and Irene left the room. He said, "Get that info to the team at the scene."

He could almost see her mentally upload the new information onto the virtual "Murder Book" that was no longer a tangible three-ring binder. She notified Fitz about the details provided by Laila.

Gabriel saw Dr. Miller standing by the nurse's station with a grim expression. She spotted them and approached.

"I'm sorry, but Jan Winter died in surgery. She had an air embolism and coded. Unfortunately, that's a common complication of blast injuries."

"Damn."

"Dr. Patton came back a few minutes ago from his scan—Room 5."

"Thank you, Doctor." He looked around uncertainly at the multitude of rooms looking for the right number.

"Down the hall to the right, Detective," Dr. Miller said, pointing.

"Thanks." Their eyes met.

She smiled.

He smiled back, his mouth dry and his pulse quickened again as he headed over to Room 5.

Gabriel and Irene found the older gentleman sitting up, his legs dangling off the side edge of the floating stretcher. He had short, white hair and bright, blue eyes behind a pair of horn-rimmed glasses with thick lenses. His pale face was lined with deep wrinkles. Tugging on the hospital gown with one hand, he clutched a small, leather-bound object with the other.

They introduced themselves.

"Dr. Patton, you work at Titan Robotics?" Gabriel asked.

"Yes," he replied and then asked in a worried tone, "Do you know what happened to Gerry—Gerry Carmichael?"

"He wasn't in the explosion," Gabriel replied.

Patton's wrinkled his brows. "But he was still sitting there when I went to the bathroom."

"How long were you in the bathroom?"

The older man flushed. "Maybe ten minutes."

"You were in the bathroom when the explosion occurred?"

"Yes, I just finished and was about to get out of the stall when the door got blown into the room. But I was protected by the stall."

"Did you see anything suspicious? Did anyone have a package or anything?"

Patton shook his head. "No, nothing. Everything was normal—seemed normal."

"What were you meeting with Carmichael about, sir?"

Patton hesitated. "Business."

"You couldn't do that at the office?"

The older man shook his head but didn't explain.

"Why not?"

"It was about something personal, too."

"Can you elaborate?"

Patton shook his head. "I'm sorry I can't, but I promise you it has nothing to do with any of this."

"Let us decide that, sir."

The old man sighed. "Look, I'm really very tired, and I want to get home. Am I cleared to go?"

Gabriel looked at him with narrowed eyes. "Yeah, but we'll need to talk to you again. Can you help us with IDs on the other patrons?"

Patton shrugged. "Whatever I can do to help, but I'm not really good with faces."

"You might remember more than you realize. We can have a police artist here very soon."

"It's been a rough day, and I really need to get home. Can I come in to your office tomorrow?"

"All right." Gabriel gave him his contact information. Then he and Irene headed back into the main ER.

Dr. Miller saw them and approached. "Dr. Patton is cleared to go home. Miss Harvey will be taken to the Observation Unit."

"Thank you, Doctor," Gabriel replied.

They bade her good-bye and headed toward the exit. He glanced back, his eyes meeting Dr. Miller's again. She smiled and looked away. Irene looked at her partner and back at the attractive young doctor. One brow arched, she gave a small, knowing smile.

Outside the ER, Gabriel updated Fitz on the plan to have a police artist meet with the two survivors.

"We're still at the scene, but we got a lead on who might've gone after O'Malley. We'll check it out in the morning. Can you go interview his wife first thing tomorrow? She probably won't know anything since he was undercover, but you never know," Fitz said.

"I assume his Captain or L-T already notified her?"

"Yeah, I heard several people from Gang and Narcotics and the brass are all over there tonight, so let's wait until morning after the circus dies down."

"All right. Good night." Turning to his partner, Gabriel asked, "You want me to drop you off at the station?"

"Yeah, my car is there," Irene said as they approached the Raptor. "Uh, can I drive?"

Gabriel laughed and shook his head, "I'm senior partner—my rules. I always drive."

She sighed.

CHAPTER 4

Tuesday Morning

Gabriel woke with a start. His throat tightened and his heart ached as he remembered what happened yesterday afternoon. He would never again hear Adeline's delighted squeals, never eat Aahad's heavenly baklava nor share Arabic coffee with Ahmed. Ahmed was like the brother he once had. And they'd treated him like part of their family. He sat up on the edge of the bed, head in his hands, staring down at the floor until the alarm went off. He gave a deep sigh and got up. He didn't have the luxury of grieving until the person responsible for the bombing paid for what he did.

On the way to Beck Tower, he absently listened to the daily morning broadcast on National Public Radio. It often walked the tightrope between factual reporting and what was officially acceptable to the DNS censors. Gabriel focused on driving when an alert tone sounded.

"We interrupt your regular program for an important special segment from the Onion News Network."

Gabriel grinned. Now we get to hear some real facts.

"Today, eleven years ago, on "The Day," multiple bombings occurred simultaneously in several major cities across the United States. Hundreds of thousands were killed. Unlike 9/11 in 2001, where the lack of coordination among intelligence and law enforcement agencies contributed to our lack of preparation, this one happened despite the supposed best efforts of the Department of Homeland Security.

That day, Congress and the President signed the National Security Emergency powers Act, conveniently and immediately proposed by a small Congressional group. This law consolidated all intelligence, law enforcement and security agencies into the Department of National Security—combining Homeland Security, Justice, all seventeen members of the U.S Intelligence Community, the Office of the Director of National Intelligence, and all branches of the military. Each of these agencies quickly appointed a few very well-prepared staff, which curiously somehow managed to swiftly and efficiently implement the consolidation process. The Emergency Powers Act repealed the Posse Comitatus Act of 1807 and gave the newly formed DNS very broad scope and powers on both international and domestic fronts.

The DNS's first task was to locate and prosecute the terrorists responsible for "The Day." An anonymous tip pointed the investigation to a well-known Muslim charity that presumably smuggled the bombers disguised as recent Middle East refugees to carry out the bombings—a charge the charity vigorously denied before it was shut down and its trustees never heard from again. All of the suspects and conspirators, including their children, were subsequently killed in DNS raids on their safe houses in several states, so there were no trials—ever. Thousands of simple encoded electronic messages planning the attacks were later discovered. Why our multiple intelligence agencies had not detected these before the bombings remains unanswered. Since then, all refugees from the Middle East were banned from entry into the U.S. and legal immigration severely—"

There was a brief moment of silence. "Uh, we apologize for that unscheduled interruption," the NPR host said, clearing his throat. "Obviously, that was not an approved message. Uh, let's return to our coverage of the severe flooding in South Florida and all along the Atlantic Coast. . . ."

Gabriel chuckled. Well, at least they were able to appropriate a couple of minutes of the news this morning. Hopefully next time it would take the DNS longer to restore the signal. ONN often hijacked official news broadcasts with uncensored reports. Therefore, it had to move its broadcast base every day, thus far thwarting DNS attempts to shut it down and imprison the last independent journalists in the country.

Gabriel picked up Irene at Beck Tower and headed out to speak with Detective O'Malley's widow. They flew northwest through the San Fernando Valley to Chatsworth. It was most notable for being the burial place for Fred Astaire and Ginger Rogers, who were pretty much unknown to the present generation except for the few remaining classic movie nerds, like Gabriel—and Ahmed.

Gabriel descended to street level as they approached O'Malley's neighborhood. The cookie-cutter houses were typical of post-Big One construction, made from light, 3-D-printed carbon-fiber epoxy for strength and durability, especially useful in earthquakes. Before The Big One a decade ago, Chatsworth had some large lots. Afterward, with limited habitable space in and around L.A. and the widespread bankruptcy of the state earthquake agency and homeowners, many lots were subdivided. New homes were built narrower and higher to conform to the smaller footprint. The three-story O'Malley house was tucked behind the two houses that fronted the street.

Gabriel set the Raptor down on the street. An unmarked police car occupied the driveway in front of the O'Malley garage.

"What's the name of the widow?" he asked.

"Evangeline," Irene said, quickly retrieving the information from the OmniNet. He was starting to recognize when his partner was interacting with her HDI; her eyes would glaze over briefly.

On the left side of the front door, there was a camera in addition to the usual RFID scanner that came with most newer construction houses, which automatically unlocked the door for those with authorized chips. O'Malley must have added the camera.

He knocked. After a moment, a tall, good-looking man opened the door. He was six foot two with sculpted muscles and light brown hair, dressed in jeans and a black tee shirt with a logo of a famous rock band. He sported a gel bandage on his right cheek. Gabriel immediately pegged him as a fellow cop.

"What do you want?" the man asked with an almost hostile tone, blocking the entrance with his impressive physique.

Gabriel flashed his badge. "Gabriel Furst. Robbery-Homicide. My partner, Irene Bolton. We need to speak with Evangeline O'Malley about her husband."

"She's not up to talking to anyone right now." His tone was protective. "And you are?"

"Uh, yeah, sorry. Finn Roberts. I'm Rick's—was Rick's—partner at GND." He shook hands with them. Being undercover in Gang and

Project A

Narcotics explained why he wasn't in the standard LAPD camo tactical suit.

"Tell us what you and Rick were working on."

"We're between cases. And I already spoke to somebody from RHD last night—Fitzsimmons. Told him everything I know."

"Yeah, well, you can tell it all to us again." Gabriel found himself disliking the younger man. He expected a little more professional courtesy from a fellow detective, especially toward someone trying to figure out who murdered his partner.

The younger man scowled.

"Can we talk inside?"

Roberts hesitated, looked toward someone inside the house and stepped aside after a moment. Seated on the couch was a very attractive blonde woman in her early thirties cuddling a young girl, who appeared to be about four. Both had red, puffy eyes.

Gabriel introduced himself and Irene. "Mrs. O'Malley, we're so sorry to bother you at this time. We're looking into the incident at the café yesterday." He glanced down at the little girl, not sure how much she knew about her father's death.

"I told them you weren't up for talking yet," Finn said.

"It's all right." Evangeline looked at Finn and then said to her daughter, "Sweetie, why don't you go in the kitchen and get some cereal? Finn will take you."

"Are you sure?" Finn asked and received a nod from Evangeline. He gave Gabriel and Irene a warning look and then hoisted the little girl up on his shoulders and headed to the back of the house toward the kitchen.

Gabriel sat on the couch beside Evangeline.

"As a cop's wife, I always knew that this day might come, but…" Evangeline covered her mouth to suppress a sob but broke into tears.

"I'm sorry, Mrs. O'Malley. I know this is a very difficult time for you," Gabriel said.

She sniffled and dabbed her tears. After her sobs subsided, she asked, "Are you married, Detective?"

Gabriel shook his head. "Divorced. My dad was on the force. He died on the job when I was eight."

The widow nodded. After a moment, she said, "Go ahead and ask your questions."

He patted her shoulder gently. "Do you know anyone who might've wanted your husband dead?"

"He's LAPD—probably everyone he's ever arrested."

"Anyone in particular?"

She frowned. "He never mentioned anyone, but he didn't talk much about the job, you know. Finn would probably know more. Do you think the bomb was meant for Rick?"

"We don't know the motive yet, ma'am. We're covering all our bases."

She nodded and wiped her cheek with the back of her hand.

"How were things between you and your husband?"

"We have our up and downs, like every married couple. He's been away the last seven months in deep cover, so we haven't seen much of him. He just got back last week."

"And in the last week, how were things between you?"

"That's enough," Finn said, entering the room. "It's none of your damn business. She's not a suspect."

Looking up at Finn with narrowed eyes, Gabriel said, "We're just getting a more complete background on everyone who was at the café, so we need to ask these things." Using his comms, he quickly texted some instructions to his partner, who was standing behind him. Turning back to Evangeline, he asked, "So, how were things between you this past week?"

"Well, a little tense," she admitted. "We just had to get used to each other again."

Gabriel leaned forward. "Where were you yesterday afternoon, Mrs. O'Malley?"

"I was here all day except when I picked up my daughter from school."

"Your daughter attends a private school?" Most public school students attended on-line classes while only some private schools were still brick and mortar institutions.

She shook her head. "No. My sister runs a homeschool."

"Can she verify your whereabouts?"

Evangeline hesitated and glanced at Finn, who gave a barely noticeable shake of his head. "Of course. Then we came straight home."

"What time was that?"

"About 3:45."

"And you stayed here the rest of the time?"

"Yes."

"And you, Detective Roberts, where were you yesterday afternoon?"

"I was driving around."

"You used the city car out front?" Gabriel asked and then glanced down at his comms at Irene's reply to his inquiry.

"Yeah."

"All afternoon?"

"Yeah."

"When was the last time you saw your partner?"

"Yesterday at lunch. We had tacos at Tito's."

"You sure you didn't last see him at the coffee shop—where you had a fight with him?"

"What do you mean?" Finn looked wary, his eyes darting back and forth between Gabriel and Irene.

"We have a witness who saw you fighting."

Finn was silent at first. "It was nothing. We just had a little minor disagreement."

Evangeline studied her fingernails.

"What was it about?" Gabriel asked.

"You know—things between partners. We disagree about how to do things from time to time."

"Do you know of anybody that would come after your partner? Maybe someone you guys put away recently?"

"Well, like I told your guy last night, we just wrapped up a case with a South American gang. They're known for using some pretty brutal methods—but usually not bombs. They don't have an explosives guy. And I'm pretty sure Rick didn't get made. He got arrested along with the rest of them to keep his cover."

"All right." Gabriel turned to Evangeline. "Mrs. O'Malley, again we're so sorry for your loss. If you think of anything that might help, please contact me or Irene." He beamed his contact info to her comms and stood up.

She nodded, got up and limply shook their hands.

"Detective Roberts, if you would please walk out with us?" Gabriel asked.

"Uh, sure." Gabriel saw Finn's hand casually brush against Evangeline's lower back as he walked past her to the front door.

Finn accompanied Gabriel and Irene to their car.

Chapter 4

"So, what were you doing with your partner's wife yesterday afternoon?" Gabriel asked.

"What do you mean?"

"City cars have GPS. It says you were here from about three to midnight yesterday when your partner was busy getting blown up."

"I just stopped in to see if she was okay, that's all. And then I stayed after we heard about Rick and while the brass and our unit were here last night."

"Did O'Malley know you were having an affair with his wife? That why you guys fought at the Rialto?"

Finn opened his mouth to protest but then seemed to understand the futility. After a moment, he said, "I had nothing to do with that bombing. I left a long time before that."

"No, but his sudden demise is rather convenient for you and the grieving widow."

"You fucking bastard! Take that back!" Finn snarled, staring down at Gabriel, their noses inches away from each other. He clenched his fists.

Gabriel stood his ground without flinching, calmly looking up at the other man. "Yeah, I am, but I'm not the one fucking my partner's wife."

Finn Roberts had the grace to look slightly ashamed and backed away.

"Look, if you actually want to help solve the murder of your partner and can think of anybody else who might have it out for him, you know how to reach us." Gabriel turned around and got into the Raptor. His partner followed suit.

The car lifted off, leaving Finn standing, glaring at them.

"Did you really need to say that?" Irene asked.

"He's got a temper. I wanted to see his threshold. Besides, he betrayed his partner. Partners gotta have each other's back, and he violated that trust in the worst way."

She nodded. "How'd you figure he was the one in the fight at the cafe?"

Gabriel shrugged. "Laila said that one guy left. Finn has a band-aid on his right cheek. O'Malley had a wedding ring with sharp corners. And Roberts' knuckles looked a little pink, too. The way he and the widow were looking at each other and touching each other—they're a little too familiar for his just being her husband's partner. And the GPS data confirmed it."

She raised an eyebrow.

"Thanks for getting that GPS info so quickly," Gabriel said.

"The advantages of having an HDI."

"Yeah, well, I still prefer to have my brain without all that Borg tech in it. The comms is already enough for me."

"It comes in handy."

"Yeah, maybe," he said, sounding skeptical.

"You're a Luddite!"

He shrugged. "I'm not against new tech. I just want to see it function without a hitch for at least ten years before I use it."

She laughed. "Definitely a Luddite."

Chapter 4

CHAPTER 5

Tuesday Late Morning

Back at Beck Tower, they met Fitz and Smiley on the parking ramp of the twenty-first floor, where RHD was based. The usually cheerful Fitz looked hot, sweaty and grumpy in his black camouflage tactical suit. Walking between him and Smiley was a muscular Latino teen with menacing tattoos that covered every inch of exposed skin. Fluorescent blue electronic cuffs bound his wrists and ankles. Gabriel recognized the tattoo of the South American gang that O'Malley infiltrated. The detectives nodded to each other.

The security scanner on the sliding duraglass doors allowed them into the restricted level. All unauthorized visitors entered Beck Tower through the first floor visitor's center. Smiley locked their guest into an interrogation room.

Outside the room, Fitz said, "That kid is José Martín. O'Malley's partner, Finn Roberts, told us that he was their contact in the gang. The gang was busted last week. José's just a grunt, so he was allowed out on bail a couple of days ago. Most of the bigwigs are still sitting in Metro." The Metropolitan Detention Center was the largest central jail for the LAPD and one of the first facilities rebuilt after The Big One.

"What's with the leg cuffs?" Gabriel asked.

"He tried to rabbit when we picked him up, so we used the bird. Don't know why people still think they can outrun us." Fitz said. Every LAPD vehicle was equipped with a drone. All officers carried drone marker guns, which fired nanoparticle tracers, labeling the target the drone tracked. Some of them also had light weaponry and other custom modifications.

"So, Suit, you got the privilege of chasing after Martín while Smiley drove the car?" Gabriel guessed. Fitz was slightly overweight and not exactly the most athletic or fastest of the RHD I detectives. Luckily, Robbery-Homicide detectives rarely had to chase down a suspect. Gabriel chuckled as Fitz scowled at him.

"We got Forensics looking at his pad for signs of explosives. You get anything from O'Malley's wife?" Fitz asked.

Gabriel shook his head. "No, but his partner was banging Mrs. O'Malley at the time."

The other detective snorted in derision and shook his head.

"The GPS in his city car places Roberts at the O'Malley residence with Mrs. O'Malley."

"You think O'Malley knew?"

"Yeah. They had a scuffle at the coffee shop a while before the bomb blew."

Fitz wrinkled his brow. "Could Roberts have placed a bomb with a timer or remote?"

"Possible, but I doubt it. It happened over a half hour after he left, and he couldn't be sure O'Malley was still going to be there."

"Unless he planted it on him."

"Yeah, but I don't think so. I don't think he knew that O'Malley found out about him and the wife before they got to the Rialto, so he wouldn't just happen to have a bomb with him."

Fitz shook his head with obvious disgust. "You go undercover and ask your partner to look out for your family while you're gone…"

"Yeah," Gabriel agreed.

"Hey, can you and Irene start on the video from the cameras while Smiley and I talk to our gangbanger?" Fitz asked them. "The copies are in my office."

Gabriel retrieved the bags of data chips copied from the bank and street cameras and handed them to Irene. She inserted the bank's data chip into her desk unit's digital reader. The bank's entrance appeared on her monitor with the café entrance just visible on the left, through the large duraglass windows. The time and date code appeared on the bottom right-hand corner. The time on the bottom right corner read 10/18/60 06:06 a.m.

"Forward to 2:30 p.m.," he said.

Using her HDI, Irene had the reader jump to that time frame. They watched the scuffle between O'Malley and his partner start inside the Rialto and end up outside the coffee shop at 2:38 p.m. Ahmed came out to break up the fight. Finn Roberts left while Ahmed accompanied O'Malley back into the café to a table on the left. A few minutes later, an African-American preacher in black robes entered the coffeehouse. He carried a bible and was flanked by two husky guys dressed smartly in suits. They stood guard on either side of the entrance, constantly surveying the surrounding area. A couple exited together. One of the other victims entered. Patton entered at 3:05. The preacher left at 3:11, accompanied by his bodyguards. A few minutes after that, Carmichael approached the café from the right, looking at something in his left hand. He tucked it carefully back into his pocket. He paused, looked around and brushed his hair back with the same hand before entering the Rialto.

"What is that?" Gabriel asked. "Go back, half-speed," he said. The video jumped back and played again.

Carmichael had stuck something slender and about six inches long into his jacket pocket.

"I can't tell." Irene said.

"Can you magnify and get a clearer image?" Gabriel asked.

Irene zoomed in on Carmichael's hand, but the image deteriorated. She shook her head. "That's the best I can do. Unfortunately, the café sidewalk is not the bank camera's focal point. It's only a small part of the visual field, and there's not enough resolution to get more details."

Gabriel was disappointed. "All right. Let's see the rest of the video."

Irene resumed playback.

Gabriel propped his chin on his hand, his forefinger stroking his lower lip as they reviewed the scene. "Why'd he stop before going in? Does he seem nervous to you?"

"Yeah, that seems odd."

They watched, noting who went in and out, and at the 3:31 p.m. mark, Carmichael came out alone, looked back into the café and walked briskly away. A couple of minutes later, just as O'Malley was exiting, the explosion rocked the café, shattering the duraglass and ejecting chairs and tables and body parts. The shock wave reverberated down the street, creating ripples in the duraglass windows of the bank and shaking the camera inside the bank. They watched in silence for a few more minutes, but no one exited from the shattered café. Several people gathered outside in morbid curiosity.

"Let's look at the video from the street cameras on Spring Street," Gabriel said to his partner. "It looks like the blast came from that side of the café and not where O'Malley was sitting. Did we get any footage off the street cams?"

With her HDI, Irene sampled the street camera recordings, quickly finding the one with the clearest view of the café's interior. Irene started the video. "Here we go—around 3:05."

They watched as James Patton sat down at the table with the preacher. The two spoke with their heads close together. The preacher put his hand on Patton's forehead, bowed his head, placed something on the table and then got up to leave.

"What was that?" Irene asked.

"Go back and slow it down."

They watched it again frame by frame.

"Can't tell. Something straight and slender," Gabriel said.

They resumed the video. A few minutes later, Carmichael entered the café. He briefly stopped at Patton's table and then disappeared out of view. After a few minutes, he came back with a cup and sat down across from Patton with his back toward the entrance. They huddled together for several minutes, apparently in an intense conversation. At one point, Carmichael wagged a finger in Patton's face. Patton got up and disappeared from the camera's view. Carmichael sat alone for a few minutes, He then pushed himself up using the tabletop and then left the Rialto. Two minutes later, the café exploded.

Suddenly, Irene was excited. "There!"

"What?"

"I'll go back to just before the explosion and play it frame by frame."

Gabriel saw what his partner with her optical implants noticed at full speed. The explosion clearly originated from the table where Patton and Carmichael had been sitting.

CHAPTER 6

Tuesday Afternoon/Evening

When Irene discovered James Patton had not arrived to meet with the police artist, she called Titan Robotics and found that he also did not show up at work that day.

"What do we know about Patton?" Gabriel asked as he steered the Raptor west toward Patton's home in Bel Air.

Irene was quiet while mentally consulting the OmniNet. "Here we go—James Edward Patton, PhD, born in 1993—that makes him sixty-seven now—one of the co-founders of Titan Robotics, along with Edgar Carmichael. Well, that explains why he lives in Bel Air. Attended MIT when he was only twelve. Has PhDs in Robotics, Mechanical Engineering and Electrical Engineering. Wow—triple doctorates!" She paused. "He studied robotics in China for two years as well. Married for forty-two years. Wife died two years ago in an accident. One daughter, Brandi Arnott, married, lives out in Loma Linda with a husband and two kids. Retired two years ago and then went back to work a few months later, right after his wife died."

"Didn't he meet Edgar Carmichael in grad school?" Gabriel asked, recalling the fairly well-known bio of the Carmichael magnate.

"Probably. Let me check . . . Yes, he and Patton started Titan in 2019, just when they were completing their graduate work. Carmichael got an MBA from Harvard. Initial research funding from DARPA. Oh, this is interesting—Patton sold his shares of the company to Carmichael after just five years." The US Department of Defense Advanced Research Projects Agency often initiated and funded the development of emerging technologies in industries of use to the military.

"Before Titan got its first contract?"

Irene checked the Titan website. "Let's see. Titan received its first contract in 2025 from the DOD for battlebots. Bought out the biggest firms in China and Japan and began making domestic robots in 2035. Now has ninety-five percent of total global market share."

"So Patton sold out just before the company grew big, therefore losing out on trillions."

Irene nodded. "That'd be motive for murder."

"Yeah, but why go after the son rather than the father? The father was the one who made it big on his sweat—sounds like Patton was the brains of the company."

Descending to street level, Gabriel turned into the cul de sac toward the Patton residence, one of the few on the small street. All the estates had high walls with gated entrances, topped with faintly shimmering, electrified security fields. Unlike most of L.A., affluent estates in wealthy areas like Bel Air, Pacific Palisades and Beverly Hills were not subdivided after The Big One. Most of these owners rebuilt their houses without declaring bankruptcy.

Although the overhead security field was activated, the massive wrought-iron front gate of Patton's property stood open. The Raptor cruised along the long, circular, stone driveway, hovering a few feet above the ground. The driveway encircled a large, three-tier fountain, which was dry. Gabriel drove up to the limestone steps leading to the marble entrance of the mansion. As he stepped out of the Raptor, he surveyed the front of the house and property. The Patton estate encompassed several acres with a large forest in the back. Another driveway branch led to a large, detached garage in the back, barely visible around the right side of the house. The Tuscan-style two-story mansion with ochre-colored walls with brown trim had an understated elegance with curved terra cotta tile roofing and arched windows.

They knocked on the door and rang the doorbell, loudly announcing themselves, expecting a robot to answer, but all remained quiet. Most newer buildings and houses had electronically-controlled security doors, designed to recognize voices, passcodes or RFIDs, but Patton's door still used a key. Funny for a guy on the forefront of technology. Receiving no answer to repeated knocks, Gabriel tried the handle. It turned, and the door swung open. They looked at each other.

"I got a bad feeling about this." He unholstered his 9 mil Glock, another relic, as almost all LAPD officers and detectives now carried the more powerful hand blasters. Gabriel didn't like the recharging lag time between shots. He preferred his dependable semi-automatic.

Irene unholstered her blaster.

On the side of the foyer, he saw the control panel of the alarm system was unarmed.

"Dr. Patton! LAPD! We're coming in!" he yelled.

It was dead quiet. Gabriel signaled to Irene that he would go first. She nodded. Gabriel moved through the large living room and dining room, filled with dusty furniture. Methodically they cleared each room on the main floor, heading towards the back of the mansion. Irene entered the study first and stopped just inside the entrance. She began taking photos with her comms.

Gabriel couldn't see what she was looking at until he entered the room, following carefully in her footsteps. The first thing he saw were shelves packed from floor to ceiling with books. Then he turned the corner. James Patton slumped forward towards his left onto the desk in front of a monitor. His head was drenched in a pool of blood, brains and skull fragments. The blood that dripped down to the plush, ecru-colored carpet was dark and congealed. Patton had been dead a while. A Ruger lay on the floor below his dangling right hand.

"There goes our prime suspect," Irene said, sighing.

Walking carefully over to the dead man, Gabriel donned gloves and tapped a key on the keyboard to wake the monitor. The translucent, paper-thin screen displayed the words "I'm sorry." Dried blood tails and brain matter speckled the screen. Activating the light on his comms, he cocked his head at an angle to check the palm of Patton's right hand. It was spattered with blood. He gingerly checked the other hand, also without touching the corpse. Stippling and soot surrounded the star-shaped wound on the right side of Patton's head behind the ear.

"Contact wound. The bullet entered here," he said.

"So he shot himself."

"Or someone held it against his head. We'll see what the GSR shows us when Forensics gets here. Call it in and get a warrant," Gabriel said. Forensics Science Division would perform an official gunshot residue test later.

Irene nodded and spoke into her comms.

The slug that went through Patton's head splintered. Some bloody shell fragments were embedded in the bookcase near the door. Unlike most people, Patton seemed not to have worn a wrist computer; there was no pale strip of skin on either wrist. Many people without comms usually carried around a portable data chip and a tablet. No tablet was found. Gabriel looked around the monitor, searching for a chip but only found the empty slot where it would have been inserted. The slot was dusty.

"We got the warrant?" Gabriel asked.

"Yeah, we're a go."

Still looking for a data chip, Gabriel opened the drawers, finding one stuffed with odds and ends, metal clips, several short sticks of varying lengths with dark cores and worn-down rubber tips at the other end. There were other metallic tubes with pointed tips.

"What are those?" Irene asked.

"Pencils and pens—I remember these from when I was a kid."

"Really? That's what those look like?"

"I haven't seen one of these in over twenty years. Didn't know anybody still used them."

"Maybe he didn't. These drawers are full of old stuff. He probably hasn't cleaned anything out in those twenty years."

"Yeah. You see an appointment calendar?"

"No, maybe it's on the missing portable chip," Irene suggested.

He would check with the Medical Examiner later to see if he or she found a data chip since only someone from the ME's office was allowed to rifle through the corpse's clothing or touch the corpse.

Gabriel grunted in reply. "Let's clear upstairs. Forensics should be here soon."

Irene nodded. They went up to the second floor, but given the congealed blood, were not expecting to find anyone. The rooms were empty. Reaching the master bedroom, Gabriel stepped into a time warp. The bed was an old-fashioned four-poster walnut California king with a damask rose-covered spread. Nightstands stood on either side of the bed. The walk-in closets contained mostly women's clothes, covered with a thick layer of dust. A few men's shirts and pants hung in one less dusty corner.

There were two sinks in the large bathroom, one with many dusty toiletries around it and the other with a cup, a comb, a shaver, an old-fashioned manual toothbrush and toothpaste.

"Didn't even know these existed any more," Irene commented, indicating the toothbrush. Gabriel nodded, suspecting Patton stockpiled these since the last one rolled off the production line decades ago.

The shower had an old-fashioned spray head, not the sonic-powered head used in all post-Big One construction. It meant this house actually withstood the devastating quake relatively intact. Most houses or buildings in Los Angeles suffered major damage during The Big One and its multiple aftershocks.

Gabriel looked under the bed and found years' worth of dust bunnies. He stood at the foot of the bed and surveyed the room slowly. Patton seemed to have left the house, and especially this room, exactly like it was before his wife had died. Several picture frames hung on the wall, dissolving from one family picture into another, some with a flame-haired baby growing up into adulthood. An old-fashioned photographic portrait showed a happy bride and groom. He studied the wedding photo; a beautiful young woman with red hair, porcelain skin and smiling, blue eyes in a white, lacy dress and a somewhat gaunt, nerdy-looking young man with thick glasses and untamable dark hair gazed adoringly at each other. In all of the pictures, Patton appeared very happy, a man very much in love with his wife and family. Why would this man bomb the Rialto Café, killing all those people? Did he bomb the café? If he did, was he after his boss or someone else who was there?

They headed back downstairs to the study.

"Wow, are these real paper books?" Irene exclaimed, looking around the library.

"Yeah, haven't seen many of those recently. My grandparents used to have them at their house."

"I've never seen anyone with printed books."

Gabriel looked at the titles of the older, hard-covered books—*David Copperfield*, *A Tale of Two Cities*, *The Iliad*, *The Odyssey*, *I, Robot*, *Dune*, *Stranger in a Strange Land*, *Children of Men*, and *Harry Potter and the Deathly Hallows*. He gingerly opened one and then another and then another, flipping gently though the delicate, yellowed pages. "Amazing," he commented, holding *Harry Potter and the Philosopher's Stone*.

"What?"

"These are first editions."

"Is that good?"

"They're collector's items—if people were still collecting books. This one is probably worth over a million. There were only five hundred first editions."

"Does he have anything that's not over fifty to a hundred years old?"

Gabriel smiled briefly. "Sometimes the old stuff's better than the new stuff." He received a skeptical snort.

"How is anyone supposed to get through these? What is that one—" she asked as she peered over his shoulder, "—223 pages! It would take forever to read one of those."

Gabriel smiled to himself. We're only a little more than ten years apart, yet it seems like an entire generation.

He heard some noise from the front of the house—probably the Forensic Science Division team—confirmed as he looked out the window at the driveway. The stone pavement was now filling up with arriving police vehicles, the Medical Examiner's van and a FSD van.

Gabriel spoke briefly with the FSD lead, Phil Zimburg, an absent-minded-looking, balding middle-aged bachelor with a noticeable potbelly. If there was anything to find, Phil would find it. He was renowned for staying up all night looking for answers to explain the most minute trace evidence found at the scenes, which made him very popular with LAPD and the District Attorney's office. In addition, he was also a hacking genius, a secret talent known only to the select few he considered close friends, Gabriel being one of them.

"Who's the ME here?" Gabriel asked.

"Toller Cranston," Phil replied with a grimace that only Gabriel could see.

Gabriel had to restrain himself from scowling. The LAPD and the District Attorney's Office all disliked Dr. Cranston. He tended to be less than definitive as to the manner of death, especially in high-profile cases. Several wealthy and influential murder suspects remained free due to his testimony. Gabriel suspected Cranston's powerful political connections kept him employed in the Medical Examiner's office. Despite the Chief ME's significant political clout, even he could not fire or transfer his unpopular deputy.

Chapter 6

Discussing with Phil what they needed to work up was almost a mere formality since they worked many cases together. Phil was extremely thorough and proactive.

"Let's go look through the grounds and the garage," Gabriel said to his partner.

It started sprinkling outside as he and Irene headed out to the detached garage in the back. They could not get in without the remote for the garage door or the key to the locked side door. Gabriel grabbed a crowbar from his trunk and within a minute was inside. Turning on the light, he scanned the large room. On one side, a long, dusty workbench was covered with ribbon cables, circuit boards and other electronic equipment. In the far corner adjacent to the counter, a few containers sat on the floor. Rummaging through the chaos, Gabriel found a vaguely familiar leather-bound notebook in a drawer. Where have I seen this before? He flipped through the journal, noting many drawings and notes scribbled in illegible writing. He placed it in an evidence bag and logged it into the case file on his comms.

"What do you think he was working on?" Irene asked, looking at the dusty equipment.

"Don't know. The notebook had a drawing of some kind of robot, but nothing here that looks like a prototype. And it's dated over two years ago."

"So nothing here explains why he would set a bomb to kill his boss."

"Mm-hmm. We'll need to test for traces of explosives here of course."

Irene pulled open one of the drawers. On top of some tools lay a matte silver pen.

"Another one?" Irene asked, reaching for it.

It suddenly hit Gabriel. "Stop! Get away from there!"

Irene froze and pulled her hand back slowly. She looked at him.

"Sorry, I didn't mean to scare you. It has the same texture as that sliver of metal that contained the explosives at the café," he explained. "Go get the Bomb Squad to check this."

Her eyes wide, Irene stared at him and then quickly retreated outside. Gabriel examined the containers on the floor in the far corner. One had a block labeled pentaerythritol tetranitrate—PETN, he recalled—and another container was labeled cyclotrinitromethylenetrinitramine—which he vaguely remembered might be RDX—both components for making Semtex.

Oh, fuck! We're at a bombing suspect's place. Should've checked those out earlier and gotten the hell out of here! Could've gotten both of us killed! Heart pounding, he strode outside away from the garage. After consulting with Phil, who had worked bomb forensics, they thought the FSD team would be relatively safe working the scene inside the house.

After almost an hour, Irene returned with two Bomb Squad techs in their bomb suits with their equipment. Gabriel told them about the suspicious pen as well as the chemical containers on the floor. One nodded and instructed Gabriel and Irene to get clear of the area but agreed the house was probably safe since it was over three hundred feet away.

Rain pelted Gabriel and Irene as they headed back into the house. Good thing these camo tacs are waterproof. It took them a few more hours to finish working the crime scene. Dr. Cranston and Phil Zimburg discussed the case with the detectives before the ME left.

Gabriel and the coroner greeted each other with barely concealed contempt. "Contact wound consistent with the 9 mil Ruger. Time of death around eleven to one last night. After the post, we'll know for sure, but it looks like suicide at this point," Cranston said.

"No other fingerprints on the computer or in the room besides his. His fingerprints are on the gun, and there's blowback on it, so it was fired at close range," Phil said.

"What about the angle of the shot? It seemed like it went in from just behind the right ear and out the left front?" Gabriel asked.

"Not the usual angle people shoot themselves, but certainly not impossible," Cranston replied. "Maybe he turned away from the gun at the last moment."

"GSR?" Gabriel asked.

"Negative," the ME said.

"What about the blood spatter in his right palm?" Gabriel asked.

"What about it?"

"You can't get that if you're holding a gun."

"We'll get a better look at the autopsy. Anyway, we'll do the post tomorrow afternoon."

"Did you find a data chip on him?" Gabriel asked.

"No, not much in his pockets. Just a pen and a pencil." He pointed to some evidence bags. "No explosives residue on that pen. Good night, everyone," Cranston said as he picked up his bag and exited.

Chapter 6   **43**

Gabriel went over to the evidence bags that held the contents of Patton's pockets. There was a gold pen and a pencil stub. Facing Phil, he asked in a quiet voice, "So what do you really think?"

"Well, he could've offed himself, but there're a few things that bother me," Phil replied slowly.

"Yeah, me, too. Any prints around that door?" Gabriel pointed to the door leading to the backyard.

"No fingerprints, but there are a few footprints on the carpet besides your 12s, Irene's 8½s and Patton's 10s—maybe an 11 to 11½ and a 12½. Smooth soles though. We'll run microbe and particulate scans on them— Irene's and yours for elimination, too. And run touch and aerial DNA analyses. As usual, we got quite a backlog, so it may take a few days." Zimburg motioned for Gabriel to lift his foot so he could swab and scrape the soles of his shoes. He also got samples from Irene's soles. Shoes had unique combinations of microbes and particulates, which could be used for identification. They were a record of everywhere the owner walked and were as unique as fingerprints if they ever got a suspect sample to compare.

One of the Bomb Squad techs came in to update the group. "Looks like the pen is a completed device on Xray, so we're going to have to destroy it if our robot can't disassemble it safely. It has traces of high-grade gel explosive material on the outside, probably Semtex K. We'll do a chemical analysis to see if it's identical to the café bombing. And you're right—those containers had ingredients to make Semtex. But we didn't find blasting caps, any kind of detonator or primary explosive. No explosive residue anywhere on the floor or workbench."

"Were you able to lift any prints off the pen?"

"Yeah, very carefully. One of the FSD techs talked us through that. I think he forwarded it to Zimburg."

"All right. Thanks for your help."

The Bomb Squad tech left.

"So, Patton could've made the explosive for the café bombing?" Irene asked.

Phil shrugged.

"Fingerprints on the pen?"

"Yeah," Phil replied. "Patton's."

Gabriel looked at the time on his comms—already 11:48 p.m. "We still have to go see his daughter."

Irene nodded. Having worked in the Homicide unit at the West L.A. Station, she would be accustomed to late hours. "She lives out in Loma Linda."

"Oh, shit," Gabriel said, groaning. They had to fly past some of the NMLs, or No Man's Lands, at night.

Chapter 6

CHAPTER 7

Tuesday Night

The NMLs were a byproduct of the major 7.9 earthquake along the San Andreas fault in 2050. The tremblor devastated Southern California, destroying hundreds of thousands of homes and buildings as well as the freeway system, the electrical power grid, water supply, sewer pipelines, and land-based communications infrastructure. Subsequent super-fires, fanned by the Santa Ana winds, swept through hundreds of city blocks. Hundred of thousands died. Over a million were injured. Nearly two million lost their homes in the region. Rebuilding was slow and never seemed to come to the poorer, gang-riddled areas, leading to a series of riots. Under martial law, these riots and protests were quickly and brutally subdued.

Containment walls were hastily constructed around these riot-affected areas and officially designated as numbered Sections, but everybody called them "No Man's Lands," or "NMLs." Section Two really meant NML-Watts, and Section Five was NML-Compton.

Within the walls, the law of the jungle ruled, especially at night when gangs fought over territory. LAPD learned the hard way. One night, in the early hours, a patrol car was sent into an NML to investigate a disturbance. Metro Dispatch received a distress call from the two officers before their comms went dead. Three additional patrol cars were called in, but they fell silent as well. Early in the morning, when the LAPD SWAT team arrived, all they found were bloody remnants, identifiable only with DNA, scattered around the stripped patrol car carcasses. Remains of two of the officers were never found. Police now only responded to calls within the NMLs during daylight and in force.

Insurrections in NMLs were punished by withholding deliveries of food, medicine, and other supplies for two weeks after each incident—with the threat of an extension if the misbehavior persisted. Non-residents of NMLs were allowed in for humanitarian purposes, but residents were not allowed out. Medical care was provided by clinics inside the NMLs, staffed with volunteers. Since the residents had no official housing, they had no official address and were therefore ineligible to vote.

When the President and Governor declared martial law during the riots, the DNS, the LAPD, the California State Police and private security firms hired by the federal government used lethal force over the strenuous but futile objections from civil rights organizations and certain news agencies. The media were quickly and ruthlessly silenced and restructured by the DNS to broadcast only officially sanctioned news, a policy that continued post-riots and was implemented throughout the country. Very few alternative news venues, like the Onion News Network, dared broadcast uncensored news. The DNS pursued the ONN and those who cooperated with it.

The history of NMLs played back in Gabriel's head as they flew past one of the them. Bright floodlights completely illuminated the outer perimeter of the six-foot thick and thirty-foot tall concrete walls, studded with broken glass on the inside face and topped by another four feet of an invisible but lethal field between the electrified posts. Inside the walls, darkness reigned, broken by an occasional campfire or flashlight. Residents charged their batteries using daylight or hand cranks, as there was no electricity service inside the NMLs. Scrap wood was almost nonexistent after ten years of scavenging.

"Thank goodness for those walls," Irene commented as she looked down onto the NML as they flew beside it.

Gabriel glanced at his partner's face in the dark, partially illuminated by the dashboard to see if she was joking. "If they'd spent money on building homes rather than walls in the first place, perhaps we wouldn't need them."

"Those types of people cause trouble no matter what," she replied, echoing the popular sentiment among many Angelenos. "At least, they can't bother the rest of us now."

"Walls won't keep people in or out forever."

"Look at the wall at the Mexican border. It solved the illegal immigration problem."

"It also doesn't hurt that these people can be hunted down and shot if resisting arrest. And that everybody's tagged in the United States," he said. The DNS implanted RFID chips into the base of the skull of everyone legally in the U.S.

"What's wrong with that if it makes us all more secure?" Irene asked. "There've been no more major terrorist incidents since the RFIDs were placed in everyone."

Gabriel shook his head. "You're too young to remember what it was like before all that and before the DNS controlled everything."

"I prefer being safe. The DNS helps keep us all safe."

"That's what they would like us to think. They control everything we see or hear—the OmniNet, the media, all sources of information."

"You're paranoid."

Gabriel shook his head.

"We're still a democracy. We still get to vote. That's better than anywhere else in the world," Irene insisted.

Gabriel was silent. Was it a democracy if the same party somehow always managed to win control of the White House and Congress with heavily gerrymandered districts for the past several decades? The laws and policies heavily favored wealthy family dynasties and private corporations. The opposition made barely a whimper. The lone voices brave enough to protest were eventually silenced, except for ONN.

They passed through the San Gabriel Valley, Pomona and Ontario and approached Loma Linda. The GPS suddenly decided to work and directed them to the upscale house of James Patton's daughter, Brandi Arnott. In contrast with the NMLs, these streets were paved after The Big One. Gabriel descended to street level and parked in the driveway.

Street lamps illuminated the endless rows of tract housing, all relatively new, made with the same 3-D-printed carbon-fiber epoxy materials as the O'Malley house. These pastel McMansions had Mediterranean-style tile roofs and boasted well-manicured lots. Obviously constructed after The Big One and definitely under the iron-handed guidance of the Architectural Nazis—the Community Regulatory Committees.

They stepped up to the doorway, triggering the motion-activated porch light. Irene pressed the door buzzer and flashed her badge to the security camera mounted on the right above the door.

A man answered the door and identified himself as Jeff Arnott, Brandi's husband. The detectives identified themselves, transmitting their credentials, apologized for the late hour, and asked to see Brandi.

"Bran! Some detectives here to see you!" Jeff yelled as he stepped aside to allow the detectives inside. "She'll be a minute. We've been trying to get the baby to sleep," he explained. He motioned for Gabriel and Irene to sit on the couch in the living room.

"What's this about?" Jeff asked.

Before Gabriel could answer, an attractive young woman with red hair appeared, looking tired and frazzled in her wrinkled shirt and jeans. "Shhh! The baby just fell asleep," she said to her husband. She was obviously the girl and young woman in the pictures at Patton's house. "Have you seen my comms?" she asked. "I still can't find it. I think the battery died, so I can't use the remote locator." Her husband shook his head. She sighed and sat down in a plush chair across from Gabriel and Irene. "How can I help you, detectives?"

Gabriel introduced himself and his partner. "We would like to speak with you about your father."

"My father? Is something wrong? Did something happen to him?"

"Did you hear about the bombing of the Rialto Café yesterday?"

"Yes, of course. Was my father in that? Is he all right?" she asked, her eyes widened in alarm.

"He was in the café but wasn't hurt. We're looking into everyone who was there," Gabriel said. "When's the last time you spoke with him?"

"Last week. We're going to see him this weekend."

"Did he seem upset or different?"

"Ummmm, a little, but then again, he's been different since Mom died."

"How long ago was that?"

"About a couple of years ago next month. He and Mom were very, very devoted to each other. He was terribly upset when she died in the accident."

"What happened?" Irene asked.

"She was killed by a hit-and-run driver on her morning walk near the house. They never found the guy. My dad never got over it. He always blamed himself."

"Why?"

"He was supposed to walk with her that day, but he stayed home to tinker with a project instead. He went back to work soon after that."

"He'd already retired?" Gabriel asked.

"Yes, he wanted to spend more time with Mom. Working for Titan all those years took up a lot of his time. He spent most weekends at the Lab while I was growing up."

"What does he do at Titan?"

"Well, Dad didn't give us much details, but he was in charge of developing the robotic control systems until he retired. I'm not sure what he's been working on after going back. He never speaks about it. I just assumed it's the same thing as before. You should ask him yourself."

Gabriel asked, "Has he been behaving differently at all lately?"

"He just seems more anxious than usual—that's all. Especially after he joined that church a few months ago. What's it called?" She turned to ask Jeff, who was standing beside her.

"The New Light Church. The feds are investigating them for fraud and racketeering." Jeff sneered.

Brandi frowned at her husband. "He's trying to help them straighten up their computer system after the feds started investigating. Someone really messed with their accounting data. He loves that church."

"Did he attend any churches before that?"

"No, not really. He only believed in science and technology—until my mother died."

"Does he own a gun?"

"Yes, a 9 mil Ruger from the late twentieth century. My dad likes old-fashioned things, which is ironic considering he's always at the leading edge of robotics at work."

"Does he own a robot?"

"Well, that's the other funny thing. He did up until my mother died. He said it helped her do the housework, but he didn't need one for himself. He really should've kept it to clean the house."

"Did he ever work with explosives?" Irene asked, followed by a sharp, admonishing glance from Gabriel.

"Explosives? Why?" Her voice rose. "What are you getting at? Why are you asking these kinds of questions?" Her eyes widened, and her brows furrowed. "Do you think he was responsible for that explosion? That's ridiculous! My father is a wonderful and gentle man—an inventor, a thinker—not a killer! How could you even think that?" Brandi's voice quavered with anger as she rose to her feet.

"It's getting very late. You're upsetting my wife. Leave. Now," Jeff said with overt hostility. He stepped between his wife and the detectives and spread his arms to usher them out as they stood up.

"We're just looking into the background of all the victims in the explosion," Gabriel said, holding his hands up, palms open, attempting to soothe them. "We're not accusing your father of anything."

Brandi calmed down a little. "I need to call him to see if he's OK." She reached for the house videocomms.

Gabriel raised his hand and placed it over her hand on the phone. She looked at him.

"I'm sorry to tell you this, Mrs. Arnott. Your father was taken to the ER yesterday afternoon after the bombing and was medically cleared and sent home. This afternoon, we went to his house and found him. He'd been shot in the head," he told her gently.

"Whaaaat?" All color drained out of her face. She staggered and would have collapsed onto the floor, but Gabriel caught her. He and Jeff helped her to the couch. "Oh, my God. How did it happen? Is he dead?"

Gabriel nodded. "I'm sorry."

She started sobbing in her husband's arms. "I can't believe he's gone, too!"

"What happened?" Jeff asked, ashen-faced.

"We're still looking into his death," Gabriel said. "I'm sorry, but I have one more question for you. Did your father have some kind of portable data device that he might have used to record his schedule? We didn't find one among his personal effects."

Brandi shook her head. "He never used those. He had a leather notebook and wrote everything down in that," she said in between sobs. "He carried it everywhere with him."

Gabriel got up to leave. "If you remember anything else, you can reach us here." He transmitted their contact information to Jeff. "Again, we're very sorry for your loss," he said with a gentle voice.

Brandi nodded and continued sobbing, though more quietly. As Irene and Gabriel headed toward the door, she managed to say, "The last time we spoke—before he hung up, he said that he was sorry for some things that happened and that were going to happen. He said that I'd understand. Oh, my God, did he mean the bombing?" She broke into a fresh round of sobbing.

As Gabriel and Irene got into the car, Gabriel said in a curt tone to his partner, "Next time, let me finish the interrogation. We almost lost her."

"I just got—never mind. I'm sorry," Irene said.

Gabriel felt his face flush. He reminded himself that it always took a few weeks, sometimes months or even longer, for new partners to get in sync.

It was long past midnight. He took a deep breath before saying, "It's getting late. We'll pick this up tomorrow. At least, she gave us a place to start. That church—the New Light? Laila Harvey mentioned that a preacher had been in the café before the explosion."

"Do you think he was from that church?"

"Guess we'll find out."

CHAPTER 8

Tuesday Late Night

They drove in silence to Beck Tower where Irene parked her personal car. She got out and flew away in her luxurious, shiny, new Quetzal. Using the RoboApp on his comms, Gabriel remotely activated his domestic droid, a model D-7000. "Robert, make me some dinner. Anything will be fine. I'll be home in about ten minutes."

"Yes, sir," replied his constant servant of eighteen years and definitely his best wedding present—considering Robert had so far lasted twice as long as his marriage and was far more faithful, too. Yes, the D-7000 series might be considered ancient and obsolete. It had a contoured metal face with red lights for eyes and a stiff walking motion. The newer models had near-perfect humanoid faces, natural walking gaits, and came integrated with the Automated Home Systems. A brand new dom-bot came with the condo, but Gabriel preferred keeping Robert. Although finding repair parts for it was nearly impossible, Gabriel was rather attached to it, regarding Robert more like an old friend. He figured that would be in his favor when the robots become self-aware, rise up against their human overlords, and take over the world.

Gabriel approached a luxurious, gleaming, blue and gray cylindrical high-rise in central downtown. He flew through the secured entry in the reinforced duraglass dome protecting the parking area and dropped down to his fifteenth floor condo. With the sensor recognizing his RFID, the interior force field temporarily disengaged to allow him access to his carport. Some condos, like Gabriel's, had extra security measures, a force field allowing access for pre-authorized people and vehicles. Visitors parked in designated areas in the central core of each ring after being cleared through security. Two security bots monitored the parking area at all times while four security guards surveilled the rest of the complex.

At the entrance to his condo, the Automatic Home System recognized his RFID and silently slid the door open and then closed it behind him.

"Welcome home, Gabriel," the AHS greeted him in a seductive female voice. "You have five new messages."

As he entered, the ever-dependable Robert placed a steaming bowl of beef stew on the table he set for Gabriel. "Good evening, sir. I hope this is to your satisfaction."

"Robert, have you been cooking all day? You couldn't have done this in ten minutes." Gabriel still liked his food cooked the old-fashioned way—without food synthesizers. It just tasted better. Although it was quite a bit more expensive to buy fresh groceries than the hydrocolloids or whatever toxic chemicals they use in those machines, Gabriel refused to have one of those food printers in his unit and instead had an old-fashioned range installed.

"I anticipated you would be late and hungry and tired this evening, sir."

"I told you to stop calling me 'sir,'" Gabriel said, sighing, as he removed his gun and utility belt and stripped off the camo tactical suit down to his underwear. He pulled on a pair of sweats that hung on a rack by the door.

"Yes, sir, I try, sir, but it is in my programming."

"I know." Gabriel chuckled. He tried and failed several times to reprogram that particular response out of his droid. He sat down and inhaled the aroma of real homemade beef stew. He took a bite and savored the flavor. "Mmmm. You've outdone yourself. This is even better than the last time!"

"Thank you, sir."

"Play messages," Gabriel said to the Automated Home System.

"Message one. Seven sixteen p.m.," replied the AHS in the husky voice he had selected. " 'Gabriel, will you pick up? Oh, are you still at work? You haven't changed,'" his ex-wife Jacquie whined on the vid-message. Her buxom figure in a low-cut sequin top appeared on the screen, her hands on her hips. " 'I'm going out of town, and I need to speak with you. Call me tonight,'" she demanded in an imperious tone.

Gabriel scowled. That was another reason they divorced. Besides her infidelity, she was bossy and treated him like her servant, especially after meeting her very wealthy, future husband.

Gabriel was a hormonal nineteen-year old when he met Jacqueline Rouze. He and Jacquie got married in his second year of college after a brief and very passionate courtship, mostly spent in the horizontal position. On a weekend trip to Vegas after some heavy partying, they found themselves legally attached. Jacquie envisioned herself the pampered wife of a very wealthy lawyer. Two months later, the honeymoon was over. Gabriel announced his decision to join the LAPD after graduation instead of going to law school when his defense attorney mentor was murdered. But by then, Jacquie was already pregnant.

She kept busy during the first few years of their marriage with their daughter Gabby and then their son Jonathan. Bored after the kids were in school full-time, she decided she needed a surgical touch-up, courtesy of a small inheritance from her father. That was how she met renowned local plastic surgeon, Dr. Edward Monroe. She started out as the receptionist at his Rodeo Drive office. Her dedication to her job and apparently to the doctor himself facilitated her eventual promotion to office manager and then to wife—never mind that the position was already filled. The childless Edward lived with his wife of thirty years in a gated Beverly Hills mansion and socialized with the A-listers from all over the state. Now with her second marriage, Jacquie could get all her little surgical touch-ups for free.

"Would you like to return this call?" the AHS asked in a come-hither voice.

He looked at the clock. It was almost half past midnight. "No. Next message."

"Message two. Nine oh-four p.m. . . . 'Gabriel, are you ignoring me? Pick up! I need to speak with you . . . Oh, for God's sake! You're not *still* at work, are you? Call me *now!*'"

"Would you like to return the call?" the AHS asked again.

"Again, no." Sighing, he wished the AHS had been programmed with common sense. "Next message."

"Message three. Ten thirty-two p.m. . . . 'Dad, Mom is having a fit over nothing. We didn't do anything. Don't worry, everything is fine.'" His seventeen-year-old daughter Gabrielle batted her eyelashes at him. " 'Bye. Love you.'"

OK, now I'm worried. The only time Gabby uses that sweet, innocent act on me is when she wants something or to get out of trouble. She inherited her mother's looks and figure, which was a walking magnet for hormonal, teenage boys, which her dad knew only all too well.

Although younger brother Jonathan had an IQ that could blow all his peers out of the water, he preferred to loaf and daydream his way through his private school, assisted by mood- and/or mind-altering pharmaceuticals whenever possible. Unfortunately, Jacquie saw no problem with her son's use of chemicals to get through life since she herself took multiple drugs every day and was therefore disinclined to enforce the drug-free policy that Gabriel tried to set.

"Would you like to return this call?" the AHS asked, interrupting his reverie.

Gabriel shook his head. "No, it's still too late. Next message."

"Message four."

"Eleven oh-seven p.m. 'Are you *still* not home? I'm so glad we're not married anymore! I'm going to bed. Call me! I'm leaving tomorrow afternoon.'" Gabriel saw Jacquie popping some sleeping pills into her mouth before she disconnected.

I'm really glad we're not married anymore either. He sighed and clenched his fists. Going away again—that's the fourth time this year and in the middle of the school year! As usual, Jacquie never lets trivial things like school schedules interfere with her travel plans. She never takes them along anyway. At least the kids have Marta. She was the very capable and nurturing live-in nanny in her late fifties who had been with them ever since the divorce. Jacquie had wasted no time becoming Mrs. Edward Monroe; her lavish, high-society second wedding took place only a week after her divorce was finalized.

Jacquie was awarded primary custody of the children, as she'd had the best lawyers her future husband's money could buy. Gabriel's policeman's salary might have been able to afford a public defender if this had been a criminal case. Instead, he got Aaron Feinstein, a sometimes shady but occasionally brilliant lawyer who had been a good friend of Jon Frieze, Gabriel's murdered mentor. Unfortunately, Gabriel had not been the beneficiary of one of Feinstein's brilliant moments in the custody battle. Though, truth be told, with his work schedule, Gabriel really was not able to care for two children on his own and couldn't afford paid help.

"Would you like to return this call?" the AHS asked.

"Still, no." Gabriel rolled his eyes even as he savored the last delicious morsel. "Thanks for a great dinner, Robert. You can shut down after cleaning up."

"Yes, sir."

"Message five. Eleven-thirty-nine p.m. A disconnected call. It originated from the residence of Dr. Edward Monroe," continued the AHS. "Would you like to return this call?"

Gabriel sighed and shook his head. "No, it's still too late to call anybody."

"Messages complete."

"Thanks." Gabriel snickered. "Go to stand-by."

"Yes, Gabriel," replied the sexy voice of the AHS, completely missing his sarcasm. He wondered if he should pick a more intelligent-sounding voice. Then again, the current AHS setting was essentially the only regular adult female company in his non-existent private life.

"On the other hand, display the bio for Dr. James Edward Patton of Titan Robotics."

The information appeared on the floor-to-ceiling screen in the living room. He walked into his bedroom, where another screen, its sensors picking up his presence, activated and displayed the same data. The AHS had a text-to-speech capability, but he liked to read things himself. He liked pondering between sentences or paragraphs and let the information sink into his eidetic memory.

Gabriel placed the sonic hydrobrush in his mouth to clean his teeth for the requisite five seconds and then spit out the small amount of cleaning fluid into the bathroom sink. He resumed reading.

Patton was an only child whose parents died in an accident shortly after he started college at the age of twelve. He attended MIT for both his undergraduate degree and all three PhDs. During that time, he published over a dozen landmark papers in major journals.

"Display bio for Linda Elaine Farmer Patton." Her biography was fairly unremarkable relative to her husband's. Born in 1994 to a very wealthy, upper crust family in Minnesota. Graduated from Yale with a B.A. in Classical Literature. Attended Harvard for a master's program but never completed because she met and married James Patton in a whirlwind eight-week romance in 2016. Gave birth to their only child Brandi in 2017. Went to China with husband for two years while he pursued post-graduate research in Robotics. Brandi lived with maternal grandparents for two years from 2024-2025. Moved into present Patton estate in Bel Air in 2026. Killed in a hit and run accident in 2058.

Gabriel's eyes returned to the fact that Brandi lived with her maternal grandparents for a couple of years. Come to think of it, in the pictures displayed on the digital photo frame in Patton's bedroom which seemed to encompass Brandi's childhood, there are no pictures of Brandi with her parents—no, just not her mother—when she was around seven to eight years old. There's a picture of Brandi with her father playing in deep snow around that time with a huge brick mansion decorated in Christmas lights in the background—obviously not L.A., so it must have been taken in Minnesota at her maternal grandparents' house. There are several pictures of Brandi around that time with an older couple in different seasons; that must have been when she lived with her grandparents.

"Show me the house that Linda Patton grew up in." It took a few seconds as the AHS searched the OmniNet for the address and then retrieved satellite photos of the property—a huge estate with a large brick mansion identical to the one in the picture but without Christmas lights. Why would a loving, adoring mother send her child away for two years? Maybe she was unable to care of her?

"Find any information about Linda Patton in 2024 and 2025. Access medical records as well." Results from the health information database, accessible only to law enforcement agencies and medical personnel, appeared on the screen after a few moments. Gabriel sat on his bed. She had leukemia diagnosed in early 2024. Received intensive, experimental treatment at a private clinic in Germany for two years.

Gabriel instructed the AHS, "Show me the history of James Patton with Titan Corporation." James Patton had sold most of his Founder's shares of Titan in spring of 2024 to his partner, Edgar Carmichael. Patton must have used the proceeds to pay off what was sure to have been astronomical medical bills. Early the following year, in 2025, Titan received its first major contract from the Department of Defense. Years later, Carmichael made billions and eventually trillions with his shares of company stock based on multiple military contracts as well as global sales of industrial, commercial and residential robots. Patton lost out on his fifty percent share of trillions.

"Screen off," he commanded, satisfied at finding Patton's possible motive for revenge on the Carmichael family. He lay down to sleep. The AHS dimmed the lights automatically. He glanced at the time on his comms—past three in the morning. Damn, gotta get up in four hours! Exhausted, he drifted off, dreaming of what eight—no, six—hours of sleep might feel like.

CHAPTER 9

Wednesday Morning

Gabriel woke up to the annoying siren of the Automated Home System's morning alarm. There were less irritating sound effects, but he figured he would sleep through those, so he chose the most aggravating sound. He took a deep breath and groaned and stretched. It can't possibly be seven already!

The AHS sensed he was awake and turned on to the NPR broadcast.

"The CDC reports the number of dengue fever cases this year so far has risen to 33,264 and has been found throughout the continental United States—"

Oh, great! More happy news. Bleary-eyed, he stumbled to the bathroom into the small shower stall. He turned on the sonic mist, which jetted out from multiple nozzles all around the shower. After shampooing and turning on the overhead nozzle to rinse off, he decided to keep the high-flow mode going for another minute to help himself wake up.

"At this rate, Gabriel, you will exceed your monthly water ration in fifteen seconds," the AHS purred at him.

"Aww, shit!" Only the very wealthy could afford the exorbitant surcharges of excessive water use from old-fashioned showerheads or Jacuzzis. But Gabriel was only a civil servant. He reluctantly turned off the shower.

Listening to NPR and checking the time as he approached Beck Tower, he knew his ex-wife was not awake yet, so he postponed returning her call for a few more minutes. Gabriel hoped that Irene was not around yet. He didn't need an audience for what was likely to be a contentious and uncomfortable conversation. However, he saw her shiny, new Quetzel as he parked his Raptor and sighed.

As he entered the office, Irene glanced up at him briefly and muttered, "Good morning" before her attention focused back on the project on her screen. He placed his hand over the biometric sensor on his desk to turn the unit on, and the large, paper-thin translucent screen scrolled up out of its slot in the desk. Sighing heavily, he instructed the videocomms to connect to the Monroe residence while he slipped on and activated the visor to keep the conversation relatively private.

Marta, the housekeeper and nanny for more than a decade, answered the house videocomms. She smiled with recognition at Gabriel. He knew she would have just returned from dropping the kids off at their respective schools.

"Hola, Mr. Gabriel," she greeted him in a cheerful voice.

"Hola, Marta," he returned the greeting. "Como estas?"

"Bien. Y usted?"

"Bien, bien. How are Julio and Juanita?"

"They good. Juanita looking for homecoming dress. Julio still love job at Mr. Giotta office. He thank you."

"Bueno. Is Jacquie there?"

"Mrs. Monroe—I think she awake now. I get her for you."

He hoped his ex had taken her Wakers. She tended to be especially unpleasant to him when tired or half-sleep and in between pills.

His ex-wife appeared on the screen—a stunning blonde with perfect facial features, even without makeup. She was barely dressed in a cream-colored, lacy, diaphanous nightgown, which was unbuttoned and flaunted much of her surgically-enhanced attributes all the way down to the hairless triangle between her legs. Once that view would have enthralled him. Now, he just wondered whether she answered all videocomms calls virtually naked.

"Well, finally! It's about time! Don't you care about your children at all?"

He resisted the overwhelming urge to yell back at her. Instead, he took a deep breath and counted to ten before replying. "I was working late last night. Good morning to you, too. What's the problem?"

"That daughter of yours is going to be the death of me yet! She was out until midnight the night before—on a school night! She was with that no-good, loser boyfriend of hers—Charlie What's-his-name! You have to

Chapter 9   **61**

talk to her! I know they were doing more than just kissing, which is what she said they were only doing. You know what can happen when kids are having sex!" She was obviously referring to their shared past.

"Have you talked to her about protection?"

"No, of course not! She's not even supposed to be doing that at her age!"

Determined to avoid an embarrassing, drama-filled confrontation at work, Gabriel swallowed the almost irresistible temptation to remind Jacquie that she lost her virginity at fourteen, three years younger than Gabby was now. She was very sexually active and not particularly faithful, neither before nor after their wedding. "I'll have a talk with her when she gets home today," he promised.

"Good. I'm leaving for Monte Carlo this afternoon."

Gabriel gritted his teeth. "Why do you need to go again in the middle of the school year?"

"I'm meeting friends there, and this is the only time they could go. The kids will be fine. Marta will be here."

He clenched his jaw and forced a casual tone. "When are you getting back from Monaco?"

"I don't know—maybe a month or two. Edward is coming with me for a week."

His blood boiled at the thought of her leaving their children again for that long—during the school year no less. Sadly, they were used to it by now. Marta was almost more like their mother than their own mother. How he wished he could care for them full-time.

Gabriel forced a "Have a great trip" through stiff lips.

"Thanks," she replied. She got up and took off her nightgown directly in front of the camera, so he received an eyeful of her nude, leggy, voluptuous figure before she walked to the videocomms and leaned over to turn it off, her large breasts filling the screen before the visor went dark. He gave a tired sigh, yanked off the visor, covered his eyes with his hand and shook his head slowly. What he really needed was a primal scream.

Irene looked at him across the desk. "The ex?" she asked.

He nodded.

"Sorry I wasn't quite awake when you came in. The Wakers hadn't kicked in yet. I was updating the vic list."

He nodded again. Personally, he refused to take Sleepers or Wakers ever again—not since his brother's accident.

"All the bodies were finally ID'd." She transmitted the list to his monitor and comms. He studied the list. "No hits on NCIC—or CODIS for those we could get DNA," she added, referring to the federal law enforcement databases, National Crime Information Center and Combined DNA Information System.

He looked at the time. "Let's go have a chat with that preacher from the New Light Church before the DNS arrive and take this off our hands."

"Reverend Light is the senior preacher at that church," she said but looked at Gabriel as if wondering why he was looking for other suspects when Patton seemed the obvious perpetrator.

Gabriel acknowledged her skeptical gaze. "Call it gut instinct, but I don't think this is all it appears to be."

"Gut instinct?"

He nodded. "Just humor me, okay?"

Irene regarded him for a moment and nodded.

Artie Fitzsimmons poked his head into their office.

"Shit, the feds are already trying to take over. They're in with the Captain right now," Fitz said, referring to the Department of National Security agents.

"The bombing or Patton's death?" Gabriel asked.

"Both."

"You get anything from that gangbanger?"

Fitz shook his head. "Don't think the gang had anything to do with the café."

Gabriel looked at his partner. "We'd better get to the Church before we get called off."

Irene followed her partner to the Raptor, deftly skirting past the Captain's office while the latter was absorbed with the DNS agents and didn't see them. They heard muffled shouting coming out of the office.

It was a quick trip to the New Light Church, a shining, white marble building located in Culver City where an International Spiritual Center had once stood until The Big One leveled it and many buildings in L.A. ten years ago. The congregation had been very generous to their church. The ongoing water shortage and higher temperatures in the entire Southwest necessitated xeriscape landscaping. In front of the two-story high, dark wooden, double doors stood a large, black marble sculpture of a preacher in robes with his arms outstretched looking up to the sky.

"Who's that?" Gabriel asked.

Irene shrugged. "Probably some New Age preacher quack."

Gabriel eyed his partner.

They used the heavy, brass doorknocker and heard it echo inside the church. They glanced around the entrance, noting a small, discreet camera. No one responded. Gabriel pushed open the door, admiring the pivoting mechanism that made it so easy to open. Inside were rows of faux wood grain pews that led to a grand apse in the front. The space was light and airy and colorful with sunlight streaming down through the large stained-glass windows. He noticed they depicted scenes from various religions.

"May I help you?" a lilting voice asked from behind. The beautiful, brown-skinned young lady appeared out of nowhere. Over her left shoulder, Gabriel saw a hallway behind her.

Gabriel introduced himself and his partner. "Who's in charge here?" he asked.

"Reverend Light," she said.

"We need to see him."

"Yes, of course. Is there some problem?" Her dark, doe eyes widened.

"We just want to ask him some questions about a case we're working on."

She nodded. "Follow me." She turned back toward the brightly lit hallway from which she had appeared. They turned the corner and stopped just outside a closed wooden door. "I'll tell him you're here, Detectives Furst and Bolton." She entered, shutting the door behind her. She returned less than a minute later, holding the door open for them.

They entered an office with two desks on either side of an interior door, which was blocked by two massive, scar-faced hulks. Ex-cons. Gabriel noticed the prison tats on the back of the hands. Each had a bulge underneath his black, leather jacket. They were the same men on the bank camera videos standing outside the café. They scrutinized Gabriel and Irene slowly up and down, eying the latter's holstered weapons. On one desk, Gabriel saw views of the front entrance and parking lot on a screen.

One of the behemoths held out his hand. "Weapons," he said in a cold, deep voice.

"We're LAPD," Gabriel said.

The big black man kept his hand out. "Policy," he said.

Gabriel and Irene looked at each other. "We're LAPD," Gabriel repeated firmly, calmly looking into the other man's eyes.

The two bodyguards looked at each other. The other bodyguard wordlessly reached under the desk. Gabriel heard the loud click of the inner door unlocking. The first bodyguard stepped aside to allow the detectives past, shutting the door behind the visitors.

A bald, black man in his sixties, dressed in a light gray suit, greeted them with a welcoming smile and open arms. "Welcome! Welcome!" Both detectives were enveloped by warm bear hugs. "I am Edward Light, pastor of this great church," he said in a rich, warm baritone. He invited them to sit down in the big, plush chairs facing his desk. He sat down behind his mahogany desk.

Gabriel introduced himself and his partner.

"What can I do for you, detectives?"

Gabriel noticed the Bible on the bookshelf behind the Reverend, along with other religious texts, the Koran, Tao de Ching and Bhagavad Gita among them. "We're here about a parishioner called James Patton. You know him?"

He visibly tensed at the mention of Patton's name. "Of course. I know all my congregation. He's been coming here the past several months and helping us out."

"When was the last time you saw him?"

"Yesterday. We met at a coffee shop downtown—the Rialto Café—the one that was bombed."

Gabriel nodded.

"Is James all right? Was he in the bombing?"

"He was not hurt in the bombing."

The Reverend looked relieved. "So, what do you want to know about him?"

"What did he do for your church?" asked Gabriel.

"He's been helping us with the computers. An associate pastor embezzled some of our funds and messed with the accounting on the computers. James is trying to help us sort it all out. Why do you ask?"

"What time did you leave the cafe?"

"About three or a little after that."

"Do you know why Dr. Patton stayed? Was he meeting someone?" Gabriel asked.

Chapter 9

Reverend Light's face became carefully neutral. He paused, fiddling with a marble on his desk before replying, "I'm not sure."

"Why were you meeting with him?"

"We talked and I returned a pen to him. He's always misplacing them."

"What did you talk with him about yesterday?"

Reverend Light looked down, straightening items on his desk. "Oh, just things about family and work. He's been under a lot of stress lately." He looked back up at them. "You know, the usual things."

"Anything in particular?" Gabriel asked.

There was a pause. "Work, in particular, I guess. He's on a project that's causing him a lot of stress."

"Do you know what it's about?"

The Reverend was quiet. "Although I'm not a Catholic priest, we still honor the sanctity of a confession. You have to ask him yourself."

"We'd like to, but last night he shot himself," Irene said.

"What?" The Reverend paled beneath his dark skin as he sank further into his plush, winged chair. He closed his eyes for a moment and then opened them, looking at the detectives. "That's not possible."

"What do you mean?" Gabriel asked.

"When we spoke yesterday, he was looking forward to spending the weekend with his daughter and grandchildren. It's just not possible that he killed himself."

"Do you think he could have caused the explosion at the café?"

"Absolutely not! He is—he was—a man of peace and just found himself spiritually in the last few months, you could say. He could never take someone else's life—intentionally, that is."

"Intentionally? Do you mean he may have been capable of doing it unintentionally?"

The Reverend searched for his answer. "No, no. What I mean is that in his present spiritual state—before he died, I mean—he could never take another's life, directly or indirectly."

Gabriel continued. "Do you know of anyone who might want to hurt him?"

Reverend Light was quiet. "I can't say." He looked at Gabriel with a solemn expression. "I've probably already said too much. I'm truly sorry I can't help you more." He stood up to his full six-foot plus height, indicating the interview was over. The detectives stood up and shook his hand.

"Thank you for your help. By the way, who's the statue of in the front?" Gabriel asked.

"Ah," the Reverend said, his face beaming. "My mentor—Dr. Michael, the great visionary and founder of the church on whose grounds we stand. The original church was destroyed during The Big One, but we built it again—even bigger and better than before."

Gabriel nodded. "By the way, what color was the pen you gave back to him?"

"It was gold. He usually had either silver or gold pens. He was running low on them, you know. They don't make those anymore, so he liked to get them back."

"I see." He paused. A gold pen had been found on Patton's body, which had no trace of explosives. But he had to ask, "Do you or either of your bodyguards have any training in explosives?"

The Reverend shook his head. "No. You don't think we had anything to do with the bombing, do you?"

"We think the explosive was in one of Patton's pens."

Gazing steadily at him, the Reverend said, "Then you need to test us for explosives residue?"

"Yes. You and your bodyguards." He hoped the Reverend wouldn't assume it was just because of his and his men's skin color. "To eliminate you all as suspects."

Reverend Light's lips narrowed, as if undecided whether to be offended. After a moment, he said, "All right. We have nothing to hide." He held his hands out for Gabriel to swab. "Darlene will show you out after you finish testing my men."

The door opened as if on cue, and the young woman they met earlier appeared. The guards looked angry and offended to be bombing suspects but quietly cooperated after a gentle word from the Reverend.

After they finished, Darlene led them through the hallway to the front door. "Reverend Light is a great and wonderful man. He adopted me after I lost my parents in The Big One. Because of him, I get to try out for the Olympics next year. He worked day and night for six years to get the funding to rebuild this church. It was finally completed just two years ago. It's a shame they're trying to bring him down now."

"You think someone is out to get the Reverend? Why?" Gabriel asked.

Chapter 9

"He gives us hope and shows us the true meaning of freedom. They don't like that."

"Who doesn't like that?" Irene asked.

"The government, of course. They're the ones behind the audit."

Only Gabriel could see Irene roll her eyes as they followed behind Darlene.

"Why does he have bodyguards?" Gabriel asked.

"They've been with him for years. He goes into some areas that are not always so safe—you know, behind the walls. He holds sermons in some of the NMLs since they can't come to him. Today, he'll be going to NML-Watts."

"He mentioned someone had stolen some funds?"

"Yes, Reverend John Burke. He was the assistant pastor here for a few months, and he disappeared afterwards and left a huge mess in the accounting data. That's what Dr. Patton is helping us with."

"How did the Church find Dr. Patton?"

"One of the other parishioners works with him and recommended him to help us. He came to work on the computers but later joined our Church. The Reverend can be very persuasive." She smiled.

"Yes, I see." Gabriel smiled back. "Thank you. Do you remember the name of the person who referred Dr. Patton to the Church?"

"Yes, of course. Chuck Coffer—he's been coming here for several years."

Gabriel and Irene thanked their guide, exited the large double doors and headed toward the Raptor.

"Do you think she's paranoid or what?" Irene asked, rolling her eyes.

Gabriel grunted in reply, deep in thought.

"His bodyguards look more like ex-cons. I just FACE'd them. Here, let's see . . ." Irene looked at her comms running the Facial Analysis, Comparison and Evaluation system, used by law enforcement agencies. "One did a nickel for burglary—got out five years ago. No arrests since then. The other looks like he was a juvie—several arrests for drugs, robbery, then did a dime in the pen for armed assault. This supposed holy man surrounds himself with such nice guys."

"How about the Reverend himself?"

Irene consulted her comms. "Nothing criminal. Wanna bet he's just a master con artist, getting all that money from his followers. Do you know how expensive all that marble and real wooden doors are?"

Gabriel nodded and looked at his partner. "Not very spiritual, are you?"

"I go to church every Sunday!" she replied with indignantion.

"And your preacher doesn't ask for money from your congregation?"

"That's different! We would never have something so—so —so ostentatious!"

Gabriel eyed his partner with a skeptical brow and then asked, "Does the Reverend or his bodyguards have any military training?"

The general biographies available to the public on the OmniNet did not include details on military service. That information was restricted to law enforcement over a secure network to Department of National Security servers. More sensitive information for DNS intelligence and law enforcement agents and certain military records were often classified Top Secret, not readily available even to local or state law enforcement agencies.

"Looking for training in explosives?" Irene asked.

"Yeah."

Irene took a few minutes to check. "The Reverend was a Marine chaplain for two years, and one of his guards was in the Marines—same unit as the chaplain."

"What was the guard's rank in the Marines?"

"He was just a grunt."

"So, not a sergeant or above?"

"Yeah, why?"

"In the Corps, only sergeants and above get to handle explosives."

"Oh, how do you know that? Were you in the Corps?"

Gabriel shook his head. "No, I went to college." All men and women who turned eighteen in the past twenty years were eligible for the draft. Most draftees from wealthier families avoided military service with medical exemptions or college or graduate school attendance. "How did the other guard not get drafted?"

"He was already a guest of the state at Corcoran for burglary."

"Did he come into contact with any inmates there with bomb-making skills?"

"I'll check." After several minutes and an extensive search on the OmniNet in the California Department of Corrections records, Irene said, "Not that I can tell. There were bomb-makers at Corcoran at the same time, but they were always housed in different wings. The records don't indicate he met any of them."

Gabriel's comms vibrated softly. There was a message to go to the Captain's office.

On their way back to Beck Tower, Gabriel asked, "What do you think about Patton's death?"

"It looks pretty clear-cut to me despite what Reverend Light thinks. There's a suicide note, and no one else was inside the house."

"A suicide note on a monitor. Anybody could have written it."

"But no other fingerprints were on the keyboard," Irene pointed out.

"They could have worn gloves or forced Patton to type it."

Irene shrugged. "Nothing we can take to the DA."

Gabriel was quiet for a few moments. "Or he may have been the target of the explosion, not the instigator."

Irene looked at him speculatively. "How's that?"

"Why stay in the café, even the bathroom, and risk getting killed if he planted the bomb in the first place? And if he were trying to kill himself with the bomb, why go into the restroom?"

"What about the pen in the drawer in his garage with explosives residue and all the chemicals we found to make a bomb?"

"The workbench was completely cluttered and dusty. Nothing's been moved for a while. No self-respecting bomb maker would make an explosive device in all that mess. You'd blow yourself up. And there were no measuring utensils or mixing containers."

"But his fingerprints were on that pen."

"He only used pencils in the notebooks found in the garage. That pen could have been his. According to the Reverend, he loses them frequently. So it could have been planted to frame him," Gabriel theorized.

Irene looked doubtful.

"Someone tried to kill him twice in one day and succeeded the second time. There may be something going on at his job that has him stressed—that's worth getting killed for. Just bear with me a couple more days, all right?"

Irene paused, looked at her partner and then nodded slowly.

CHAPTER 10

Wednesday Late Morning

The new Captain of Robbery-Homicide, Ken Yokino, was an Asian-American in his early fifties. He had a reputation for being a stickler for the rules, which made Gabriel a little apprehensive since he didn't always color inside the lines. But Yokino was also known for not playing the usual political games that helped promote those who were less qualified. He was highly respected by Robbery Special where he was a lieutenant prior to his well-deserved promotion to Captain of RHD.

As they entered Captain Yokino's office, Gabriel saw the usually amiable Lieutenant Corwin glaring at two well-dressed federal agents standing around the Captain's desk. The older agent looked at them with a cold, humorless expression beneath his receding gray hairline. The smiling younger man was blond, handsome and probably in his early-thirties. His dark blue suit clung to his athletic frame.

Captain Yokino introduced them. "Detectives, these are Special Agents Steve Harmon and Sam Weston from the DNS," he said, indicating the older man and then the younger. "Detectives Irene Bolton and Gabriel Furst."

They shook hands and exchanged contact info via their comms, per protocol. Gabriel noted they were from the Anti-Terrorism Division of the Department of National Security.

Yokino addressed his detectives, "The DNS is taking over the case at the Rialto Café. Turn over any evidence you have, and give them your full cooperation. Fitz has already transferred the case file, but they still need to go to Evidence and FSD to pick up the physical evidence."

"We want it all," Steve Harmon, the older agent, demanded.

Gabriel could feel his blood pressure rising.

"Of course," Irene said. "Let's go to our office and review what we have so far."

"Lead the way," the younger agent said warmly to Irene, eyeing her up and down.

"If you don't mind, Special Agents, I'd like to speak with my detectives alone for a moment," the Captain said.

The DNS agents nodded and stepped out of the office. The heavy duraglass door closed softly behind them.

"So, was Patton's death a suicide?" Yokino asked in a low voice.

"It appears that way, but there are several inconsistencies I'd like to clear up, sir," Gabriel replied.

"Bolton?" Yokino asked.

Irene glanced at her partner and bit her lip before nodding.

Yokino looked at the two detectives and then at Lieutenant Corwin, who worked in Homicide Special for the past few years. Corwin nodded. The Captain said, "All right. The café bombing is theirs—unfortunately. But the death of the prime suspect is in our jurisdiction and still our case for now. Close it—quickly—before these assholes find an excuse to take that away from us, too."

Gabriel looked at his new captain with new found appreciation. He might end up liking him after all.

Gabriel and Irene nodded and filed out into the hallway where the DNS Special Agents waited for them. Together, they headed to their office where Irene reviewed the Rialto Café case with the Agents. It seemed to Gabriel they barely listened or looked at the evidence. On a hunch, he glanced down at their shoes.

Harmon said, "Since Patton is our main suspect, his death is ours, too."

Gabriel replied firmly, "No, you've already discussed this with our captain."

"It makes more sense—"

"It's in our jurisdiction."

"If he's the bomber, then his death is in our purview," Harmon insisted. "Why waste your time with a suicide? I'm sure you've got more important things to do."

"For. The. Last. Time. No," Gabriel said, enunciating every syllable,

Project A

looking Agent Harmon in the eyes.

The older man opened his mouth to speak again, but Gabriel shook his head, his eyes narrowed and his jaw set. The DNS agent backed off.

Irene looked at her partner and at the older Special Agent and then offered to go to Evidence and the FSD with the DNS agents, leaving her grateful partner behind. He worked with agents from the DNS before, of course, and liked very few of them—okay, none that he could recall. Usually, they were arrogant with very little respect for local law enforcement. Their idea of mutual cooperation usually meant a one-way flow of information. He really missed the FBI.

Irene returned about an hour later, humming softly.

Gabriel looked at her with a raised brow and then asked, "How about a field trip to Titan Robotics for a chat with Gerry Carmichael?"

"Sure," she said eagerly.

Titan Robotics occupied nine square city blocks southeast of downtown L.A. The massive building gleamed like a golden pyramid. It even had an internal, enclosed parking structure not found in most post-recovery buildings.

The Raptor hovered outside the massive main gate, level with the base of the giant, black "T" embossed on the massive, golden, sliding doors. The two security guards, in an enclosed duraglass booth, verified their credentials. The three-foot thick doors silently glided open and closed behind the Raptor. Gabriel parked in a space designated for visitors. Beyond the visitor parking, he saw another closed, large metal door that was labeled "Employees Only" in red.

An attractive woman wearing a navy blue business skirt suit and five-inch heels approached them as they stepped out of the car. "Welcome, Detective Furst and Detective Bolton. I am Roberta, and I will be your guide today. Please follow me," she said in a warm, welcoming voice.

He did a double-take when he realized she was a droid—the most human-like gynoid he'd ever seen. She walked with a slight swing of her hips, like a real woman. Her smooth, lilting voice was amazingly life-like. Her wavy, blonde hair bounced naturally with each step. He realized that she actually had real hair. Following behind Roberta, Gabriel looked at his partner in wonder. She gaped back at him, equally wide-eyed.

Roberta told them they were expected at the Director's Office. Somebody at Titan anticipated their visit to the CEO, Gerald Carmichael.

"Please have a seat," Roberta said as they stepped into a golden elevator. Padded, gold damask-covered benches lined the golden walls. There were gold, overhead hand holds. It was like a lavish subway car completely gilded with gold. Noiselessly, the elevator first took them horizontally, deeper into the building, and then straight up for what seemed an eternity. It finally glided to a gentle stop.

They arrived at an outer office where the executive assistant usually sat. The chair behind the large metal desk was empty. Beyond the secretary's desk was another, even more luxurious, golden elevator. They took the brief ride up one floor. The doors opened up into a spacious executive office with a panoramic view of L.A. through the gold-tinted duraglass windows that formed the peak of the pyramid. The two detectives stepped out, looking around, a little in awe.

The Pacific Ocean filled up the west-facing windows. Orange County and parts of San Diego County were visible to the south through the haze. A colossal, wall-size, drop-down screen blocked the eastern view. Mostly of NMLs anyway, Gabriel smirked to himself. Overhead, clouds wafted gently in the gold-tinged, blue sky. The afternoon sun gave the room a warm, golden glow, but the special insulated duraglass, similar to those installed in all police cars, prevented it from getting hot.

"Beautiful, isn't it? I love the L.A. skyline at this time of day," came a voice behind them. They turned to see the famous, handsome, blond man in his early forties. He wore an expensive, dark gray, silk suit. "Gerry Carmichael." He firmly shook their hands as they introduced themselves. "You're here because of Jim's untimely death—poor man. Please, have a seat." He indicated the lush, gold-trimmed, upholstered chairs opposite his expansive, mahogany desk.

Real mahogany, I bet. Gabriel inwardly drooled. Real wood was scarce and ultra-expensive these days.

Behind Carmichael, the detectives saw the gray haze emanating from the fires in Ventura County, fanned by the annual Santa Ana winds.

They all sat except for Roberta, who stood beside Carmichael's desk facing the detectives.

Gerry asked. "Would you like some coffee? We have espressos and lattes as well."

"A latte, please," Irene replied.

"Coffee—black," Gabriel said.

"Roberta, two lattes and a black coffee," Carmichael ordered.

With a serene smile, Roberta walked over to the espresso machine near the elevator.

"Now, how may I help you?" Gerry Carmichael asked.

"We would like to ask you a few questions and look at where Dr. Patton worked," Gabriel replied.

"Of course. However, his work area is rather sensitive, as I am sure you understand. You will need to clear everything with Roberta before you open anything or look at anything."

"Will we need a search warrant?"

"I am sure you can get one, but you know as well as I do that it will be limited under my terms anyway." He smirked as he brushed his forelock back with his right hand.

Gabriel understood and nodded, gritting his teeth. This man was powerful enough to dictate the limits of a search warrant. Although the court weighed heavily toward law enforcement after The Day, somehow powerful business interests still managed to get their way.

"Titan's legal department needs you to sign a Non-Disclosure Agreement since everything is proprietary information."

"Of course," Gabriel said.

Gerry tapped a few buttons on the comms and retrieved the NDA, which was delivered to the detectives' comms.

Gabriel e-signed his NDA and saw his partner do the same.

Roberta returned with a tray with two gold demitasses and a gold mug, all emblazoned with a large, black "T."

Carmichael sipped on his latte with an extra thick layer of whipped cream on top. "Ah," he sighed. "There is nothing like the real thing. None of that synthesized stuff!"

Gabriel tasted his drink, savoring the rare and rich flavor of coffee beans. Real coffee beans were a scarce and very expensive luxury. Only a few protected coffee plantations had access to the nearly extinct domesticated bees. Most high-end coffee shops, like the Rialto, used a mix of real beans and synthetic coffee. The chain shops used mostly artificial coffee. Carmichael's was made from pure coffee beans.

"This has real cream, too. Nothing beats lattes with cream!"

Irene nodded enthusiastically as she sipped her latte.

"Now, where were we?" the CEO asked.

"When was the last time you saw or spoke with Dr. Patton?" Gabriel asked.

"Last week—here at work."

"You didn't meet with him two days ago at the Rialto Café?" Gabriel asked.

"No, as I said, I was here on Monday until about seven p.m. I heard about poor Jim on this morning's news," Gerry Carmichael said.

"What if we told you we have witnesses and video placing you at the scene?"

"You are very much mistaken. I was here."

"Was anyone else here with you?"

Carmichael hesitated for just a moment. "No, I was here alone. But everyone who comes in and out of Titan is registered in our security logs. You can check."

"We'll do that. Where did you go afterwards?" Gabriel asked.

"Home."

Irene asked, "Do you know what Dr. Patton was worried about the past few weeks?"

"Everyone here is stressed. We have deadlines. We are in a very competitive industry. But I know of nothing in particular at work that Jim would have been concerned about."

"He and your father started the business together?"

"Yes, but Jim sold most of his founder's share of the company to my father."

"Therefore, losing out on trillions," Irene said.

Carmichael nodded. "Although he still made billions from his remaining shares."

"Do you know why he sold his shares to your father?"

"Not really. He was more my father's friend. I was just a little kid at the time. But what does any of this have to do with his suicide? Why did he bomb the café?"

"What makes you think he caused the explosion?" Irene asked.

"That is what I heard on The News a few minutes ago."

"What?" Irene and Gabriel looked at each other. They turned over the case to the feds less than an hour ago.

"Watch." Using his comms on the left wrist, Carmichael retrieved the news video from the archives and displayed it on the large, ceiling-height screen.

"Breaking news! Authorities released more information about the explosion at the Rialto Café at First and Spring yesterday afternoon in downtown L.A. Thirteen people were killed, and two later died at University Hospital. The only survivor was Dr. James Patton, later found dead at his home along with a confession taking responsibility for bombing the Rialto Café.

"Dr. James Patton was the co-founder of Titan Robotics, along with Edgar Carmichael . . ." the reporter continued, but Gabriel stopped listening.

Two died at the hospital? Gabriel mentally reminded himself to check on that later. He asked Carmichael, "How do we get a hold of this security log?"

"I will have Roberta download it and transmit it to you before you leave."

Roberta gave them a serene smile.

"If there is nothing else—" Carmichael began.

"Would you show us his office, please?"

"Of course, Roberta will take you there. Remember, she needs to examine anything you want to touch. And, of course, you may not copy or remove anything—since everything is proprietary information."

Gabriel nodded.

"Oh, and Detectives, if you would like to upgrade your domestibots to our newer models, I can arrange it for you—on the house for you fine public servants. Or, of course, if you prefer, there is our brand-new model—the Pleasurebots 6. They are our most life-like models yet. Roberta is our prototype. And we have a male line also." He directed the latter comment to Irene, who stiffened.

Pleasurebots were intended for sexual gratification and had been nicknamed "sexbots" by the public. Reputedly, the latest models were very realistic in their presentation and performance with adjustable volume controls. In fact, some up-scale escort services were already using them since they were legal and much easier to disinfect and reprogram, therefore perceived as safer. One of the detectives from Vice told Gabriel that some customers couldn't even tell the difference. Gabriel was skeptical until he met Roberta today.

Resisting the urge to punch the robotics tycoon, he declined his host's generous offer in a gruff voice and followed Roberta to the elevator. The elevator doors opened, and a man in a white lab coat stepped out, holding a Titan demitasse in his right hand, his sleeve barely covering his comms. His build and coloring were similar to his brother Gerry except for the disheveled hair with a left forelock, a mustache and an absent-minded air about him. One shirt collar peeked out from under a frayed, cream, cashmere sweater. Brushing a stray lock back with his other hand, he glanced intently at the detectives as he stepped aside to let them into the elevator, which retained the pungent aroma of his espresso.

"Ah, Harold, there you are . . ." Gabriel heard the elder brother say as the elevator doors silently closed.

They followed Roberta to a different part of the vast complex. The completely white hallways were disorienting as it was difficult to tell where the walls ended and the floors began. It looked so sterile that Gabriel was certain no speck of dust or bacteria would dare land on any surface anywhere in Titan. They walked past several identical frosted duraglass doors until they arrived at Patton's lab.

At the entrance was a three-part biometric security system—with retinal, facial recognition, and handprint scanners. Roberta bypassed it and activated the sliding, frosted duraglass door labeled in gold lettering, "Robotic Chip Design Laboratory—James Patton, Ph. D, Director." Inside the lab, several employees busily worked at their stations. Some glanced up when the detectives entered behind Roberta.

"These are Detectives Furst and Bolton from the LAPD here to investigate the unfortunate passing of Dr. Patton," Roberta announced in an eerily pleasant voice, reminding Gabriel of the Stepford wives. He noticed that she, like her boss, didn't use contractions, making her speech slightly stilted—or haughty. "Please give them your full cooperation."

The employees looked at Roberta, then at the detectives and nodded.

They first interviewed Andrea Lisle, an attractive, red-head in her mid to late twenties, who was Patton's primary research assistant. The young woman headed to an office in the back of the lab.

"This was Jim's office," she said. "You can do your interviews in here."

"Thank you," Gabriel said.

"I can't believe what happened to Dr. Patton," she said, wringing her hands.

"What did you hear?" Gabriel asked.

"That he set off the bomb at the café, and then he killed himself."

"Do you think that's what happened?"

She was quiet and looked down. "Of course. That's what they say happened."

Gabriel eyed her, suspecting she was being less than forthcoming. He went on, "Has there been anything unusual in his behavior recently?"

"No, not particularly. He was an absolute genius but always—you know—sort of odd."

"Was Patton supposed to meet anyone yesterday afternoon at the café?"

"Well, he was going to meet Gerry Carmichael."

"Did he?"

"Yes, as far as I know."

"Did Patton keep a calendar or notebook of some sort?"

"He was very absent-minded. He wrote everything down in one of those journals and stuffed everything inside. He didn't like using digital devices," she said with a smile that Gabriel noticed didn't reach her eyes. "He even used those old-fashioned lab notebooks to write his experiments down."

"Do you know where his journal might be?"

"He always kept it with him."

"Where are his notebooks on the experiments?"

"Oh, they're right here." She pointed toward a drawer in Patton's steel desk.

"May we see them?"

"Of course." Andrea unlocked and pulled open the drawer. She removed two thick notebooks to hand over to the detectives, but they were intercepted by Roberta. Andrea flushed but said nothing.

Roberta scanned through the pages before handing the notebook to the detectives. "These contain proprietary information covered by the NDA. You may read these here, but do not take them with you or make copies."

Gabriel handed them to Irene. He acknowledged her Human Digital Interface gave her a huge advantage here. She began scanning the pages quickly, much faster than he could possibly read.

"Are those all of them?" Gabriel asked.

"Yes, everything he's been working on in the past few years," Andrea replied.

"Do you think he planted the bomb?" Gabriel continued.

"Well, he must have, otherwise they wouldn't have said so on The

Chapter 10

News."

"Thank you, Miss Lisle. If you should think of anything else, please contact us." He beamed her their contact information. She nodded and exhaled deeply, seemingly relieved to be done. She left the office and sent in the next employee.

Many of the other employees echoed the same sentiments, except one, Charles Coffer, a balding man in his fifties.

"You've worked with Patton how long?" Gabriel asked.

"Since he came back from retirement. Brilliant man. Can't believe this happened."

"Have you noticed any change in his behavior lately?"

Without moving his head, Coffer's eyes darted in Roberta's direction. She was standing slightly behind and to Gabriel's right. He hesitated. "He seemed unhappy lately, like something was bothering him," he replied in a quiet voice. "But he never said what it was."

"You attend services at the New Light Church and recommended him to fix their computer system?"

He nodded.

"Do you believe he caused the explosion and then killed himself?"

Coffer was quiet. "That's what they're saying," he said, his eyes again glancing in Roberta's direction and then back at Gabriel.

Gabriel knew everything was being recorded by the gynoid and understood that Coffer didn't feel free to speak. He nodded. "Well, if you think of anything further, here's our contact info."

After Coffer's departure, Gabriel asked, "Roberta, may I look through the rest of Patton's desk?"

Roberta acquiesced. Gabriel rummaged through but didn't find an organizer or anything else of interest except more pens and pencils. He looked over the shoulder of his partner, who was still perusing Patton's lab notebooks.

"Find anything?"

She looked at him and replied, "Not really," but her eyes belied her words. He understood. She said she needed a few more minutes to finish with the notebooks.

Once they were done, Roberta led them through the maze of Titan's hallways to their car in the visitor's lot.

"Here are the entry logs you requested," Roberta said as she beamed them to the detectives' comms.

"Thank you, Roberta," Gabriel said.

"Of course. It was my pleasure," replied Roberta with her Stepford smile as the door of their Raptor closed.

Gabriel maneuvered the car beyond the surveillance system of Titan's garage into the bright sunshine of the city, "What do you make of all that?"

"Obviously, everyone's been told what to say."

"You'd think Carmichael would've told Andrea to say that he cancelled the appointment with Patton."

Irene asked, "Does he really think he's going to get away with lying about not being at the café when there's video and eyewitness evidence?"

"You mean, there was an eyewitness until Laila died," Gabriel said.

"We still have the video."

"The DNS has the official video now."

"Let's find out what happened to Laila," Irene said. She called University Hospital and spoke to a nurse in the Observation Unit who informed her that Laila Harvey passed away last night, probably from an air embolism caused by the explosion.

Gabriel frowned.

"Why would Carmichael offer the logs as proof since he went to meet Patton?"

"He may've had them altered. So, what'd you find in the notebooks?" Gabriel asked.

"Well, most of the notes—and there're a lot of them—are about experiments done over two years ago. There were only about fifty pages on stuff he'd done in the last two years—after he came back from retirement. But it didn't really say anything."

Gabriel pondered that. "What has he been up to the past two years?"

As they headed toward the Medical Examiner's Office, Gabriel turned on some classical music—Rachmaninoff Piano Concerto Number Two, performed by Vladimir Ashkenazy with André Previn and the London Symphony.

Irene looked at him and didn't say anything, but he could tell she was sighing to herself.

CHAPTER 11

Wednesday Afternoon

The ME's office was never one of Gabriel's favorite places. Regardless of how much the air was filtered or how much air freshener or disinfectant was sprayed, he was always on the verge of throwing up. And, unfortunately, the putrid odor of rotting corpses stubbornly persisted in his nostrils for several hours despite his futile attempts to wash it out. Somehow, crime scenes never smelled as bad as the ME's office.

Dr. Cranston greeted Irene with a smile but barely acknowledged Gabriel's presence. The ME proceeded to do a seemingly cursory external examination of James Patton. Then the corpse was put into the Virtual Autopsy Scanner, which scanned the body using advanced CT imaging. They watched each millimeter-thick slice appear on the large quantum dot display as the VAS progressed down the body. The computer compiled the images into a highly detailed 3-D virtual rendition of Patton's corpse. The whole process took about half an hour. Then it analyzed the results and recommended areas that needed to have actual tissue samples taken. Many police officers and detectives, like Gabriel, considered the noninvasive VAS a faster and much less nauseating experience than the blood and gore of traditional autopsies that some medical examiners still preferred.

Cranston manipulated the composite image, zooming in on a few areas of interest, like the head. Gabriel saw the bullet's destructive path— starting behind the right ear, traversing through the center of the brain, scattering bone and bullet fragments along the way, before exiting out the left temple. Some pathologists liked to discuss and explain the details of the images, but Gabriel knew from past experience that Cranston wasn't one pf those, even when asked.

"Well," Cranston began. "It looks like suicide, cut and dried. The stellate contact wound behind his right ear is consistent with a close-contact and probably self-inflicted gunshot wound. No other signs of trauma. No need to do further tests on the body itself. Tox screen should be back in a couple of weeks."

"What about the GSR?" Gabriel asked.

"The scope confirmed no GSR on his hands, just like the field tests." Earlier that day, the forensics lab used the scanning electron microscope to confirm the absence of gunshot residue.

"Isn't that unusual for these types of guns?"

"GSR is negative in ten to twenty percent of suicides," the ME said and shrugged. "That's all, detectives."

Stalking away from the Autopsy rooms, Irene whispered, "Well, that was a total waste of time. Is it just me, or did it seem like he was just going through the motions? That was the most pitiful excuse for an autopsy I've ever seen, especially on such an important case! How does this guy stay an ME?"

"He's got better connections than his boss."

"Sort of makes you wonder whether somebody told him what to find."

"You're catching on," Gabriel said, nodding. "I've got to take care of something before we go."

She followed him to the office of the executive assistant for the Medical Examiner, who scheduled all the autopsies.

"Hi, Madge," he said in a cheerful voice. "How are you doing today?"

The older, no-nonsense woman glanced up. "Detective Furst," she acknowledged briefly and looked back down at her monitor.

"Would you please check and see when the autopsies will be done for some friends of mine?"

"Names?" she asked without looking up.

"Ahmed, Aahad and Adeline Haddad."

The harried assistant checked the schedule. "Three days at the earliest. Maybe a week or two."

"They're Muslim and need to be buried ASAP."

"We're really backed up—you know—it's L.A. Some others coming in have higher priority."

"I understand. It's really, really important. Would you please see if they can be moved up on the list?" he cajoled.

She was silent.

Then he remembered. "You like cabernets, right? I've got a bottle of Stag's Leap Cab that has your name on it if you can somehow manage to have it done sooner."

She eyed him. "You know I can't be bribed," the stern, gray-haired woman said, "but I'll see what I can do. It says here you'll be responsible for the disposition of their remains?"

"Yes."

"Then, I'll give you a call when they're ready."

"Thank you, Madge. I'll have that bottle of wine for you."

Gabriel thought he might have imagined a small, fleeting smile on her lips before her attention returned to her computer screen.

As Irene and Gabriel headed to the Raptor, Irene said, "That's pretty pricey. Good wine is so expensive these days."

"Yeah, but Islam requires Muslims to be buried as soon as possible."

"Buried? That's going to cost a small fortune for three spaces." Most people cremated their dead due to the paucity of available land for burials, but Islamic tradition forbade cremation.

"Yeah, I got a little saved up." He would have to stay in town for the next vacation or two, but the Haddads were Muslims. He would honor this last ritual out of respect and affection for his adopted family.

"You're a really good friend."

"You sound surprised."

She shook her head. "Didn't mean it like that."

"Loyalty is everything in friendships—and partnerships," he said.

She regarded him without speaking. She was probably wondering just how far he would go for his partners. Her father was in the Force Investigation Division years ago and investigated a case involving Gabriel and a fatal shootout.

A newly minted detective in Hollywood Division, Gabriel and his partner were investigating dealers of highly addictive, designer drugs sold to schoolchildren at a local community center. One suspect turned out to be the only son of a very wealthy and powerful L.A. businessman. The underage drug pusher and his fellow teenage entrepreneur pulled out illegal assault rifles when they saw the detectives pulling up to the boy's mansion. The driveway shootout ended before backup arrived with the teenage miscreants dead, both shot by Gabriel. His partner was severely injured and ended up on desk duty for the remainder of his LAPD career. Gabriel walked away unscathed but bore the brunt of the LAPD investigation and the wrath of the teenager's well-connected father. Irene's father, now the Deputy Chief of the department that included Internal Affairs, suspected Gabriel lied during the investigation. He wasn't wrong, but it wasn't to protect himself.

"So, where do we go from here?" Irene asked.

"We need to find that notebook. I think Patton had it with him at the hospital, but it disappeared sometime after that."

"If you're right and Patton was murdered, then maybe his killers got it."

"Yeah," he said, his lips tightening. He thought hard for a few moments. "Did our guys find Patton's vehicle yesterday?" he asked.

"No. I checked the evidence list before transferring all the info."

"What kind of car did he have?"

Irene checked the DMV records on the OmniNet. "A '51 gray Cadillac."

"Let's go find it. Hopefully, the feds haven't confiscated it already," Gabriel said. "Can you locate its GPS?" All modern vehicles were equipped with GPS tracking.

"Yeah, it'll take me a minute to get the code and access its position." She paused for a few moments. "Looks like it's still near the café."

They headed toward the remnants of the café. The immediate area was still cordoned off. Outside of the restricted area, it was packed with cars parked end to end and side to side. They located the Caddy three blocks away and set down the Raptor beside it. Gabriel deactivated the alarm and unlocked the door of the Cadillac with a unique access code. The car's on-board computer recorded his police ID number in case someone needed to find out who accessed the vehicle.

They searched the Caddy and its trunk but didn't find anything resembling Patton's journal, just a few bags and food wrappers from some fast food restaurants. They swabbed the passenger compartment and the trunk. FSD could test the swabs for explosives residue later even though LAPD was officially off the bombing case. They could still get unofficial field tests done on these and the ones they took of the men at the Church, which Gabriel hadn't turned over to the DNS agents. Oops, must have forgotten since those guys were such dicks.

Chapter 11

Irene scanned the car's GPS. "During the past two weeks, Patton drove home fourteen times, to Titan Robotics twenty times, an address on Figueroa Street ten times, his daughter's house once, the New Light Church twice, and a few different restaurants."

"Check out the Figueroa address. What is it?"

Irene consulted her comms. She looked up. "It doesn't say."

"I guess we'll have to go there and find out. Let's see what remote access codes he has." Gabriel's comms stored the three codes. "Well, probably one for his house—could've used that last night—and one for Titan. What's the other one for?"

"Maybe his daughter's or the mysterious place on Figueroa?"

Gabriel nodded. "I think you're right. Let's have this vehicle towed to FSD before the DNS gets their hands on it, and they can go over it more thoroughly."

Irene nodded and made the arrangements. They locked Patton's car and headed towards the mystery address on nearby Figueroa. There, they found a large, nondescript, windowless, concrete building with only a single entrance, a heavy, gray garage door. Gabriel tried the third of Patton's remote access codes first. The large parking garage door slid open silently. He had barely maneuvered the Raptor inside when klaxons went off.

"UNAUTHORIZED ENTRY! UNAUTHORIZED ENTRY," blared a deep electronic voice over the loudspeaker repeatedly as the Raptor set down on the concrete floor. Four gun-metal gray, robotic guards approached them with blaster rifles raised.

"You are not authorized to be here," one of the security bots informed him in its cold, electronic voice.

"We're from the LAPD. We're investigating the death of James Patton," Gabriel informed it. "We need to speak with someone in charge about him."

"Only pre-authorized visitors are allowed. You are not authorized to be here," the guard repeated, raising its weapon and aiming it at Gabriel. The other three guards also pointed their blaster rifles. "You must vacate the premises."

"All right, all right," Gabriel raised his hands, wondering what they were doing with blasters. "How do we get authorization?"

"You must vacate the premises," the first sec-bot repeated.

"We're leaving right now." Gabriel noted the logo on the inside wall—a black triangle with a red eye enclosed within. He carefully lowered his hands to the steering wheel, turned the Raptor around and headed toward the exit. His rear view mirror showed their egress being followed closely by four pairs of cold, red, laser eyes and the tips of their blasters.

"What do you think all that was about?" Irene asked after Gabriel eased the car into street traffic as the gray door closed behind them.

"And how'd they get blasters?" Gabriel asked.

His partner glanced at him. "Government?" Blasters were restricted to law enforcement, which included local police and sheriffs, as well as federal agents and the military in the Department of National Security. None appeared on the black market—yet.

"My guess is DNS."

"Let's head back to the station," Irene said.

"What? Got a hot date or something?" he asked.

She blushed.

"Who is it?"

"It's none of your business, Furst."

"Okay, okay." Gabriel grinned like the Cheshire cat.

"Just drive," she said. As he turned on his classical music, she asked, "Can we listen to something else?"

"What would you like?"

"Preferably not a dirge composed by someone who's been dead for centuries."

"OK. You choose something, and I'll see if I like it."

Irene requested a song from a modern electronica band.

Gabriel tried to tolerate it, but it was too noisy and gave him a headache. "No, sorry, can't do that." He turned it back to classical.

"Hey, when do I get to choose the music?"

He glanced at her. "When you get to drive."

"But you won't let me drive."

"Nope."

She let out a huffy breath, leaned back in her seat and crossed her arms with a frown.

CHAPTER 12

Wednesday Late Afternoon

At Beck Tower, Irene hurried to her car while Gabriel headed down to the Forensic Science Division to find Phil Zimburg, whom he knew would still be around after hours. Phil, like most tech wizards, lived, breathed and—many suspected—slept for his job in FSD. In all the years Gabriel had known him, the forensics whiz had never even mentioned going on a date, which would have been difficult anyway as he often didn't leave work until the early hours of the morning. As expected, he found Phil zooming in on a sample in the digital microscope displayed on a large monitor.

Phil looked up when he entered. "Hey, Mav, what's up?"

"I knew I'd find you here."

"My home. It really sucks those Do No Shitters took away everything," he fumed.

"Did you get anything back before they stole our case?"

"Very little. Just confirmed it was Semtex K."

"Could the Semtex be inside a pen?"

Phil looked thoughtful. "Yeah, that metal shard could've come from a pen. Now that you mention it, the pattern on the metal is a lot like the pen from Patton's garage, but we didn't get time to work on that before the DNS showed up." He frowned.

Gabriel nodded. Holding out the swabs from Patton's car and the men at the New Light Church, he asked, "Can you test these for explosives residue? Just a field test would be fine."

"So, no paper trail?" Phil asked.

Gabriel smiled and nodded.

Phil took the swabs, headed over to a different room, and pulled out the explosives detection field test kit from one of the cupboards. He rubbed each of the swabs onto explosives residue test strips, labeled the samples, and then scanned them with the hand-held detector.

"All negative," Phil said when he finished.

"That's what I thought. Thanks, buddy."

"Where were these from?"

"The case that we're not supposed to be on anymore: Patton's car and some men from Patton's church, who were at the café before it blew."

"Ah," Phil said.

"Get anything back from Patton's house?"

"Well, the DNS took the pen and all the chemicals from the garage, but we still have the evidence from the study. The aerial and touch DNA should be done in a couple of days at best—maybe longer, depending on how many cells we get and whether they'll need amplification. The other two shoeprints in Patton's study were an 11½ and a 12½. Smooth soles, so no good prints on that carpeting. I'm running the shoe microbial profiles and particulates right now, but we probably won't get a preliminary until the morning. We need to catch the suspects in the next few days before those microbial profiles change too much."

Gabriel nodded. "Yeah. You said the shoes were 11½ and 12½?"

"Yeah."

"Hmm. Patton's car, including the steering wheel and start button that you just tested, is negative for explosives." He paused, thinking. "He was found dead in the clothing he wore at the explosion. Can you test his clothes in his laundry hamper—what he was wearing before the day in the coffee shop—for explosives residue? If he made those explosive pens, then something he wore while making them should show residue."

"Unless he made those exploding pens right before work that day or long before, and his clothes had already been washed."

Gabriel nodded. "Yeah. But if he had made them right before going to work that day, where are all the measuring tools he would have needed? Would he have gotten rid of those but not the chemicals? Why are there no traces of explosives on his workbench or on the floor? And wouldn't there be residue on the steering wheel?"

Phil inclined his head. "Glad I'm just the forensics tech and not the detective."

They both laughed. Gabriel whistled as he left.

Back in the office, Gabriel remembered the promise he made to Jacquie about talking to their daughter. Shit! What do I know about talking to a teenaged girl about sex? He took several deep, calming breaths and called the Monroe residence on his comms. Gabby answered the house videocomms.

"Hi, Dad," she answered—her voice a little too cheerful, maybe trying to put him in a good mood?

"Hi, Gabs. How was your day?"

"Oh, the usual. How about you?"

Gabriel shrugged. "You know, the usual. People getting murdered."

"Hey, I heard the genius guy who blew up the Rialto killed himself, and the case is being handled by RHD. Are you on that one?"

He nodded.

"Cool. So, did he really do it?"

"You know I can't talk about active investigations."

"But how am I going to follow in your footsteps and become a police detective one day if you won't share these insights with me?" she cajoled.

Gabriel chuckled. "Nice try, Sweetie. We can talk about it after the case is closed, but in the meantime no insider info to share with your friends at school."

Gabby gave a loud sigh. "You're no fun at all, Dad."

"You'll have to find some other way to impress them."

She stuck her tongue out at him.

"Did your mother get off okay?"

"Yeah," she replied, her voice tinged with bitterness. "Doesn't she always?"

"I'm sorry, Gabs. I know you hate it when she leaves you for such a long time."

"Well, it's better this way. All we do is argue."

"How's school?"

"The usual. Easy."

"How's your brother?"

"The usual," she said, shrugging. "I know you want to ask me about Charlie. Mom told you, didn't she?"

Gabriel smiled despite himself. Kids were just too smart. "Yeah, she mentioned you were out really late on a school night. She was worried you were doing something you shouldn't with a boy with raging hormones. So," he mentally took a deep breath and asked in as casual a tone as he could manage, "were you having sex?"

His daughter looked down, studying her fingernails intently. The silence stretched. She'd know better than to try to lie to him since he was damned good at detecting lies, even better than the machines. After a full minute, she cleared her throat and replied in a small voice without looking up, "We're being careful."

Gabriel put on his best impassive, nonjudgmental parental face despite the urge to grab his shotgun and pay a not-so-friendly visit to the young man. "I'm sure you are. I'm supposed to tell you not to do it, okay?"

Gabrielle looked up and smiled. "Okay, you told me."

"You know you've got to use birth control. It's something that can screw up the rest of your life."

"I know, Dad," she said, and by the tone of her voice, probably rolling her eyes on the inside at him.

"You know you can come to me with anything, okay?"

"Yes, Dad. Love you!" she said.

"Love you, too, Gabs. No staying out past eleven on school nights, though, OK?"

She sighed. "Okay, Dad." He could tell she was hoping he had forgotten that point.

"Hey, is your brother home?"

"No, he's at Luke's. They're playing PUBG—again!" she replied, rolling her eyes. Gabriel had played Players Unknown Battleground on his gaming system with his friends when he was a kid. Now with the simulators, like the holodecks on *Star Trek*, his son roamed the virtual reality battlefield, trying to stay alive in the Playzone, shooting at the enemy, and hiding behind rocks and in bombed, damaged buildings that felt only too real.

"Tell him to give me a call, okay?"

"Yeah, right," Gabby said. Her brother Jonathan never picked up a videocomm if he could help it.

"Good night, Gabs. Love you."

"Good night, Dad. Love you, too."

They disconnected. Gabriel leaned back in his chair, buried his face in his hands and gave a loud groan of frustration. The thought of some boy,

Chapter 12

91

even one he liked somewhat, messing with his little girl made his blood boil. But there was nothing he could do about it. Forbidding her to be with him would just drive her towards the boy, not to mention close the line of communication that she had only recently reopened with her dad. *How am I ever going to survive the kids' teenage years? How had my mom survive my teenage years? Karma really sucks!*

Gabriel propped his feet up on the desk. *How can we find that notebook? What was Patton really working on? What is the company with the triangular logo all about, and what did Patton have to do with it?*

The videocomms buzzed, displaying "Unknown Caller." *A burner?* Gabriel connected.

"Hello? Detective Furst? This is Chuck Coffer—from Titan."

"Yes, Mr. Coffer. Good to hear from you."

"Uh, can we turn on channel encryption?"

"Sure." Gabriel pressed the appropriate keys on his videocomms to establish a secured, encrypted line with Coffer's comms.

Coffer then continued. "Thanks. I was thinking. You asked about Jim's troubles."

"Yeah."

"Well," he hesitated. "Jim was worried about something, all right. He wouldn't tell me what. But I got the feeling it was about the project he was working on."

"What project was that?"

"I don't know. He mentioned something about it when he first came back, but I don't remember the name. He didn't say much about it. Anyway, he wasn't here very much."

"He wasn't at work very much?"

"Well, no, I mean he wasn't working here at the lab most of the day."

Gabriel took his feet off the desk and sat up. "Where was he?"

"I don't know. He wouldn't tell us."

"How about his assistant, Andrea? Would she know?"

"Well, probably, but she might not tell you if it's a security issue. Plus, she's—uh, never mind."

"She's what?"

"Look, I don't know for sure, but there are rumors that she and Carmichael are—uh—very, very close if you know what I mean. He's had lots of girlfriends in the past, so that's usually no big deal, but things are hush-hush now because he's thinking about running for U.S. Senate."

Leaning back in his chair, Gabriel paused for a moment. "Do you know who Patton might have confided in?"

"Well, if anybody, it'd have been the Reverend."

"Reverend Light?"

"Yes, Jim got close to the Reverend these past few months."

"Thanks, Mr. Coffer."

"Call me Chuck."

"Of course, Chuck." Gabriel was about to disconnect but decided to play a hunch. "Hey, by the way, do you know of a company with a triangular logo with an eye inside it?"

"Is it a red eye inside a black triangle?"

"Yes." Gabriel sat up again, his heart pounding.

"Well, it sounds like Kyriarchia Tech's logo."

"Kyri—what?"

"Kyriarchia. K-Y-R-I-A-R-C-H-I-A."

"Kyri-ar-chia?" he pronounced slowly as he typed it into his deskunit. Sounds Greek. Where have I heard that name before?

"We know them better as K-Tech. They make the RFID chips that's inside everybody's noggin."

Ah, that's it. What's up with the Carmichaels' fascination with the Greek language and mythology? Titan Robotics was named for the Greek deities that preceded the Olympian gods. "Would Patton have been involved with them in any way?"

"Not that I know of. Jim was a robotics guy. He did the work on the chip design and software updates for our advanced products. K-Tech is a subsidiary of Titan, but that's not public knowledge. I used to be the employee rep to the Board of Directors of Titan."

"How do you get into the building? There's no front entrance, just a garage with some very unfriendly guards."

"I don't know. I've never been there. I guess you could ask Carmichael."

Gabriel thanked Coffer for his help, disconnected and contemplated the link between Kyriarchia Technologies and Patton. He looked up the meaning for the word. It was Greek for "dominion." No, nothing sinister about that. He searched the OmniNet for more information on the company, but he could not find a direct connection to Titan on their website or in state or national financial records. And the information he did find was surprisingly sparse for a company with such a ubiquitous presence.

The RFID system had been implemented after The Day. RFID chips were inserted into the scalp at the base of the skull of everyone legally in the U.S. DNS agents implanted chips into all babies born in the U.S. whose parents were legally in the country. People entering the U.S. at any port of entry had chips inserted with their identities and dates they were legally in the country. Those with invalid or overdue chips were considered illegal aliens, subject to being hunted down and subsequent detention, deportation or at worst immediate execution if they resisted arrest. Only agents from the Immigration and Naturalization branch of the DNS carried portable units that could change these dates on the RFID chips.

The chips were used everywhere. Each chip contained a unique ID, permanently assigned and immutable. The mutable part of the chip was used to store personal data. RFID scanners were pervasive—schools, companies, stores, restaurants, law enforcement, hospitals, banks, and many other places—used not only to verify identities but also to keep track of consumer preferences, financial accounts, and pretty much all aspects of everyday life.

Gabriel spent a frustrating hour and a half on the 'Net trying to dig out more information about K-Tech before surrendering to his headache and calling it a day. Hopefully, Irene, with her digital interface, would have better luck tomorrow.

CHAPTER 13

Thursday

Gabriel groaned loudly when the siren on his alarm sounded. It was one of those mornings he wished he hadn't sworn off all consciousness-altering drugs.

Most Americans took several pills every day—to wake up, be happy, get more energy, relax, or get to sleep. His brother Wesley was in a coma because of those pills. His brother Wesley was in a coma because of those pills. He never regained consciousness from the severe head injury suffered in a car accident. . Gabriel reminded himself to go visit his brother at the long-term care facility—after he found the real bomber and got justice for his friends.

Arriving at the office, Gabriel found Irene already at her desk smiling and humming as she was searched the 'Net.

"If you're looking into that logo, it's for a company called K-Tech, short for Kyriarchia Technologies," Gabriel remarked casually.

"Couldn't you have told me that earlier?" she grumbled and frowned his way.

"I messaged you last night."

She looked at her messages on her comms. She sighed. "Shit! I forgot I turned off notifications—and I forgot to reset it this morning. I never do that!"

"Really hot date last night, eh?"

Irene blushed but was silent.

"Chuck Coffer called back yesterday evening. He used to be the employee rep on the Board of Directors at Titan and said that K-Tech is a subsidiary of Titan. But I couldn't find anything about Titan being affiliated with it when I searched the 'Net last night."

"Hmmmm," Irene acknowledged as she studied her screen.

The videocomms buzzed. The caller ID displayed "University Hospital."

"Hello, Gabriel Furst here."

"Detective Furst, this is Katherine Miller. I was the doctor who treated the café bombing victims in the ER the other day."

"Yes, of course." His pulse quickened. "How can I help you?"

"Please don't tell anyone that you spoke with me."

"Of course. What can I do for you?" His interest was piqued.

"That second victim who died in the hospital—Laila Harvey. I—I don't understand how she died."

"They told us it was an air embolism."

"Yes, that's what I heard, but she shouldn't have gotten an air embolus. She didn't have any signs of blast lung. She shouldn't have died."

Gabriel was silent.

"Something's not right. I know I sound like I'm trying to not blame myself. But she only had a mild concussion, perforated eardrums and a few minor scratches. Her scans were completely clear. In the Observation Unit, her records showed no signs of respiratory distress right up to the point she coded. It just doesn't make sense."

"Are they doing an autopsy?"

"Yes, our pathologist is performing one here later today. He's a licensed forensic pathologist. Since the ME's office is so backed up, they asked him to do it. I plan to watch."

"Let me know what it shows, okay?"

"All right. I'm sorry. I have to go. Someone's coming." She disconnected.

"Who's that?" his partner asked, looking over at him.

"Dr. Miller, the ER doc at University Hospital, who took care of our bombing survivors. She's upset about Laila Harvey dying and wants to let us know that they're doing an autopsy."

Irene nodded and went back to her research.

"Did you turn over those security recordings from the bank to the feds?"

"Yes."

"Did you happen to keep our copies?" Gabriel asked hopefully.

His partner smiled, opened her desk drawer and held up a few memory chips. They were not supposed to keep copies of anything related to the café bombing case as it was now out of their jurisdiction. Gabriel was pleasantly surprised that Irene disobeyed the order.

"It seemed like a good idea at the time," she said, shrugging.

"And so it was." He smiled widely. "I spoke with Phil Zimburg last night. No trace of explosives on the samples we collected from the guys at New Light Church and Patton's car."

"None from his car?" She leaned back in her chair and chewed on her thumbnail.

"That's right. So, if Patton carried the pen onto the scene, it had to be in something since there's no trace in his car. He'd also need to wear gloves and change clothes since we didn't find residue on the steering wheel, start button or any surface inside the vehicle—and even then, it's difficult not to leave some trace."

Irene silently nodded.

Gabriel propped his feet on the desk. "And why take so much effort to cover his tracks if he planned to die in the explosion?"

She said slowly, "So you think somebody else brought in the pen and therefore the explosives?"

"Yes."

"Who could it've been? Not the Reverend or his bodyguards since they also tested negative for explosives."

"Right. But what about Gerry Carmichael?"

"You've got to be kidding! He's the CEO of one of the biggest companies in the world. He wouldn't risk his life like that."

"Unless it was worth it."

Irene shook her head. "What could be worth that kind of risk?"

"I don't know, but maybe it's something at K-Tech."

They updated the Homicide I team at the morning conference, which they missed the last couple of days. Back at the office, Gabriel and Irene spent the rest of the morning in frustrating pursuit of a definitive link between Patton and K-Tech. Although he hadn't said it directly, Yokino's tone at the team meeting reflected his growing impatience with the lack of usable evidence as the DNS was breathing down their necks.

After lunch, Gabriel asked, "If that leather-bound book Patton had with him at the ER is his journal, what did he do with it between the ER and his house?"

"Well, if he didn't off himself, maybe his killer took it."

Gabriel sighed, leaning back into his chair. Suddenly, he sat up. "How did he get from the hospital to his house? We know it's not in his Caddy."

"Well, he could've called a friend or maybe used a ride service."

"Let's check the ride services," he said. "I'll take the first half of the list."

A few minutes later, Irene hit pay dirt.

"U-Ride-We-Drive reported picking up a fare at University Hospital and ending at Patton's house on Bel Air Road with a five-minute stop at . . ." she began and paused while speaking with the service, ". . . a self-service parcel delivery kiosk." She contacted the parcel service and discovered Patton sent a package to University Hospital but under no specific name. "He just came from there. Why would he send something back?" Irene asked.

They looked at each other, puzzled.

"Well, let's see if it arrived. Did they give you tracking info?"

Irene checked and told him it had been delivered to the hospital. Unlike residential deliveries carried out by drones, deliveries to hospitals and secure facilities still went through the internal mail systems within these organizations.

Gabriel called the hospital and spoke with the mail reception clerk.

It took a while for the videocomms to be answered. "Yeah, sorry, we're in the middle of upgrading our tracking system here. The whole thing crashed yesterday," the clerk said, looking frazzled. "And the upgrade screwed up two of our delivery drones because of some fucking software incompatibility."

"Is there any way to find out where a certain package was delivered?" Gabriel asked.

"Look, I'm here by myself. And we get hundreds of packages and flowers every day. With the system down, I can barely get all the flowers and some of the packages out, much less keep track of where they all went."

"So you can't tell me if you still have the package with you?"

The harried clerk sighed. "No, sorry."

"Well, can you be on the lookout for a package from someone named

James Patton?"

"Yeah, right," replied the clerk in a skeptical and less than enthusiastic tone.

"It's very important and involves a terrorism case."

The clerk grunted.

Gabriel disconnected.

"I've yet to see a smooth upgrade," Irene remarked.

Sighing, Gabriel said with reluctance, "We probably should we go over there and look for our package." He wasn't looking forward to rummaging through hundreds of packages in the bowels of a hospital but knew this could be vital to their case.

Irene nodded. They decided to head over to University Hospital separately since she had plans for dinner.

"Another hot date?" Gabriel asked.

Irene's face flushed. "Same guy."

"Who is it? Anybody I know?"

"Still none of your business," she said, waving him off as she got into her car.

Gabriel grinned. It must be getting hot and heavy. He got into the Raptor, following her snazzy, new Quetzyl into the late afternoon traffic.

They arrived at University Hospital and found their way to the mail-sorting center in the basement. The overworked and over-stressed clerk from the earlier call informed them he was done for the day. "But you're welcome to search what's there. Good luck!" he said as he sailed out the door.

Shaking his head, Gabriel said, "Nothing like citizens eager to do their civic duty."

Irene grunted in agreement.

They surveyed the hundreds of haphazardly stacked, undelivered packages. Irene began sorting through the packages on one side of the room, Gabriel the other. An hour later, both sighed in frustration with still a quarter of the packages left to comb through.

"Look, why don't you get going for your date, and I'll keep looking?" Gabriel suggested.

"Are you sure?" Irene asked.

He nodded.

Irene looked at her partner gratefully. "See you tomorrow. I owe you one."

Shrugging, he said, "Have a good time."

She smiled on her way out.

He continued searching through the remainder of the packages without success. That meant it had already been delivered. Damn!

His comms buzzed. He looked at the caller ID. It was coming from inside the hospital. "Detective Furst here."

"Hi, it's Katherine Miller. Can we meet somewhere?"

"Um, sure. I'm here at the hospital."

"Where?"

"In the mail room."

"That'll do. I'll be right down." She disconnected.

What did she mean by "That'll do"?

Ten minutes later, he heard a knock on the door, which was locked from the inside. He opened the door. Katherine looked down both sides of the hallway before entering.

"What's going on?"

She looked around the room before answering, "Good. No cameras."

As she faced him, she was even more beautiful than he remembered but obviously anxious. Like the other day, her dark hair was pulled back in a bun. She wore a white blouse with lace trim and a modest, gray skirt under her white doctor's coat.

"I wanted to give you this." She pulled out a package wrapped in white paper from inside her white coat. "It's from Uncle Jim—Dr. Patton."

Gabriel gaped. "Did you open this?" he asked.

She shook her head. "Just the outside wrapping."

Gabriel put on gloves and unwrapped the sealed package carefully. It was the leather-bound journal. "We've been looking all over for this!" Flipping through the pages, he found a removable calendar inserted inside the front cover. The rest of the journal contained notes. Gabriel looked at the calendar entry for the date of the explosion. "3:15p GC. Rialto" was written in Patton's barely legible cursive, unlike his lab books in which he used print lettering. "How did you get this?"

"Uncle Jim sent it to the hospital without an addressee, so it went to Administration. When they opened it, there was another package on the inside addressed to me. So I just got it late this afternoon. There was a message with it." She handed Gabriel the note. The tips of their fingers briefly touched. Their eyes met. His heart pounding, Gabriel reluctantly pulled his gaze away and looked down at the barely legible note.

My dear Kathy,

Thank you for taking such good care of me today. I'm sorry I had to leave in a hurry. Please give this to the LAPD but not the DNS. I know how things will look. In the name of your dear father, my good friend, I swear I did not do what they will say I did. Please tell Brandi if I cannot.

Yours,
Uncle Jim

"I thought it'd be better if I didn't open the package—chain of evidence and all that."

He looked up at her. "Years of being the daughter of the Chief of Police?"

She smiled. "Dad taught us a lot of things about police work and even had us undergo special training."

"Such as?"

"I'm quite handy with a gun—any gun—handguns, rifles, shotguns, blasters—you name it. And he had us take hostage training and survival skills. As the family of the chief, we were always at risk for being kidnapped or worse."

"He prepared you for any bad stuff that could happen."

"Yes, well, thank God I never had to use any of it."

Gabriel nodded. "So, you knew Patton well?"

"When I was a child, Uncle Jim and my father were close friends. Then he didn't come around anymore. Brandi was like an older sister when I was really little, but after that we never saw each other again. I don't know what happened," she replied, pausing. "I really didn't remember much about him until the other day when they brought him in."

Gabriel nodded, looking down at the journal, anxious to examine its contents. He logged it into Evidence on his comms and slipped it into an evidence bag, along with the packaging.

She fidgeted and looked around and seemed to hesitate before asking, "Um, I'm off-duty now. How about going to grab some dinner?"

He looked from her to the journal and back. He really wanted to study the journal they'd spent so much time looking for. But here was a beautiful

Chapter 13

woman asking him to dinner . . . "OK. What do you feel like?"

"Do you do sushi?" she asked. Katherine pulled her hair out of the bun and let it drape softly past her shoulders. She slipped off her white coat, revealing a slim but shapely figure.

He grinned and replied, "Sushi is my middle name. But how are we going to get in without a reservation?" Sushi was a rare delicacy these days. Reservations at the few remaining sushi restaurants usually took weeks to finagle.

She smiled. "I saved this guy in the ER once who just happens to own a sushi place . . ."

CHAPTER 14

Friday Morning

Seated at his desk at home, Gabriel looked over at the beautiful, naked woman, asleep in his bed. He tried to focus on the journal in his hands, but his thoughts kept returning to the evening they spent together. They talked easily over sushi about many subjects and found they shared common interests. They were saying good night when the intended casual kiss quickly and unexpectedly turned very passionate. Gabriel was thankful they didn't end up creating a public spectacle in the parking lot. They decided on his place since it was closer. They barely made it inside the door.

Reluctantly, he refocused his thoughts on the journal. Patton's cursive shorthand was difficult to decipher. Gabriel was glad that he learned cursive handwriting in Catholic grade school before everything nearly became exclusively digital. From what he could figure out, the notes started two years ago after Patton returned from retirement. Some entries reflected his deep sadness and guilt over his wife's death. Most entries were related to something he kept referring to as "Pr A." He recorded his reluctance to proceed with it, especially after discussions with RL. This discomfort increased in the last few months as the project neared completion. The final entry, dated the day before the explosion, said, "Mst tll C—cnt fin, no mtt wh th do to me or fam agn. Mst warn B."

"That must be fascinating reading," came a sleepy voice from his bed.

He replied but didn't look over, "Yeah, I just don't know what most of it means yet."

Katherine got up and walked over to him. "I heard you were a workaholic." She looked over his shoulder.

He could feel her naked breast resting against his shoulder blade. "Did you check up on me?" he asked, turning towards her.

She maneuvered herself into his lap, straddling him. She wrapped her arms around him and kissed his cheek. "Of course. My father had a few friends in the LAPD."

He smiled and kissed her throat, fondling one breast. "And you still went out with me? Maybe they didn't tell you everything."

"Oh, I definitely don't know you well enough," she said, reaching down between his legs. With a moan, he dropped the journal onto his desk and gave up studying it for the night.

The Automated Home System alarm rudely woke him up.

"Ah, no, it can't be morning yet," he groaned, hugging a pillow over his face. "I just need another couple of hours."

"Wake up, sleepyhead," a sexy voice said, the owner of which removed the pillow and sat down on the bed. Kathy already took a shower and was dressed, looking very proper in her blouse and skirt.

He ogled her and pulled her into his arms. He kissed her and rolled on top of her.

"I can't. I'm going to be late for work," she protested and then moaned with pleasure as he unbuttoned her blouse, freed one of her breasts and teased her nipple with his tongue.

They were both late for work.

Arriving late at the office, he saw Irene sitting at her desk, looking very content but also sleep-deprived. She glanced at him while he casually pulled out the evidence bag with the journal and waved it in front of her. She sat with her mouth open. "You found it!"

He replied, nodding, "Sort of. Patton sent it to the doc who took care of him in the ER. He was an old family friend of hers."

"Dr. Miller? Did she read any of it?"

"No, she left it in the package. He wrote her a note though," Gabriel said as he transmitted a copy to Irene's screen.

She looked at it. "It looks like chicken scratch. What the hell does it say?"

He read it to her.

"Sounds like he's denying he did it."

"And he sounds like he's scared and that someone's after him."

"So, what's in the journal?"

Gabriel handed the bag with the journal inside to her. "From what I can decipher, he was working on some project he referred to as 'Pr A.' Whatever it was, it seems he was getting more and more uncomfortable with it." He showed her the last entry. "I think he meant 'Must tell C—can't finish, no matter what they do to me or family again. Must warn B.'" He paused. "He was going to tell C—I assume Carmichael—that he was stopping his work on the project. That was the last entry, and it's dated the day before he died."

"So, you think he was killed for this?"

"Maybe. Whatever that project is, it seems like he was willing to die for it. So, if he was willing to die for it, maybe somebody else was willing to kill for it."

"But what does 'what they do to me or family again' refer to?"

At that moment, Gabriel received an incoming videocall identified as Brandi Arnott. "Detective Furst here."

"Oh, Detective, I just got a call from my father—I mean, from the day he died. I lost my comms, and the battery died. I finally found it and got it charged up this morning," she began, sobbing.

"Mrs. Arnott, I'm so sorry. Take a few slow breaths and tell me what he said."

Irene looked up from the journal at the mention of Brandi's name.

He could hear Brandi taking several deep breaths before she continued. "He said 'Backwoods.'"

"Does that mean anything to you?"

"Yes, that's our secret code. It means to drop everything and go into hiding immediately."

"You had a previous arrangement for that? When did you set that up?"

"Two years ago around the time he went back to work. He bought a cabin in Montana far away from everything under a different name. He had new identities and bank accounts all set up just in case. He said then that we should go there if he ever told us that word and that he would join us later."

"What time did he call you?"

Brandi looked down at her wrist computer. "It was from his office—2 p.m. the day he died."

Gabriel absorbed the information.

"Another thing—someone broke into our house and ransacked it," she said in an agitated tone.

"When was that?"

"Yesterday afternoon after I left to pick the kids up from preschool."

"Was that after the mail came to your house?"

Brandi was silent for a while. "Yes, I brought in the mail before I left and then went to pick the kids up."

"Anything missing?"

"No, but they opened a package that had just arrived. We're still going through things to make sure."

"What was in the package?"

"It was a book I ordered for my father."

Gabriel was quiet and then said, "I think I know what they were after."

"What?"

"Your father's journal."

"We don't have it."

Gabriel paused for a moment. "Are you going to leave town?"

"No. I can't leave before his service," her voice broke. "No matter what they're saying about him, I know he didn't blow up that café. He wouldn't do something like that!"

"When is the service?"

She told him the location and time. Before she disconnected, he warned her to be very careful during the next few days.

"What's this all about?" she asked.

"I'll tell you in a few days. I promise." He disconnected.

His partner looked at him. "What happened?"

"Apparently, Patton had a contingency plan for his family, and he activated it the day he was killed."

Irene was quiet, her mouth agape. "He thought that he and his family were in danger."

Gabriel nodded. "In the journal, he also said 'again.' I wonder if he's referring to his wife's death. That was supposed to have been an accident, right?"

"Yeah." Irene searched for information on the OmniNet on the death of Patton's wife. She skimmed through a few articles. "It was a hit-and-run in their neighborhood. No wits, no suspects, and no one was ever caught."

"Also, Brandi said that someone broke into her house."

Her eyes widened. "Thinking that Patton sent the journal to her."

Gabriel nodded. "For now, let's keep Kath—Dr. Miller's role in this to ourselves, okay? Even here."

"Of course. By the way, I reviewed the security logs for Titan on the day of the explosion. It says that Carmichael left at 2:47 p.m., came back at 3:56 p.m. and then left for the day at 7:06 p.m."

Gabriel stroked his chin. "So, he's got no alibi for the time of the explosion, and we have him on security cameras from the bank. You'd think that before he committed a crime, the CEO of a high-tech company would've thought of all this and covered his tracks better."

"Well, rumor has it that he's just the figurehead at the helm."

"In the journal, Patton mentioned that he'd told RL about the project. I'm thinking RL could be Reverend Light."

"Maybe we need to pay him another visit," Irene suggested.

"That's what I was thinking."

Irene's comms buzzed softly. She connected and was speaking with a smile in a low voice to the caller when one of the other detectives poked his head in and informed them that the morning team meeting was starting.

"OK, we'll be there," Gabriel replied, indicating to his partner where he was going.

She nodded and told him she'd be right behind him.

Gabriel headed to the conference room. Captain Yokino, Lieutenant Corwin and the other Homicide I team members were sitting around a large U-shaped conference table discussing another case with a virtual whiteboard on the front screen as well as several individual roll-up monitors around the table. After they were finished, Yokino indicated to Gabriel that it was his turn. He projected the evidence and other particulars from their case file onto the main screen as well as the computer monitors.

Irene entered and leaned against a wall.

Gabriel passed the journal to Fitz, who slipped on gloves to remove it from the evidence bag and perused it with several of the other detectives looking over his shoulder. Gabriel summarized the case.

"As you know, James Patton left the ER with minimal injuries from the bombing at the Rialto Café. He stopped at a parcel service to send that journal," he began, indicating the journal in Fitz's hands, "to the hospital to be forwarded to us. The journal has his personal notes from the past two years as well as his appointment calendar."

"Why didn't he just send it to you here?" Fitz asked.

"Maybe he didn't remember our names and contact info since he didn't have a wrist computer," Gabriel replied, deliberately omitting Katherine's involvement. He continued, "He went home and was shot in the head. There's a note on the monitor saying he's sorry. There are size 11½ and 12½ footprints in the study that are not his, but we don't know whose they are or when they were left there. Aerial and touch DNA are pending. Microbe and particulate scans of those footprints are pending. Patton has no GSR on his hands and is shot from behind the ear on the right with the exit wound on the left front of his head."

The room was quiet.

He took a breath and continued. "There are no fingerprints on the gun except Patton's and no fingerprints anywhere else in the study except his. There's a small amount of blood spatter on his right palm, which was supposedly holding the gun. The chemicals found in his garage are for making Semtex. There is a pen in the garage with explosives inside, possibly like we found at the café. The chemical bottles don't have any fingerprints on them, although Patton's are on the pen. There's no explosives residue on the workbench, which is also cluttered. No blasting caps or primary explosives were found."

"What's your take on all this, Mav?" Lieutenant Corwin asked.

"I think that someone framed Patton for the bombing and is trying really hard to make it look like he killed himself"

"Or it really is suicide," Irene countered.

"But why not kill himself at the café then if he really wanted to commit suicide?" Gabriel asked.

"Maybe he chickened out and then was wracked with guilt afterwards," Fitz said, playing devil's advocate, a common practice in team meetings to cover all the bases. "Look, there's no evidence that anyone else was there with him when he was shot."

"There's no GSR on his hand, and there's blood spatter in his right palm, which he wouldn't have if he were holding the gun."

"Usually," Irene added. "And they were very small specks. And what about the suicide note? There were no other fingerprints on the keyboard besides his."

Gabriel nodded. "Whoever typed the note could've been wearing gloves, or they could've forced Patton to type it."

"And the chemicals in the garage?"

"The bottles of chemicals had no fingerprints. If they were Patton's, why would he wipe off his fingerprints but leave them in his own garage? And what kind of self-respecting bombmaker would make explosives in the midst of all that clutter on his workbench—which also had no explosives residue, either of Semtex or its components or of any primary explosive? And there were no measuring tools—no scale, spoons, cups, scoops, mixing tools or containers—nothing."

"What if he just didn't get around to disposing of the chemicals?" Fitz asked.

"But if he took the time to wipe his fingerprints . . ." Gabriel trailed off.

"And the pen with explosives? It had Patton's prints," Irene said.

"Someone could have picked up a couple of his pens. The Reverend said Patton was always leaving them around. Then, the real bomber could've filled them with explosives to frame him."

There were a few nods around the room.

"Also, there was no trace of explosives in his car. And somebody broke into Patton's daughter's house, possibly looking for this journal," Gabriel added.

"What's in this journal that's so important?" Corwin asked.

"It mentions something about a 'Pr A.'"

"What's that?" Captain Yokino asked.

"We don't know yet. But it might have something to do with his work at Titan—or K-Tech, which makes the RFID chips in all of us. His car's GPS shows him going to K-Tech every day, but we don't know what he did there. I think his last entry also says that he's going to stop the project and tell Carmichael."

"And the robo-guards at K-Tech kicked us out when we went there yesterday," Irene added. "They wouldn't even tell us who to ask for permission to enter."

Fitz turned to the last entry and looked up after perusing the journal page. "You could read this, Mav?" he exclaimed. "It looks like chickenscratch to me."

"Good thing they've digitalized everything now," Johnsen, agreed. "I haven't seen handwriting this bad since my own—in grade school."

Everyone laughed except their captain.

"You may be right, Furst. This is sounding more than just a suicide, assuming Patton didn't do the bombing," Yokino said in a grim tone. "But do you really think Carmichael might be good for the café?"

"He could have been, but who made the bomb for him? He's a businessman, not an explosives expert. And from what I remember about him, he didn't do military service. He went to college."

"Maybe someone at Titan made it for him—privately," Fitz suggested. "Or he hired someone."

"OK, Fitzsimmons, you and Johnsen check out the employees at Titan HQ," Yokino ordered. "See if anyone has a military background, especially with explosives. If we check his comms records, we'll need a subpoena, and he'll probably hear about it, so let's hold off on that for now."

"That's several thousand employees just in L.A.," Fitz groaned, which was silenced by Yokino's stern glare.

Johnsen asked, "Isn't the bombing the Feds' case?"

Gabriel replied, "Yeah, but if we figure out who rigged the explosion, we'll probably also find out who killed Patton since they were probably trying to get him in the first place."

"So you really think that Gerry Carmichael would put himself at risk with an explosive device?" Fitz asked. "He could've just as easily blown himself up."

Gabriel shrugged. "Unless he really knew what he was doing."

Yokino nodded. "Furst and Bolton, do you need any help in the field?"

"No, we're good at the moment. We'll be interviewing the pastor again and Carmichael of course."

"The pastor?"

"Yeah, Patton seems to have discussed this project with him. But he wouldn't tell us what it was when we talked with him."

"Bring him in. Hold off on Carmichael until we get something solid. He won't be going anywhere, especially if he thinks he's gotten away with it. We know where to find him anyway," Yokino said. "Everyone, this case gets priority for now. I've got a feeling our fed friends will try to take it away from us if they have even an inkling of what we're up to, so we'd better wrap this up quickly and quietly." Yokino dismissed them.

Gabriel and Irene headed back to their office and then out to the car.

"When did you get the journal from Dr. Miller?"

"Yesterday afternoon."

"Late night last night?" his partner asked.

"We grabbed some dinner together yesterday evening," Gabriel said, trying to sound casual.

"Mmm-hmm. You look like you got very little sleep last night," she said with a knowing smile.

"I was trying to decipher all that chicken scratch; you saw how bad the writing was. And you look like you got very little sleep as well."

"Hmmm," she grunted and looked away.

"Is it serious—your new beau?"

She smiled. "None of your business."

He put on Mozart's *Marriage of Figaro*.

She glanced at him. "Let me guess—yet another dead composer?"

He smiled. "Wolfgang Amadeus Mozart. One of the greatest composers ever."

She sighed.

CHAPTER 15

Friday Late Morning

He set the Raptor down in the parking lot of the church. As they headed towards the entrance, they noticed the heavy wooden door was ajar. They knocked, but no one answered.

"Reverend Light? Darlene?" Irene called out, her voice echoing in the grand nave. It was dead quiet. They looked at each other.

"Maybe the Reverend is out visiting congregants," Gabriel said hopefully despite the tingling on the back of his neck. As the door closed, he noticed a wet stain on the interior face. It looked like blood. He drew his gun and indicated the stain. Irene looked at him, then at the dark red streak and also drew her blaster.

On their guard, they walked toward the Reverend's office and knocked on the closed door. There was no answer. Inside the antechamber, just outside of the Reverend's private office, they found the two bodyguards. Each had been shot once in the center of the forehead. One was sprawled back onto his chair, his eyes still open wide in surprise. The wall behind him was spattered with his blood, brain matter, and pieces of his skull. The other bodyguard lay face down in an expanding pool of blood on the travertine tiles. His chair was overturned, and there was a matching spatter of blood and brains on the wall behind him.

The door to the Reverend's office was wide open. Inside, they found Reverend Light slumped over in his winged chair, shot twice, once in the forehead and once in the chest. The blood was still wet, dripping down the cushioned bottom onto the plush carpet. He had a smear of blood on one side of his neck.

"Aww, damn it!" Gabriel swore, saddened at the sickening sight of the warmhearted man he had met only two days ago.

"I'll call it in," Irene said, activating her comms.

They searched the rest of the church. No one else was on the premises. They found the side door ajar with pry marks. There was no camera overlooking that door.

Phil Zimburg and his forensics team arrived thirty minutes later, followed by the Medical Examiner. Gabriel discussed the case with Phil regarding what they were looking for. A few minutes later, Lieutenant Corwin arrived and examined the scene with a grim expression. He walked over to the main entrance with his detectives while FSD started collecting evidence.

"They knew we were coming," Gabriel said, his stomach in knots. "This must've happened less than a half-hour before we got here. We barely missed them."

"How'd they know? You didn't even know you were coming until just a while ago." Corwin asked.

"I don't know," Gabriel said through clenched teeth.

"So, where are we now?"

"Well, there were probably at least two shooters. For one shooter to hit both in the middle of the forehead before the second bodyguard had time to draw his weapon seems unlikely. These shooters are pros," Gabriel concluded.

"You think assassins?" Irene asked.

"Maybe, or ex-military or—law enforcement. A .45 with that kind of accuracy at that distance—and they policed their brass." No shell casings were found at the scene. There was an empty slot where the chip containing the security camera footage from the church's front entrance would have been been inserted.

Looking over his lieutenant's shoulder, Gabriel saw a large crowd gathering just beyond the electronic perimeter, attracted by the Forensics and Medical Examiner vehicles, indicating something terrible had occurred. He also saw a familiar African-American girl in a bright yellow dress coming toward the church grounds but blocked from entering the crime scene.

Gabriel approached Darlene and the officer denying her entry past the cordon. "Officer, let the young lady in," he said to the young patrolman and motioned for him to deactivate the perimeter to let her in.

Chapter 15   **113**

"You were here the other day—Detective Furst," Darlene said. "What's going on? What happened?" Her voice quavered.

They walked towards the church to get out of hearing range of the onlookers. "Darlene, I'm sorry to tell you this, but someone shot and killed the Reverend and his bodyguards," he said as gently as he could.

"Oh, my God!" she cried and would have collapsed to the ground if Gabriel hadn't caught her. Darlene clung to his arm and sobbed, "Why? Who would do this? He just wanted to help people!"

He gently touched her shoulder. After her crying eased and she could speak again, he said, " Darlene, maybe you can help us find his killers."

"How?"

"You listened to some of the private conversations in that office, didn't you?"

"Why would you think that?" she asked, not looking at him.

"You knew exactly what we had discussed with the Reverend the other day when you showed us out. You were listening, weren't you?"

She was silent, then gave a small nod. "The guards convinced the Reverend to put in a camera, so we could watch and make sure nobody was hurting him, but we were sworn to secrecy about anything that was said in that office."

"Were they recorded?" Gabriel asked.

Shaking her head, she said, "No, sorry."

Damn, he thought. "Did the bodyguards hear those conversations also?"

Darlene nodded her head. "I know most people think they couldn't be trusted because they were ex-cons, but they turned their lives around and truly found God and were absolutely loyal to the Reverend and the Church. They'd never tell any secrets that were said in that office."

"Darlene, did you ever hear a conversation between James Patton and the Reverend about a project he was working on?"

Her brows furrowed. "They talked many times about something, but I missed most of them. I was helping out in the kitchen. We serve meals every evening for the poor."

"Do you remember the name of the project or what it was about?"

Darlene looked uncertain. "I'm not sure I should tell you. The Reverend said not to say anything about what we heard," she whispered.

"I understand, but this is important in figuring out who killed Jim, the

114   *Project A*

Reverend and the guards—your friends and family. You said the Reverend was a second father to you."

She looked away. After a minute, she turned back to him, nodded and said, "Um, I think it was something that started with an 'A'—something like atrophy—no, no, not exactly. But it was something like that. One of our parishioners recently crossed over due to spinal muscular atrophy—and it was a word that sounded like that"

"Do you have any idea what the project was about?"

"Not really. Mr. Patton used to talk in technical terms a lot. It sounded like it had something to do with a chip."

"Do you know if anyone else overheard these conversations with Patton and the Reverend?"

She shook her head. "I don't remember anyone else being there at those times. I think it was just the Reverend and the bodyguards—and me a little bit."

"Thank you, Darlene. I know this is a very difficult time for you, and I appreciate all the help you've given us. If you remember any more details, here's our contact info." He sent the information to her wrist computer and started to turn away.

She nodded and looked down. "I was supposed to be here this morning." Her voice cracked, tears streaming down her face again.

Gabriel stopped in alarm. "Are you usually here at this time?"

She nodded. "I'm here every morning."

"Aren't you supposed to be taking classes?"

"I have on-line classes later in the morning. In the afternoon, I get practice time to try out for the Olympics next year."

"Why were you late today?"

"I went to the doctor's before I came in today."

Gabriel's spidey senses were tingling again. "Look, stay here for now. Don't go home yet."

"Why? Do you think they're after me too?" Fear crept in her voice.

"I don't know, but let us check it out. Who knew about the videocam?"

"Just the inner circle. It was put in about a year ago."

"Can you write down the names of all the people who know about it, including anybody not here anymore?"

She nodded. He obtained her address and had Corwin send a patrol car there.

"What's going on?" his partner asked as she approached them.

"They have a video feed from the Reverend's office to the people in the outer office. I think whoever did this knew about it and thought that the bodyguards and Darlene heard what Patton told Reverend Light. And now they're cleaning up."

Irene frowned. "Did they have recordings?"

"No, unfortunately. Stay with Darlene and make sure no one gets to her."

"Of course." She headed toward the younger woman, who recognized her and began sobbing again on her shoulder. Irene looked uncomfortably at her partner and slowly raised her hand to stiffly pat Darlene's shoulder as she guided her to a bench.

Gabriel searched the area for other cameras. There weren't any more on church property. He made his way through the throng of curious onlookers. There was a street camera a couple of long blocks away at the intersection with the main road. Someone had sprayed black paint onto the lens. It was still tacky to the touch.

"Shit!" He grimaced. He probably wasn't going to get any useful footage, but he transferred the video onto a new chip anyway. The next closest cameras were three to four blocks away at very busy intersections, and they would include a lot of extraneous traffic. He copied those videos too. Heading back towards the Church, Gabriel obtained the videocam recordings from the three adjacent businesses. The owners said their cameras didn't cover the Church entrance or much of the parking lot.

Phil Zimburg came out to report to Gabriel and Corwin.

"Looks like .45 caliber full-metal jackets for all three vics. No casings left around. Neither bodyguard drew his gun."

"Probably no time, especially if there were two shooters," Gabriel said.

Phil nodded. "We'll know better after ballistics."

Corwin stepped away to take a call on his comms. Phil went back inside.

Gabriel approached his lieutenant, who was speaking on his comms to the officers at Darlene's apartment. He looked grimly at Gabriel.

"You're right. Her place was broken into and tossed."

"We need to put her into PC. She may not know anything, but they think she does, and these guys are deadly serious."

Corwin nodded and started making arrangements for Protective

Project A

Custody through his comms.

Gabriel walked over to Darlene and Irene, sitting near the black marble statue in front of the church. His partner looked up as he sat down beside Darlene. In a gentle voice, he said, "Darlene, it looks like someone broke into your apartment."

Her eyes widened. "Oh, my God! Is it the same people who killed the Reverend?"

"Maybe. We don't know yet."

Darlene was quiet. "You know, I was thinking about the name of the project that Jim was working on. I think it was called 'Atropos.'"

"Atropos—you're sure?"

She nodded. "Here's the list you wanted me to make." She beamed it from her comms to theirs. There were eleven names on the list, including hers. Three were dead. Irene began researching the other names on the OmniNet and NCIC, the National Crime Information Center.

Corwin approached them and introduced himself to Darlene. He asked her to go with him to Beck Tower until she could be placed into Protective Custody. Gabriel remembered what Atropos was, and a cold chill went down his spine.

"Bolton," he said. "Atropos was one of the Moirai, the Three Fates, in Greek mythology."

"What are the Three Fates?"

"They were the three sisters who controlled your fate and destiny in life. Clotho spun the thread. Lachesis measured the length. And Atropos—Atropos cut the thread of life."

Both let that sink in for a moment.

"What does that have to do with computer chips and robots?" Irene asked.

"I'm not sure. Right now, robots last for many years. Maybe Titan wanted Patton to figure out a way to program the existing chips to self-destruct—planned obsolescence. Then, you'd need to get a new bot. That'd be worth billions. People have killed for less."

"Yeah," Irene said. "Makes sense."

"Let's keep this out of the report for now, okay? I think the fewer people who think Darlene knows anything, the better—for her."

"We can't tell our squad?" Irene asked, uncertainly.

"Just for one day, okay?"

Chapter 15

Bolton considered her partner's request. "You know the Captain's going to have a cow if he finds out, and we'll be suspended."

"I know. I'm asking a lot, but I'll take the heat if Yokino comes down on us."

Irene looked hesitant. "Okay—but one day only," she said slowly.

"Thanks," he said. "Also, the closest street camera has been spray-painted, and the ones from the businesses around here don't have much of a view of the Church or parking lot."

Irene sighed.

"So, whoever did this cased this area well."

"Yeah, seems so."

It was late afternoon by the time they finished working the scene with forensics. As they headed back to Beck Tower, Gabriel realized they both hadn't had any lunch yet. They both picked up food at the first floor cantina before heading to the office. Darlene sat alone in the conference room, her eyes still red and staring blankly ahead. Gabriel asked if she had eaten any lunch. Darlene gazed at him with a numb expression.

"Hope you like cheeseburgers," he said, placing his plate of burger and fries in front of her.

She gave him a wan smile. "Thanks, but I'm not very hungry right now," she murmured. Her entire world had been turned upside down in the last few hours.

"Try to eat," Gabriel said, patting her hand gently.

The teenager absently picked up the burger and began nibbling on it without enthusiasm.

"Darlene, I have a favor to ask of you," Gabriel began. "Would you please keep quiet about what you told me this morning? About the project?"

She nodded.

"Did anyone else ask you about it?"

She shook her head.

"Good."

Sitting beside Darlene, Irene opened her lunch and began eating. Gabriel went to the café to get another cheeseburger.

The lack of sleep the previous night was catching up to him. Ten years ago, he could stay up for thirty-six hours straight and still be alert. Now, he was definitely feeling his age—maybe he was too old for Katherine. He hoped not. He realized she hadn't called him yet. What would a beautiful, young doctor see in a balding, middle-aged cop anyway? He forced himself to focus his thoughts back on the case. They needed more information about what Project Atropos really was.

"Hey, Bolton, I'm going to Titan and see if I can catch Chuck Coffer before he goes home for the day. Can you stay with Darlene?" he asked after poking his head into the conference room.

Irene looked at him, then at Darlene and back at him and nodded slowly.

CHAPTER 16

Friday Afternoon

At Titan, he was greeted this time by the robo-guards, who obtained authorization from the main office before allowing Gabriel past Visitor's Parking. One of the droids then led him to the Robotic Chip Design Lab. The door sign now displayed Andrea Lisle's name as lab director. She met him at the lab entrance and invited him back to her office.

"Congratulations on your promotion."

"Due to unfortunate circumstances." She motioned for him to sit.

He looked at the scrolling digital pictures on a frame on her desk. Most of them were of her as a child or a teenager with her family at different places around the world. One was in front of the Eiffel Tower, another in St. Peter's Square with the basilica in the background, and another with a structure shaped like a large Greek letter *pi*. He picked the frame up, turned it to face her, and asked, "What's this?"

"Which one?" The digital frame had dissolved to the next picture. "The Coliseum?"

"No, the one with what looks like a *pi* structure in the background."

"Oh, that's the Monument to Fallen Miners in Mitrovica."

"Where's that?"

"Kosovo. I lived there for a few years."

"Ah." She was very well-travelled. "Andrea, did Dr. Patton spend most of the day in this laboratory?"

"Of course, he is—was—the director. He oversaw all the projects."

"Was he working on any projects himself?"

"No, his role was mostly supervisory here."

"Did he ever work at K-Tech?"

Without batting an eyelash or pausing, Andrea replied in a calm voice, "No, he worked here exclusively."

"Why did the GPS in his car tell us he went to K-Tech every day?"

"I'm sorry—you must be mistaken. Where did it say he went every day?"

Gabriel gave her the address. She shrugged. "I don't know where that is. I assure you that he was here most of the time every day, except for the hour off for lunch."

"Is Mr. Coffer around?"

"No, he's out of the building right now."

"When will he back?"

"I don't know, but I can let him know you'd like to speak with him," she offered.

"Thanks for your help," Gabriel said before he walked out of the lab. There was an old adage in policework that everyone lies. He hated being lied to and wondered why she did it, but he didn't want to confront her just yet.

As he walked to his Raptor in the parking lot, he saw another vehicle waiting for the employee garage door to open. Inside was Chuck Coffer. Gabriel flagged him down and walked over to the older man's car.

"Mr. Coffer, I was just looking for you."

"Hi, Detective. What can I do for you?"

"Have you heard of Project Atropos?"

"No, it's not one of ours. Why?"

"We think that Patton may have been working on it."

"Well, it's definitely not one of ours—I know all the projects going on in our lab."

"You said you didn't know whether Patton worked at K-Tech?"

Coffer shook his head. "No, he never mentioned it."

"You said Patton was gone for much of the day?"

"Yeah, he was usually gone in the late mornings to early afternoons. Don't know where he went."

"Thanks, Mr. Coffer." He turned away and then remembered, "Have you seen the news about the New Light Church today?"

"What news? I'm afraid I ignore reading billboards or listening to the news in the car."

"Then, I'm sorry to inform you Reverend Light and his bodyguards

Chapter 16   **121**

were killed this morning in the Church."

Coffer's jaw dropped, and his face turned ashen. "Oh, my God. Such a wonderful man," he muttered. "Such good men," he amended. "Do you think it has anything to do with Jim's death?"

"Why would you think that?"

"Well, I can't believe that Jim killed himself, no matter what's being said. He wouldn't kill others either. That means he was killed. So, it's probably no coincidence that the Reverend was also killed."

Gabriel nodded. "Yeah. By the way, watch your six."

Coffer indicated his glovebox. "I'm an old vet from the War. I always pack when I'm out. Thanks for the warning. Good day, Detective." He drove his car into the employee lot.

As Gabriel exited the parking lot, he saw movement in the security office. When he turned back to get a better look, he saw one of the robo-guards looking at a monitor.

Gabriel headed back to the office for the afternoon team meeting. The other team members were waiting for Captain Yokino. Lieutenant Corwin was on duty watching Darlene at the hotel.

Yokino entered. "All right, most of you already know that the pastor in Patton's church was murdered this morning, along with his two bodyguards. We have one witness, so to speak, in protection. We'll need to arrange shifts to cover this."

"Just what does the witness know?" one of the other detectives asked. Yokino nodded to Gabriel.

"Unfortunately, not as much as the killers think she does. The Church had a security surveillance system set up so that those trusted few in the outer office could see and hear what was going on in the inner office when parishioners spoke with Reverend Light. We think that the bodyguards and our witness overheard Patton telling the Reverend about the project he was working on. She doesn't remember much as she came in late in the conversation. But the killers somehow found out about this system and want to get rid of any witnesses or anyone they think is a witness," Gabriel informed them truthfully, albeit incomplete.

"What could Patton have been working on that'd be worth killing all those people?" Johnsen asked.

"That's the million-dollar question," Yokino said. "Any ideas, Furst?"

"We think Patton also worked at K-Tech as well. His GPS places him there every day. However, his personal assistant claims he worked exclusively at Titan."

"That's hinky. What's she hiding?" Fitz asked.

"Maybe the project is top secret. She'd know since she was his assistant," Irene said.

"Well, if we can confirm that Patton worked at K-Tech, then we can get a search warrant," Yokino said.

"Too bad we're not the feds; they don't have to worry about petty details like the Fourth Amendment or search warrants anymore," Fitz muttered. Everyone nodded—yet another reason to despise the DNS.

"What do we have on the people who knew about the tap on the inner office of the Church?" Gabriel asked his partner.

"Well, other than the people killed today, there was Darlene, two other long-time office workers, the security company who installed the system and a Reverend John Burke."

"John Burke—that was the one who embezzled from them."

Irene acknowledged. "I did a search on him but found nothing solid before two years ago when he joined the New Light Church. There was info before that, but it seemed like a poorly done backstop— only good enough for a cursory background check. I went back to school pictures and couldn't find a single one of him in any of the schools he supposedly attended."

"If he didn't really exist before, then he got a new identity," Gabriel said.

"Only the DNS can do that," Fitz said. "They create new identities all the time for the Witness Protection Program."

The furrows in Yokino's brow deepened. "Well, this just gets better and better. Bolton, see if you can get a picture of this guy and FACE him. Maybe we can find out his real identity. Johnsen and Fitzsimmons, how're we doing on the employees at Titan? Any leads?"

Fitz replied, "We're only about a fifth of the way through the list. Nothing's jumping out at us. There are thirty-two employees so far that are ex-military, but none were in any units handling explosives. Carmichael himself was business school and robotics. One interesting thing— Carmichael's brother Harold was in Military Intelligence. But his service records are redacted."

"That nerdy guy?" Irene asked with a tone of disbelief.

"Yeah, we got a kick out of that one," Fitz said, laughing. "He joined Titan five years ago."

"Keep at it. Anything else?" Yokino asked. No one spoke. "All right. Given the importance of this case, everybody's working this weekend, at least in the mornings. For those who can, sign up for protective detail. Double overtime pay," he informed them. He shoved a tablet on the conference table.

Although exhausted from lack of sleep, Gabriel tapped in the box by his name for the first shift, since Darlene was his witness. Some of the others also signed up, eager for the bonus pay. The slots filled, and everyone scattered to his or her respective office.

"Sorry, I couldn't sign up for tonight," Irene told Gabriel.

"Big date again?"

She gave an almost imperceptible nod.

"It's OK. Have a good night, then," he said with a smile.

"I promise to make this up to you," she said as she was leaving.

He was going to be joined by Smiley Johnsen, one of the first to volunteer for any extra detail. Gabriel walked over to Johnsen and Fitz's office and found Smiley talking on the visorcomm with someone who Gabriel guessed was his wife. Although Gabriel and Smiley worked in the same RHD squad for many years, he'd never met Johnsen's wife. The older detective did not socialize with the rest of the team, not even at the departmental holiday get-togethers. So, very few knew much about his personal background.

"Same to you," Johnsen ended his call as he eyed Gabriel.

"Ready?" Gabriel asked.

His partner for the evening nodded, gathering his things. "I'll meet you there."

Arriving at the hotel, they checked in with the uniformed officers in a patrol car on the street and then took the elevators up to the tenth floor. They examined the entrances and exits before heading to the room. Smiley knocked on the door.

Behind the door, a gruff voice answered, " Who's there?"

"Little Red Riding Hood," Gabriel replied with the pass phrase. He sighed. Who the hell comes up with these things? Probably some joker who secretly enjoys recording cops saying these ridiculous phrases and posts them on some video-sharing website.

The door cracked opened. Lieutenant Corwin stood in the doorway, blocking entry until he recognized them. He and another detective from the squad sheathed their blasters after the door closed behind the new arrivals. Gabriel updated them on the case. After the two left, Darlene poked her head out from her room into the sitting room of the suite and managed a wan smile when she recognized Gabriel.

"Darlene, this is Detective Dan Johnsen. He works with me. We'll be taking care of you until midnight."

Her eyes still red, she nodded without enthusiasm. "I'm getting a little hungry now. I didn't eat much of the burger you got me earlier. Sorry."

Johnsen wordlessly handed her the e-menu tablet for room service. Both detectives inspected the rooms and views from all the windows in the suite. They liked to plan for all contingencies.

While they waited for room service, Darlene stayed in the living room area with Gabriel instead of retreating to her bedroom. She seemed comforted by his presence.

"How're you holding up?" he asked, his voice gentle.

She shrugged, hanging her head.

"Do you have anyone or anywhere to go to after this?"

She shook her head. "He—the Church was all I had." Her voice broke. He put an arm around her. She sobbed on his shoulder. "Why would anyone do that to the Reverend? He was such a kind man. Why?"

He knew there were no words that could ease her pain. He caught Johnsen's eye over her shoulder. Smiley looked clearly relieved that his shoulder was not the one getting soaked.

The rest of their shift was fairly uneventful. Darlene eventually drifted back into her room after Gabriel emphasized to her to ensure she always locked and bolted her door. He gave her his contact info, including his comms and home number. He made her repeat the numbers even though she saved them on her comms.

Smiley remained quiet, although Gabriel managed to pry a little more information about the former's personal life. Johnsen's wife Candace had been ill for many years, and they had no children.

At midnight, two other RHD detectives relieved them. As they headed away from the hotel, Gabriel noted the team in the patrol car had also changed shifts.

As Gabriel walked into his apartment, the AHS informed him he had three messages. He was too tired to do anything except crawl onto his bed and fall asleep.

CHAPTER 17

Saturday Morning

The alarm blared after just a few minutes—or so it seemed. Gabriel glanced at the clock, which read "07:00," groaned and tried to muster the energy to get out of bed.

Over the hot breakfast Robert made, he listened to his messages from yesterday— one from his daughter, one from his sister-in-law and the last from Katherine. He told himself to calm down, but his heart raced like a teenager with his first girl.

"Hi, Gabriel, um, this is Katherine. I'm working tomorrow until seven. Could we get together afterwards? Please give me a call."

He checked the time. She was probably already on her way to the hospital. He took a deep breath and instructed the AHS to call her. She picked up on the first ring. He saw her sitting in her car, apparently on automatic pilot, as she looked at him instead of paying attention to traffic.

"Hi, how are you? I was worried when I didn't hear back from you last night," she began.

"Yeah, sorry. I didn't get home until after midnight," he explained.

"Late night."

"Yeah. The case is getting more complicated."

She paused, taking a deep breath. "Do you think you can make it to my place for dinner? It won't be anything fancy. I'm going to pick something up on the way home."

"Takeout—my favorite."

She smiled at his reply. "Around 7:30?"

"Sure."

She gave him the address. "See you then."

"I can't wait," he replied honestly, hoping he didn't look like the horny teenager that he felt like inside.

"Me, too," she said, her voice sultry, and disconnected.

Well, that's a great way to start the day. Gabriel beamed, energized.

Irene, as usual, was on her computer when he arrived. "I've got good news and bad news. Got a FACE match on John Burke. Turns out he's actually John Bergstrom. The bad news is that the information is classified."

Gabriel stroked his chin. "So, he's probably DNS—intelligence, military intelligence, national security, spec ops," he listed the divisions of the DNS which usually classified their operatives' service records.

She nodded. "But why infiltrate that church?"

"Well, if you think about it, the New Light Church promotes values that are opposed to those of the DNS."

"Now you're sounding paranoid." Gabriel could tell she was mentally rolling her eyes at him. "You're not a big fan of the DNS."

"I just don't think any agency should have so much—almost unlimited—power and so little oversight."

She shook her head. "Paranoid."

"Just because I'm paranoid doesn't mean I'm wrong."

She retorted, "Doesn't mean you're right."

"Did you work with the feds much at West L.A.?"

She shook her head.

"Well, you will here. When those two DNS agents came and took over the case, they didn't even bother to listen to what we had to say."

"I don't agree." Irene flushed. "They did listen."

"Well, one of them checked you out the whole time—what's his name—Weston?"

"Sam Weston."

Gabriel looked keenly at his partner. "He's the one, isn't he?"

"He's the one what?"

"He's the one you've been dating."

She looked down intently at her screen.

"Those footprints at Patton's—they're the same sizes as Harmon's and Weston's," Gabriel said.

"You're being paranoid again."

"Maybe, but I looked at their shoes when they were here the other day.

They're similar to the size and shape of those we found."

"Lots of men have those shoe sizes."

"Yeah, but how many hang out in pairs with those exact sizes *and* are connected with this case?"

She snorted.

"Just be careful, and of course I don't need to remind you not to discuss the case with him," he said.

"Of course not," she said, glaring at him. "I would never do that. We have other things to talk about."

An uncomfortable silence hung between them. Corwin appeared on the screen to remind them of the morning conference. They walked to the conference room in silence. Irene reported her findings about John Bergstrom.

Afterward, they returned to their office. Irene went wordlessly to her computer and resumed her research.

His comms buzzed, and Gabriel answered. His face turned ashen.

Irene looked across at him as he disconnected. "What's the matter?"

"That was an officer from Central. Chuck Coffer was in a car accident this morning. His autopilot malfunctioned, and his vehicle ran into a barrier. He's dead."

"His car malfunctioned?" she asked in disbelief. The automatic pilot feature of cars rarely malfunctioned. There were multiple backup systems.

"That's what they say."

"Why'd they call you?"

"I gave him my contact info yesterday. It was the last entry on his comms." Gabriel covered his eyes with one hand. "I put him in danger by talking to him at Titan."

"You think it's related?"

Gabriel sat back in his chair. "Maybe it's just an accident, but it seems everyone helping us with this case is getting killed." He suddenly went cold. "You didn't tell anyone about Katherine—Dr. Miller—did you?"

"No, of course not. You said she hadn't read the journal anyway."

Gabriel's dark brows wrinkled in thought. He paced the room, stopped abruptly, and glanced around before turning to Irene with a finger over his lips. "Let's get a snack," he said casually even as he gestured urgently for them to leave. Once they were heading down in the elevator, he said in a low voice, "It's like they know our every move."

"Do you think they're tailing us?"

"No. I think they bugged our office or worse. Let's get the techs to sweep the office and our electronics to check for spyware. I know that they can track us by GPS."

"Only the DNS has the equipment to do that."

Gabriel nodded with a knowing look.

"Oh, don't give me that again," Irene said in an exasperated tone.

They headed to the LAPD Electronics Unit in the basement of Beck Tower. It was almost deserted on weekends with a skeleton staff to cover incoming cases. Gabriel called his good friend there who said he was working.

Paul Zimburg was in his mid-thirties with disheveled blond hair and looked nearly identical to his triplet brother Phil in FSD.

"Hey, Mav," Paul greeted him.

Gabriel introduced Irene. Paul stood up straighter, brushed his hair out of his eyes and eyed her curvaceous, athletic figure.

"So, how can I help you today?" Paul asked, looking at Irene with puppy dog eyes.

"Can you check our comms for any tracking or spying apps? We also need you to sweep our office and deskunits," replied Gabriel.

Paul looked at Gabriel. "Oh, well, that's easy. Give the comms to me, and I'll run them through the scanner."

They removed their units, handed them to Paul, and followed him to the lab with the scanner. He set each, one at a time, on a platform inside a device that resembled the old-fashioned MRI machines that Gabriel remembered from childhood. There was a soft hum as Paul activated the scan for electronic surveillance devices and viruses or malware.

"Looks clean," he said after a few moments, handing Gabriel his comms. "That looks good, too," he said to Irene after scanning hers. "It'll take some time to sweep your office. I just need a few minutes to finish my current project, and then I'll come up."

"Thanks, Paul," Gabriel said. The clasps of the comms clicked softly as the detectives slipped them back on their wrists.

Paul gave Irene one last longing glance before the elevator door closed.

Irene looked at Gabriel as the elevator lifted.

"He's absolutely brilliant with computers and tech stuff. Even better than his brother. You should be very flattered; he usually doesn't notice a woman unless she's a real knockout."

"Are you calling me a knockout?" Irene gave him a teasing smile.

"No, I said Paul thinks you're a knockout."

Irene grimaced. "So, you really think we're being tailed or bugged?"

"I don't know. We could have a leak also, but I don't want to go there. Somehow, they know everywhere we've been and everybody we've been talking to and are going to talk to. The Captain's not going to be happy that we got another dead witness."

Just outside the office, Gabriel started to update the case file about Coffer's death on his comms but couldn't find it. He searched frantically on his comms. "Everything we have on this case is gone! I can't even find the case file."

"What? It was there this morning," Irene exclaimed and looked down at her comms. Then, she went to her desk. After a moment, she looked up at him with a grim expression.

He called Paul and informed him that all their electronics were compromised.

"Fuck! I'll be right up," Paul said.

The tech expert came and looked through their comms and deskunits. After a few minutes on Irene's unit, Paul looked up at the detectives with a frown. "You know when a case is closed, all the files get deleted from your devices and archived in RID. Well, somebody hacked the system and marked the case as closed, so all the files were deleted from your devices. Then they hacked into Records and erased all the relevant files—and overwrote them several times, so the original data is not recoverable."

They looked at each other in grim silence. Someone had penetrated the what-was-supposed-to-be-absolutely-secure LAPD archive servers in the Records and Information Division.

Gabriel thought furiously. "Is there any way to retrieve it? How about the off-site backup?"

Paul shook his head. "I checked. All of that was deleted and erased as well."

Irene asked, "What can we do? The DNS has all the official evidence. Most of our wits are dead, so we can't get new statements from them."

After a minute, Gabriel said, "Whoever got into the system could still corrupt anything we put in. But Patton's car—the GPS might still have the data proving Patton went to K-Tech every day."

She nodded.

"Let's go."

Paul was muttering expletives under his breath while typing away on Gabriel's deskunit as the two detectives rushed out.

They went downstairs to FSD and discovered Patton's car was not there and in fact never arrived, according to the electronic records. However, the forensic tech, who received the vehicle, insisted he personally logged it in and left the car overnight in the designated, secured bay for FSD.

Frustrated, they stared at the empty space.

"You're right. It's like somebody's sabotaging us." Irene sighed.

Gabriel blew out a sigh in frustration. They headed back to the twenty-first floor.

Paul greeted them in the hallway of their office. Several other techs were sweeping the offices of Homicide I with portable scanners.

"What did you find?"

Paul held up evidence bags with two pinhead-sized, black dots. "We found these in your office and the conference room. We're sweeping all the offices. These nanobugs are almost impossible to find, given their size. They're voice-activated and upload intermittently. Also, they use an ultra-high frequency band that channel hops with a range of two miles—cutting edge stuff. I've only heard about these on the spy boards," he told them with reluctant admiration in his voice.

Gabriel picked up a clear evidence bag with a nanobug, held it up to the light, squinting. He then handed it to Irene to analyze with her visual implants.

"They can also override most of the anti-surveillance systems in this building. There're not many of these out there. We almost missed them, but luckily I just updated our scanners last month so they could detect these."

"Who has access to them? The DNS?" Gabriel asked.

"Of course. Any intelligence service with enough money has access. You can also probably get these on the black market for a quarter to half a mil—each. That's not even including the receiver, which in itself is about five mil."

Gabriel whistled. "They spent at least six mil on bugging this office."

Captain Yokino and Lieutenant Corwin approached them.

Frowning, the Captain said, "I tried calling Agents Weston and Harmon at the DNS. Assistant Director Thurston said they're no longer working there as of a month ago." Jack Thurston was the Assistant Director in Charge of the Los Angeles Field Office of the Department of National Security.

Irene's face turned ashen. "Weston and Harmon are not working for the DNS?"

"He denied they're actively working for the DNS."

"But I reached them through the main DNS number," Irene said.

"Where did you call from?" Paul Zimburg asked.

"My office phone and my comms."

"They could have any calls from here routed to them instead of the L.A. DNS office," Paul posited.

"Thurston thinks they may have gone rogue," Yokino said.

"Or they're still working for the DNS," Gabriel said, "and the Department is covering its ass by disavowing them."

One of Zimburg's techs came up to him and handed him another evidence bag with a tiny, black dot. "The office at the corner." He pointed. Johnsen and Fitz's office.

"Weston and Harmon went in there, too," Gabriel said.

"Titan could afford these, too," Irene said.

Gabriel nodded. "But as far as we know, nobody from Titan's been here recently."

"Is there any way to tell how long they've been placed here?" Irene asked.

Paul shook his head. "Whoever was listening is probably gone now. They'll know we found the bugs. I recommend everybody set their windows on complete blockout in case they're using any optical or laser mikes. Also, we'll put in scramblers around the unit just in case we missed anything. It's ultrasonic, and most eavesdroppers won't like the effects. Your comms won't work inside this zone, of course, so you'll need to forward your calls to the videocomms. My team needs to scan the entire LAPD system for malware and see if we can find and trace the hack point." He sighed loudly.

Captain Yokino nodded, his eyes narrowed and his face flushed. He seemed to take it as a personal affront that someone was spying on them and witnesses were killed as a result.

Chapter 17

133

Within minutes, all the duraglass windows in the squad were set to total blockout mode, preventing any light or sound vibrations from coming in or going out. The silence was oppressive, broken only by the low-pitch hum of the ventilation system and the occasional ringing videocomms, which was a wired system and not affected by the scramblers. Feeling very claustrophobic, Gabriel paced around his office.

"So much for having window views in the office," he muttered to himself. Suddenly, he stopped, his eyes wide with alarm. He dashed to the conference room, trying to remember whether they mentioned the location and room number where they stashed Darlene. His partner followed closely behind him. He scanned the tablet for the schedule of detectives on protective detail. Using the videocomms in the room, he called the number for one of them. No one answered, and the call went straight to messaging. He and Irene exchanged worried looks.

Using the other videocomms, she called the other detective's comms, which also went unanswered. She then called the hotel room, but there was no response. They hurried out of the conference room. Gabriel poked his head into the Lieutenant's office.

"There's no answer from our guys in the hotel room. We're on our way there," Gabriel said in a tight voice.

Corwin looked alarmed. "I'll call for backup."

This time, Irene didn't complain about Gabriel's manual driving as he raced past the usual, heavy L.A. traffic, sirens wailing.

CHAPTER 18

Saturday Afternoon

As Gabriel drove, Irene contacted the uniformed officers parked in front of the hotel. They reported that the last check-in forty-five minutes ago had been routine. She told them to go inside to check on the witness and protective detail.

When Gabriel and Irene arrived in the hotel lobby, they saw the desk clerk hand a key card to a patrol officer. This older hotel was a favorite Robbery-Homicide safe house because of its limited access to the upper floors. Most newer hotels had a parking platform on every floor, making surveillance and protection more difficult. This was older with a parking lot just on the first floor and therefore less accessible. Most newer hotels also had doors with electronic access controlled from a central station. This one still required special key cards, which were considered more secure and unhackable.

"No one answered, and we couldn't knock the door down upstairs," the uniformed officer explained. The hotel had heavily reinforced doors and frames.

Gabriel told him to help cover the front entrance to ensure no one leaves the premises, which was already on lockdown. Another pair of patrol officers arrived. Gabriel assigned them to the back and side entrances to back up hotel security.

As the elevator doors opened on the tenth floor, they saw a young black patrol officer pounding on the door down the hall.

"There's still no answer," she said with a shaky voice.

Gabriel's throat tightened, and he drew his gun. Irene and the patrol officer drew their blasters. He unlocked the door to the suite and opened the door. Just inside the entryway, a white linen-draped room service cart sat with two covered plates of food and a carafe of ice water. An overturned plate with a hamburger and fries was spilled onto the floor, its cover lying a few inches away. The cart linen was partially pulled off. Gabriel carefully walked into the room around the cart and found the lifeless body of one detective, lying on his back about eight feet from the entrance. He had a gunshot wound in the middle of his forehead. Blood and brains created a lumpy, crimson soup around his head. The back part of his skull lay in pieces a few feet behind him. His blaster was still in his holster.

In the nook around the corner, the other detective was sprawled on the couch, also shot in the head, with his blaster on the couch beside him. The wall behind him was spattered with blood and brains, still oozing down, and embedded bone.

Gabriel grimaced. "Fuck!" He and Irene looked at each other and then at the door to the adjoining bedroom. The heavy wooden door was ajar. There were splinters around the hardware and several bullet holes through the latch bolt and the deadbolt. Gabriel did not want to think about the beautiful young girl, only slightly older than his own daughter, dying a violent and painful death. He had promised her safety. He clenched his jaw, steeled himself against what he expected to find, and entered the room.

It was empty. They swept the room but didn't find a body or any blood. Darlene's comms was on the floor by the nightstand. The room and adjoining bathroom were deserted. The sliding balcony door was open. Gabriel rushed out, gripped the metal railing, and looked down—nothing but the peaceful, glimmering blue water of the hotel pool. He closed his eyes briefly and sighed, relieved but puzzled. He looked at the balconies to either side—no signs of disturbances. Their sliding glass doors were closed. The concrete base of the balcony above him was about three feet above his head and looked undamaged. Small flecks of pink paint-covered stucco lay near the rail of the balcony. He leaned his back against the rail and looked up. No signs of Darlene, but there were possible scuff marks on the face of the balcony above.

When he and Irene came back into the main room, Lieutenant Corwin and the SWAT team had just arrived.

"The girl?" Corwin asked.

Gabriel shook his head. "She's not here, but there're no signs of a struggle or that she was killed." He looked at the bodies of the fallen detectives. They were both from RHD squad II. One just got married and was expecting his first child. The second detective had a wife and two young children. "It looks like they surprised our guys. He," Gabriel said, indicating the one lying closest to the door, "answered the door for room service. Must have put away his blaster to e-sign the check when they got him. Maybe he forgot to check the bottom of the cart before putting his piece away." He paused, swallowing the lump in his throat. "Probably at least two perps. The other guy probably hid in the bottom of the cart. Both were shot right through the head—single headshot each. Large caliber rounds. Just like at the Church."

Corwin scowled, his hands on his hips.

They solemnly surveyed the corpses of their fellow detectives.

"We're going to get these bastards," Corwin said under his breath, his voice tight. "They're not getting away with this."

The uniformed officers, tactical team and detectives all nodded. Gabriel heard someone mutter under his breath, ". . . brass verdict . . ."—meaning the perpetrators were not going to reach a trial by jury.

"None of that, guys." Corwin shook his head and turned away from them. He brushed the curtain aside and looked out the window. He gave a frustrated sigh.

One of the SWAT officers entered the suite. "Found a body in the service elevator landing down the hall. One shot through the forehead. Looks like he was Room Service." He shook his head. "Just a kid, man."

Corwin turned around, grimacing. "Start clearing the hotel," he ordered the tactical team. Then he looked intently at Gabriel. "So, why'd they want Darlene so bad if she didn't know anything?" Gabriel avoided his gaze. Corwin motioned for Gabriel and Irene to go into the bedroom and shut the door behind them. "All right, Furst, what're you not telling me?" he asked in a clipped tone. He always used "Furst" rather than "Maverick" when he was upset with Gabriel.

"I'm not sure this is a secure location, LT."

Corwin led them to the bathroom, and he closed the door. He removed a portable electronic jammer from his tac suit. Though with a shorter range and not as efficient as a standard model, it would block any electronic transmissions in the vicinity within ten feet. "Now tell it to me straight," he said with narrowed eyes. "Everything."

The bathroom was small, and Gabriel was getting claustrophobic, especially with his lieutenant glaring at him. He began, "Darlene said Patton was working on a project called Atropos. She thought it had something to do with a chip."

"And?"

"Atropos was the Greek Fate who cut the thread of life."

Corwin thought for a moment. "So, you think it was a chip to kill robots to limit their lifespan?"

"That's one possibility," Gabriel said slowly.

"That sounds like sci-fi," Corwin said. "And robots don't last forever anyway, so why do they need that?"

"If they could kill on command with a touch of a button, it would be worth billions—even trillions—to replace all those units. People have killed for less."

"So, you think Titan is behind all this?" Corwin asked in a skeptical tone. "But why kill Patton?"

"I believe he was going to end the project. He must've told Carmichael at their meeting at the Rialto. They probably knew he was getting cold feet and were ready to kill him if needed."

"So, Carmichael just blew him up?" Corwin asked in a tone of disbelief.

"It would've been just another terrorist incident if we hadn't gotten involved."

"What do you mean?"

"Remember the café bombing happened on the day of the Cal Trans bombings. CT, Major Crimes and the Bomb Squad were all tied up. Usually, they would've called the DNS Counterterrorism Team to run the café case, but the Deputy Chief called RHD instead."

"Because he hates the DNS after they blamed him for the clusterfuck last year," Corwin said, slowly nodding.

"If they'd caught the case, then the café explosion would've all been under their purview. They could blame the bombing on Patton and make it seem like he was loony. Then, if word somehow leaked about the project, no one would believe him. They'd already planted the pen and the chemicals in his garage. That should be pretty convincing since they thought they'd run the case and wrap it up quickly. But Patton survived the café, and we caught the case. So, they had to kill him at home and make it look like a suicide because of a guilty conscience. We started asking questions, so they killed the Reverend and anyone else who knew about this project."

Corwin looked thoughtful.

"There is also something else to consider," Gabriel said slowly.

"What's that?"

Gabriel took a deep breath. "If Patton also worked at K-Tech, then Project Atropos could be for them. Chuck Coffer worked with Patton at Titan. He said it was not one of theirs."

"And this means—?"

"K-Tech makes the RFID chips in all of us. Patton could've been developing a chip designed to kill people."

"But why would they do that?" Irene asked.

"It would be very useful to be able to use the chip to kill someone on command. Let's say someone is holding up a bank or committing some type of serious crime. All the DNS would have to do is press a button to eliminate him. Presto!—problem solved."

Irene looked doubtful. "You really think they would do that?"

"Absolutely. They could also activate the kill switch of anyone who did not conform to their agenda."

"But that'd be too obvious." Irene scoffed.

"Not if they make it look like a heart attack or stroke or something 'natural.'"

"I can't believe that Gerry Carmichael would take any part in that," Irene said.

"Don't let that polished charm fool you. He's a businessman first and foremost. I doubt he'd let ethics or morality get in the way of making money. And the DNS would pay big, big money for that capability."

Irene shot him a skeptical look.

Corwin was quiet for a few moments. Gabriel knew the LT might be doubtful. But his gut instinct had proven itself in many cases over the years.

Finally, Corwin asked, "Do we have any evidence or witnesses that haven't died or disappeared?"

The group was quiet.

"Get me something I can take to the D.A.," he said as he shut off the jammer.

CHAPTER 19

Saturday Evening

After he dropped Irene off at Beck Tower, the Medical Examiner's Office notified Gabriel the bodies of the Haddad family would be released the next day. On the way to Katherine's, he called the mosque the Haddads attended and asked for the senior cleric. A balding man in his sixties with an olive complexion and a neatly trimmed, gray beard appeared on the screen in the Raptor. He wore a light-colored tunic and a white *taqiyah* cap.

"*Asalaamu alaikum*, Peace be unto you," Gabriel said.

"*Asalaamu alaikum*," the imam replied.

"Imam, my name is Gabriel Furst. I'm a friend of the Haddad family."

"Yes, that was terrible—the entire family," he said in a gentle but rich voice, shaking his head. "Ahmed spoke very highly of you. He said you are a detective with LAPD?"

"Yes."

"How may I help you, Detective Furst?"

"Their bodies are being released from the Medical Examiners tomorrow, and I need to arrange for their service."

"We can pick up and arrange for the preparation of their bodies for the *salah* service. They need to be washed and wrapped beforehand, which we can do here," the imam said.

"Yes, whatever needs to be done. I understand that they will need to be buried as soon as possible."

"Yes, according to Islamic law, we cannot cremate their bodies. But it is of course very expensive here."

"I will cover the costs for the burial for the family."

The imam's expression warmed, and he asked, "You will want to be part of the service? Ahmed said you were like his brother."

"Yes. Please let me know when everything will take place and what I can do. I will let the ME's office know to release them into your care."

"Thank you, Detective Furst. I will speak with you soon."

"Thank you, Imam."

Gabriel arrived at Katherine's condo. She opened the door looking beautiful in a short yellow polka dot sheath.

Taking a look at his grim demeanor, she asked, "What happened?"

He gave her a stiff peck on the lips as he entered. "Rough day at the office."

"Do you want to talk about it?" she asked, closing the door.

He sighed. "Probably shouldn't. Seems like anybody who might know anything is getting killed or is missing."

"Oh." She paused. "Well, I'm a big girl and can take care of myself. My dad was a cop for over thirty years. And, oh, by the way, he was the chief, too, you know." She joked, then took his hand and led him to the couch. "Can I get you something to drink?"

"What do you have?"

"Beer, wine, water, tea, coffee."

"What kind of wine?"

"White or red?"

"Red."

"I have cabernet."

"Sounds good." He took a deep breath, trying to relax. They were still virtual strangers who had been quite intimate once. Recalling that night excited him despite his black mood.

She headed to the kitchen.

He looked around. The slightly cluttered condo had picture frames and mementos everywhere. Some pictures showed Katherine with her family— her parents and a boy who was a younger version of her father, probably her brother. The digital photos dissolved into others, which appeared to cover her college and medical school years. There were multiple images of her with a few girlfriends and several with two different men. One was a thin, light-brown-haired, serious-appearing young man with a much younger Katherine. The other was a tall, blond Norse god.

"Who are these guys?" He picked up one of the frames when she came back into the room with two wineglasses.

"Oh." She blushed, handing him a glass and sitting down beside him on the couch. "I really should take those out. Um, this one," she said, indicating the younger man, "is Colin, my first boyfriend, from college. We're still friends. And the other is Sven, my boyfriend in med school."

"He looks very impressive."

"He was—and quite impressed with himself, too."

"It looks like you went out for a long time."

She nodded. "Last three years of med school. I thought he was The One."

"What happened?"

"I found out he was not as—exclusive as I was."

"Oh," he said, inclining his head sideways. "Not a very bright guy then, was he?" After placing the wineglass down, he pulled her onto his lap so she was straddling him and kissed her lips and her throat. She gave a sultry laugh, wrapped her arms around him and kissed him back. Their kisses deepened. He reached under her dress.

Half an hour later, they laid naked side by side on the floor of her living room, their breathing finally slowing from their exertions. Gabriel's stomach growled, reminding him he missed lunch while working the hotel crime scene.

Hearing his stomach, she said, "Oh, I'm such a terrible hostess! The food's probably cold by now."

She reached for her clothes, but he snatched them away, shaking his head. She laughed and rose from the floor, walking to the dining table. He ogled her nude, shapely figure, making her blush.

"So, what are we having?" he asked, following her.

She opened the take-out cartons on the kitchen table. "There's Mandarin Chicken, Roast Duck, Tofu and Vegetables, and Hot and Sour Soup. I slaved away all day to make this, so you'd better appreciate it!"

"If it's not synthetic food. I like it already!"

Laughing, she said, "Yeah, I'm not a big fan of synth food either. Real Chinese food always makes me feel better—or at least makes my stomach feel better!"

"And a beautiful stomach it is, too," he stated. "You know, if you quit your day job, you could always be a model."

"Flatterer," she accused.

"I'm a cop. I only tell the truth."

She laughed. "Nice try, but I've known too many cops."

They ate their dinner and talked easily, laughing a lot. Gabriel felt the tension drain from his body despite his crappy day. He gathered the dishes, taking them to the sink, and then grabbed a cloth to wipe the table.

"Oh, I'm sorry. My dishwasher is broken, so I have to hand wash everything."

"You know, you really should get a dom-bot—and fix your dishwasher—to help you with the housework."

"Are you saying my place is messy?" she asked, hands on her hips, pretending to be insulted.

He grinned. "No, I'm saying there are better things to be doing instead of washing dishes. Here, let me," he said, coming from behind her, cupping one breast and taking the washcloth from her hand with the other. "It's the least I can do since you slaved all day over dinner."

She laughed and moved aside. "I don't know what I'd do without Chinese take-out and drone delivery."

Filling up a small sink with soapy water, Gabriel asked, "So, how did you get into medicine?"

She smiled. "Law enforcement wasn't for me, unlike my father and my brother."

"Your brother?"

She was quiet for a moment, her face dark. "Rob is a couple of years older. He was stationed at Wilshire for a few years." She stopped.

When she didn't continue, he prompted, "What's he doing now?"

She was quiet. "I don't know. He left the force—why—he wouldn't tell me. He disappeared soon after that. Once in a while, we—my mom or I—get a call from him asking for money, but I haven't heard from him in two years. I think he got into drugs."

He looked at her. They were both quiet for a moment. "I had a brother, too. I mean—he's still alive—if you can call it living."

"What happened to him?" she asked, leaning against the broken dishwasher.

"Fifteen years ago, Wes was a surgical resident and went home for the night after being on call. He took some Sleepers but got called back in for a mass casualty. He forgot to put the car on autopilot, and the Wakers didn't have time to work before he crashed into a tree. He has severe brain damage and has been in a coma ever since. Even with stim implants, stem cells and nanochips, he just lays there. He doesn't move on his own. When he opens his eyes, he doesn't talk or focus on anything. I don't see my brother in them."

"I'm so sorry."

"He was the family's golden boy—Dad's favorite and always the star athlete of whatever sport he played. He graduated salutatorian and lettered in four different sports. And, of course, he was very good-looking and very popular with the girls."

She regarded him for a moment. "So, what were you like as a child?"

He chuckled. "Let's just say that if I continued on that path, I'd have a long rap sheet and probably be serving some serious time—*if* they were able to catch me."

She laughed. "You were a juvie?" she asked, sounding shocked.

"Hey, I only got arrested a few times."

"A few times!"

"My crew wasn't very bright. They kept making mistakes and getting caught."

"So, if you worked alone, you might not have gotten caught?" she teased.

He grinned. "I'd like to think so. The first couple of times, the cops and judges went a little easy on me because of my dad. And, luckily, Jon Frieze was my lawyer the last time I got caught."

"The defense attorney that was killed?"

"Yeah—great guy. I guess he saw something and took me on as a special project. He believed in me and got me thinking about the future. I stopped hanging out with my old friends and started to take school seriously. I wanted to become a lawyer like Jon."

"What changed your mind?"

"I was in college studying pre-law and married already when he was murdered. The police never found his killer. So, I switched majors and decided to join LAPD to figure out who killed him and catch other bad guys."

"Did you ever find his killer?"

He shook his head. "Not yet. I have copies of the files from the guys who caught the case. I work it once in a while to see if there's anything new. The trail is pretty cold after fifteen years, but I'll catch his killer—someday."

They were both quiet.

"So, are you going to tell me about what happened today?"

He sighed. "I'd hoped you'd forgotten about that." He rinsed the last dish, placed it in the drying rack and dried his hands.

"If it's bothering you, I want to know about it—as long as it's not something that's classified of course." She reached out and stroked his cheek gently with her thumb.

He nodded. "I guess you'll hear about it on the news anyway. We were protecting a wit—my witness—and it got all fucked up. Two RHD detectives were killed—young guys with families. The witness is missing. God only knows what they've done with her. She's barely older than my own daughter," he said, his throat tight.

"Does this have to do with Uncle Jim's case?" she asked.

He nodded. "Whoever is behind this doesn't care about life—anyone's life—and they don't care how messy this gets." He gave a tired sigh.

She held his hands. They were both quiet for a few moments.

"That reminds me—the autopsy for Laila Harvey yesterday."

"What happened?"

"She had a coronary air embolism—that's air in the arteries supplying the heart. It's usually seen in patients with pulmonary blast injury, but she had no evidence of that kind of injury on the body scan. I just don't understand how she died. I'm sure I didn't miss anything. We didn't find anything else on her post indicative of blast lung either. She never had problems with getting enough oxygen. Her oxygen sats were normal the whole time she was in Obs. Usually signs of blast lung show up in the first few hours, and her scans were completely clear except for her perforated ear drums and of course her ASD."

"ASD—what's that?"

"An atrial septal defect—a hole between the atria, the two upper chambers of the heart. Hers was small enough where it usually wouldn't cause any problems, but the blood between the two sides can get mixed that way. If you remember from high school bio, normally, all the deoxygenated blood goes from the right side of the heart to the lungs to get oxygen and then back into the left side of the heart and pumped to the rest of the body. They don't mix. But with an ASD, the blood can get

Chapter 19   **145**

mixed in the heart, so that some deoxygenated blood can get into the left side."

"Where do the arteries supplying the heart come from?"

"They come off right at the base of the aorta—the big artery coming out of the left side of the heart."

Gabriel was thoughtful. "So the ASD showed up on her body scan?"

"Of course."

"Was that in her chart?"

"It was in the radiologist's report of the scan."

"Who has access to her chart?"

"Well, all the docs, nurses, techs working on her case. What're you thinking?"

"Is there a way someone can cause air to get in her heart?"

"Yes, if they accidentally inject a lot of air into a vein, but the nurses are very careful about that."

Gabriel thought for a moment. "Did she have an IV when she died?"

Katherine paused, tilted her head, looking up as if mentally reviewing the chart. "Yes, I believe so. It was running TKO—to keep open—which is very slow."

"What if somebody injected air into her vein through the IV, could it end up in her coronary artery?"

Katherine eyes widened, her mouth agape. "You think someone did that deliberately to her?"

"That could have caused a—what did you call it—a coronary embolism?"

"A coronary air embolism." She nodded. "Yes, it's very possible. But she was in an open unit. It would've been impossible for anyone to inject air into her IV without being seen. And cameras record everything in there."

Gabriel grinned and held her face between his hands, planting a kiss on her mouth. "That's the best news I've had all day!"

She laughed, stroking the hair on his chest, trailing it down his abdomen and then lower. "The best?"

He kissed her neck as his hands cupped her buttocks. "Well, maybe second best." He lifted her up in his arms and carried her to the bedroom.

CHAPTER 20

Sunday Morning/Afternoon

The next morning, Gabriel informed Irene about Laila's autopsy findings and his suspicions. They headed over to the security office at University Hospital to review the closed circuit recordings from the Observation Unit. Using the staff directory, they identified the nurses and doctors by Laila's bedside throughout her brief stay. Though she was not on oxygen, a respiratory therapist in scrubs and a white lab coat stopped by a few minutes before her cardiac arrest. He kept his face averted so it was never clearly seen on the video footage. Only his red hair was visible. The man's head disappeared below the top of Laila's bed for a few seconds.

"He may have access to the IV tubing down there. Look and see who that was," Gabriel told his partner. "Something about that guy is familiar, but I can't place him."

The therapist walked quickly out of the unit afterwards. A few minutes later, nurses and then doctors rushed to Laila's bed to resuscitate her. Irene had the security tech go back and zoom in on the name on the respiratory therapist's lab coat. After digitally enhancing it, they could barely make out a grainy "F. M—"

Irene contacted the Obs Unit and asked for a list of medical staff on duty at the time and who was assigned to Laila. No respiratory therapist was assigned to her, but they did find an RT, Fred Majors, who was assigned to other patients in the Observation Unit that shift. Most on the list were usually on the night shift, but they were able to speak with a few who were working the day shift. None of them could explain what happened to Laila that night.

Next, they headed to the morgue to track down the hospital pathologist who autopsied Laila Harvey. Dr. Vincente Ortiz was in his early sixties with gray peppering his wavy dark hair. The detectives introduced themselves.

"We're here about the autopsy on Laila Harvey," Gabriel said.

Dr. Ortiz leaned back in his chair and peered at them over the top of his reading glasses. Here was the second person wearing glasses in the past few days. Most people preferred corneal surgery or lens implants to correct their vision. Glasses were uncomfortable and bulky. "I wish I could help you, but they already took the body, my report and my samples."

"They who?" Gabriel asked, knowing the answer.

"The DNS—Agents—oh, what were their names?"

"Weston and Harmon?" Gabriel hazarded a guess.

The pathologist nodded. "Said not to discuss the case with anyone, too, otherwise I'd get arrested," he added in a grave voice.

Gabriel's hopes plummeted. Most people feared the consequences of defying the DNS. Everyone heard stories about people who disappeared after their arrest—except Irene, apparently.

The older man replaced his reading glasses with his regular ones from his shirt pocket. He deliberately wiped the lenses of his reading glasses. After a minute, he looked at the LAPD detectives and said, "In my day, you had something called freedom of speech and pursuit of truth."

Gabriel's heart leapt. "Was there something unusual about her death, doctor?"

"Yes. She died from a coronary air embolus. What's unusual was that she had no other signs of pulmonary trauma. I did a very thorough gross examination of her lungs and found no signs of blast injury whatsoever. I was going to do the microscopic evaluation today, but they took all the samples. Usually, pulmonary blast injury causes systemic air embolism in the acute phase or after mechanical ventilation, which did not apply in her case. But she definitely had air in her coronaries."

Irene asked, "Can you please translate that into English?"

The pathologist smiled and said, "That means, young lady, in blast injury, an abnormal connection can occur between the lung's air spaces and the lung's vessels, so that air gets into the blood directly, goes into the heart and then gets pumped throughout the body."

"And this could have caused the coronary air embolism?" Gabriel asked.

"Yes, but that occurs in the first few hours after the blast and may be exacerbated by being on a ventilator. But in Miss Harvey's case, none of those applied. And the high resolution scan of her body just before her autopsy didn't show air emboli in the pulmonary veins, which we should see if those had originated from her lungs."

"Could the air have been introduced through her IV then?" Gabriel asked.

Dr. Ortiz gazed at him with a grim expression and then said slowly, "With her ASD, something like that could explain how the air got into her coronaries without pulmonary trauma." He paused for a moment. "You're suggesting someone did this on purpose—kill this young woman— in the hospital with all those people around?"

"That's what we're looking into."

The older man shook his head and muttered, "To survive an explosion only to be murdered like that . . ."

"What did you put as the cause of death on her death certificate?"

He handed the death certificate to them. "I put down what they told me to put down—coronary arterial embolism secondary to pulmonary blast injury. Unfortunately, we no longer have the body or the scan, so I cannot confirm your suspicions."

Gabriel nodded. "Thank you, Doctor."

On the way to the car, Irene asked, "Why would he put that down as the cause of death if he suspected otherwise?"

"Because you do what the DNS says, or you don't see your family again." He settled in the driver's seat.

"Seriously! You really are paranoid! Those are just rumors. This is still a democracy. Anyway, that only happens to the illegal immigrants they catch. They can't do that to U.S. citizens."

He shrugged. "Believe what you will. But they are in this one up to their necks."

She was quiet. "I don't believe they would do that. Besides, why would they be involved in a private company's business?"

"Titan/K-Tech supplies their battlebots and RFIDs. And most of these DNS guys are ex-military, many in Special Forces. They're trained to kill using anything around."

"Sam told me about his life. He was Navy but certainly not special ops," she said, defending her new boyfriend.

"Spec Ops are sworn to secrecy for life. Most of what they do is top secret. They're trained to think they're doing their duty for the country's

Chapter 20

149

security."

"So, they're being patriotic."

"That's what they think, yes."

"And what do you think?"

Gabriel was silent. He didn't want to get into another argument with his partner. Then he realized something. "That respiratory therapist—now I know what it was about him—his bearing. He's ex-military, but there's something else familiar about him, too."

"Well, let's check him out."

They went to the home of Fred Majors, in one of the high-rise apartments near the hospital. A young, slender, blond man answered the door. He wore jeans and a T-shirt with a "Save the Earth, It's the Only One We Got" logo on the front.

Gabriel and Irene introduced themselves and asked for Fred.

"Fred's still sleeping. He worked last night and just got home a few hours ago."

"This is important. It involves the death of a patient at the hospital a few nights ago," replied Irene.

"All right," the friend said reluctantly. He went down the hallway, opened the bedroom door, and spoke to someone, presumably Fred, in a conversation indistinct to the detectives. The roommate came back and said Fred would be with them shortly.

A minute later, a muscular man with bright red hair and a hairy chest appeared in a pair of scrub pants. Rubbing his eyes, he limped down the hallway with a mobile cast on his right knee.

"Detectives, what can I do for you?"

"You're Fred Majors?" Gabriel asked.

The man nodded. "What's this about a patient that died?"

"Were you the respiratory therapist for the Observation Unit on Tuesday night?"

"Tuesday night—oh, yes, I was."

"Was Laila Harvey one of your patients?"

"Who?"

"Laila Harvey."

Fred appeared to search his memory.

"She was in an explosion and was watched in the Observation Unit."

"Oh, her—the one that coded. I was late to work that day and got to

Obs after she coded."

"You were never by her bedside before then?"

Fred shook his head. "I came in as they were working on her. One of the other therapists covered for me until then."

"We have you on video."

Again, he shook his head and looked Gabriel in the eye. "You must be mistaken. I'm telling you—I never saw her until she coded. You can ask the guy who took my place."

"What happened to your leg?" Gabriel asked.

"I busted my knee Tuesday afternoon playing beach volleyball."

"You've been limping ever since?"

"Yeah, had to go to the orthopod at the evening clinic—said it was a torn cartilage. It took 'em all damn evening to put on a fricking mobile cast, which is why I was so late for my shift. You'd think since I work at the hospital, they'd take care of me faster."

"Can I get the name of the doctor you saw?"

Fred told him.

"You have any problems bending down or kneeling?"

"Yeah, it really hurts when I do that. Luckily, most of the time, I don't have to do that for my job. But, it hurts now to run to codes."

"What do you usually wear at work?"

"My scrubs, of course."

"How about a lab coat?"

"Well, we're supposed to wear one."

"How about on Monday night—were you wearing one then?"

The respiratory therapist shook his head. "Couldn't find it in my locker. Thought I left it there, but I haven't found it."

'Where's your locker located at?"

"It's in the ICU Employee Lounge."

"Who has access to your locker?"

"Well, it's got an electronic combo lock. I guess anybody who knew the combination."

"Ever been in the military?"

Fred exchanged a knowing look with his roommate and laughed, "No, not the military type."

"All right, thank you for your cooperation. Have a nice day," Gabriel said and turned around to leave. His partner looked at him.

Chapter 20

After the door closed behind them, Irene asked, "What's up? You actually believe him? We have video with him on it. We should take him in."

Gabriel shook his head. "It's not him. The guy in the video didn't limp and could bend down below bed-level when he tampered with the IV tubing. Also, after Laila Harvey's heart stopped, when all the people were around her bed, this guy limped in without a lab coat."

"Maybe he took it off. Maybe he's faking the limp."

"Call the doc."

Irene spoke with the orthopedist and found out Fred was telling the truth—his injury had been confirmed with a scan. The doctor assured them Fred could not bend down on his knees easily.

"I still don't think he's off the hook," Irene muttered.

"You don't like him, do you? Because of his lifestyle?"

She shrugged, disapproval written all over her face. But she only said, "So, we're back to square one."

"Somebody knew the hospital routine and had access to employee lockers. Let's get the list of employees of University Hospital. And we need all the hospital's surveillance videos. Maybe another camera picked up the guy's face, or we can see his movements before or after. Let's get a warrant."

Irene inclined her head. After obtaining the warrant, she put in a call to the hospital human resources office, which sent the complete list of employees to her comms. The security department would compile and send a copy of all surveillance recordings from the relevant day to her later.

They headed back to Beck Tower and updated the Captain and LT. Fitz and Johnsen, who just finished doing background checks on Titan employees, groaned when Yokino assigned them to help Gabriel and Irene run background checks on the over five thousand hospital employees.

The Captain gave them a sharp look. "A tech from Electronics will help."

This took up the remainder of the day and promised to take a few more. However, just before they went home for the day, Johnsen poked his head into Gabriel and Irene's office.

"Mav, I got something." That was as excited as Johnsen ever sounded. "A nurse in the ICU is named Cherie Farmer. The ICU is right next to the Observation Unit, and she works there sometimes."

Gabriel looked up expectantly at the older detective.

"Her maiden name is Harmon. You remember Steve Harmon, one of the DNS agents who was here the other day. She's Harmon's little sister, though it doesn't actually say that outright, of course. But, according to her bio, her parents have the same names, dates and addresses as Steve Harmon's parents—even though her name doesn't come up on his bio or hers on his, of course."

"So she'd know where all the cameras are and could've gotten him into the staff locker area." Gabriel smiled. Things were falling into place. "Nice pick up." He saw a flash of a rare smile on Smiley's face at the compliment before he left.

Gabriel's comms showed an incoming call from Phil Zimburg from FSD.

"Hey, Mav, the aerial DNA scan from Patton's study just came back. The prelim shows five different sources—one was Patton, two from you and your partner, and two unknowns. In the final report, these two were deleted."

"DNS?"

"Probably."

"Can you match the DNA if we get a sample from a suspect?"

"If we can—" Someone interrupted Phil in the background, and there was a muted discussion. He came back on, "Uh, sorry, no, the detector totally deleted them from the system, and we're out of sample."

Gabriel swore.

Phil continued. "Sorry, pal. Hey, I've still got several hours of work here. How about we grab a snack—our usual place, the cantina?"

"Uh, we're a little busy—" Gabriel began but then stopped as he realized it was an unusual request, and Phil was trying to tell him something. "But I guess we can spare ten minutes. How about we meet in five?"

"Sounds great. See you then." Zimburg disconnected.

"You want to join us?" Gabriel asked his partner. She nodded and as they headed down the elevator, he said, "I think he's got something."

"How can you tell?" Irene asked.

"We never eat together here."

CHAPTER 21

Sunday Afternoon

Walking into the busy cantina on the ground floor of Beck Tower, Gabriel saw that the Zimburg brothers were already digging into their food. He acknowledged them with a nod and went to order his snack. As he and Irene sat down, Paul whispered he had activated a white noise generator to block any eavesdropping attempts. Anyone outside a 5-foot radius would hear nothing. He also had a signal jammer in case anyone bugged them.

The Zimburgs eyed Irene.

"Nothing we say here gets out, understood?" Gabriel asked his partner. Irene nodded. "Of course."

"She's all right," Gabriel said to Paul and Phil, vouching for his partner.

"You're sure?" said Paul.

Gabriel turned to Irene, who looked back and forth between him and the brothers. She gave a firm nod. He always trusted his instinct about his partners, fellow officers and detectives. So far, he was batting a thousand. True, there was always a first time. But he considered her trustworthy despite her romance with a DNS agent, who might be a suspect, and despite his contentious history with her father. Gabriel nodded to the brothers. "Go ahead."

"As I was saying, before Paul told me that your phone or office may still be compromised, I think we can do a DNA profile comparison if you can get a sample from a suspect."

"How? I thought you said the DNA machine deleted the results." Irene looked puzzled.

"It did. However, I took a screen shot of the preliminary results. I had a case a few years back that deleted a sample in the final report, so now I get a screenshot of all initial results. If we get the suspects' samples, I can run and compare them manually."

Gabriel grinned. Phil's ingenuity and tenacity were why fellow detectives and district attorneys all loved working with him. "What if the machine deletes it again?"

Smiling, Phil said, "I'll do it at home on an old DNA analyzer connected to an air-gapped computer, so no one can hack in. It's got its own power generator, so no one can get in that way either. It'll take longer, but I can prep a run tonight if we get a sample soon."

"You have an old analyzer at home?" Irene asked, her blonde brows arched.

"I've got lots of old equipment the department replaced. But it's unofficial, so we won't be able to use the results in court."

"But it'll give us an idea if we're on the right track," Gabriel interjected.

"So, can you get the sample?" Phil asked, palming a long, tube-shaped sample collector from his lab coat under the table.

Gabriel turned to Irene. At first Irene looked back at him with a puzzled expression. Then, as it seemed to dawn on her what he was asking, her face flushed.

"It'll prove his innocence if he's not a part of this," Gabriel said.

Irene grimaced and glowered at her partner but accepted the sampler under the table and deftly slid it up the long sleeve of her tactical uniform. She excused herself to go to the restroom.

"She happens to have a sample with her?" Phil asked.

Gabriel nodded but didn't elaborate.

"Hey, I asked some buddies about K-Tech," Phil said in a low voice despite the jamming devices. He also covered his mouth to thwart any lip readers.

"Yeah?"

"Well, I know people who stake out that building—you know, since they make the RFID chips there. They tell me that over the past few years that some people go in but never come out again."

"What're you saying?"

Phil whispered, "I mean they take prisoners there—DNS prisoners from the Fed building downtown—and no one sees them walking or rolling out of there—or anywhere else ever again."

Chapter 21

After several years on the police force in some pretty brutal crime scenes, nothing should surprise him anymore, but Gabriel's jaw dropped. "You're saying they're killing people there?" he whispered back, covering his mouth.

Phil shrugged. "You're the detective. You figure it out."

Gabriel sat back in stunned silence. Things were starting to make sense. Then something else occurred to him. "Our electronics were compromised. Irene's HDI—could someone have tampered with that?"

Paul looked deep in thought. After a moment, he replied, "Well, any tech can be hacked. If someone had her access code, then he could install malware in her HDI she can't detect. Then when she connects to any system, that malware can transfer to it, including our LAPD system. But, so far, I haven't heard any rumors of that particular hack. And they'd probably have to get pretty close to her HDI to install it."

"But if anybody can figure out how, it's the DNS and K-Tech. After all, the NSA and CIA all became part of the DNS, and we know at least one of them had no qualms about human experimentation or eavesdropping," Phil said.

The other two nodded solemnly.

Irene rejoined them, passing the sampler discreetly back to Phil, who adeptly slipped it into his coat pocket.

"How long will the results take?" she asked.

"I'll isolate the DNA tonight. If it doesn't need amplification, I can run it overnight. We might know tomorrow morning," Phil said.

"You'll see," she said to Gabriel.

"I hope for your sake that you're right."

"I am," she insisted.

Gabriel wasn't sure whether she was trying to convince him or herself.

Heading back to their office, Irene said, "We just got the surveillance recordings from the hospital."

At her deskunit with Gabriel looking over her shoulder, Irene scanned the recordings from the hallways near the Observation Unit on the night of Laila Harvey's death. A red-haired man in a white lab coat with an ID badge approached from the direction of the Intensive Care Unit and entered the Observation Unit a few minutes before Laila's code. He kept his face averted from all of the cameras. After exiting the Obs Unit, he walked briskly to the west stairwell, away from the ICU. A few minutes later, after the code blue was called, a red-haired respiratory therapist without a lab coat limped from the direction of the ICU into the Obs Unit.

"Do we have any cameras for the ICU Staff Lounge where Fred Majors' locker was?" Gabriel asked.

Irene rapidly searched through the videos. "No, it looks like the cameras monitor entrances of the units, patient care areas and the hospital entrances except the employee entrance. The footage from that west stairwell from that time period appears to be looped, so we still don't have his face."

He pounded his fist on her desk. "Shit! So he could have waltzed in through the employee entrance, gone to the ICU employee lounge, stolen Fred Major's coat and ID, come down the west stairs and exited the employee entrance without ever showing his face on a single camera!" He gave a long sigh. "Obviously, somebody told him where all the cameras are."

"Yeah. I'll keep looking through the video to see if anyone resembles the guy."

"He'd have taken off the wig and lab coat afterwards, so you'll have to look at the height and the walk. He walks like a military guy."

"Yeah, that should narrow it down." Irene groaned, slapping her forehead.

"See if you can find Harmon's sister Cherie Farmer on video. Maybe she helped our suspect get in. If she's really involved in this, then it might be Steve himself."

Gabriel received a skeptical glance and a scowl. She was probably rolling her eyes at him but not to his face.

"We'll need to find out who has access to these recordings and how they got looped. I'm going to check to see if the guys in III are in."

She grunted at him, her eyes focused on the screen.

Gabriel headed down the hall to the offices of Robbery-Homicide Squad III, assigned to investigate the deaths of the two RHD II detectives at the hotel as well as Darlene's disappearance. Squad I, Gabriel and Irene's squad, was too closely involved, so the Captain assigned the investigation to Squad III. Although it was Sunday, Gabriel found the two detectives in their office, dedicated to finding their colleagues' killers. The senior partner, Grant ("How") Howard, a tall, rugged, black man in his late forties, had curly, dark hair peppered with occasional streaks of gray. His partner, Lucia ("Lucky") deSoto, was a Hispanic woman in her late thirties.

Early in their partnership, they survived a shootout with a drug cartel faction. Howard was shot five times, twice in the chest. "How in hell had he survived?" became his tagline, quickly shortened to his "How" nickname. DeSoto escaped unscathed and became "Lucky." Both had reputations as solid detectives.

How and Lucky acknowledged him with a nod as he entered their office. How sat in front of his monitor, with Lucky looking over his shoulder. Gabriel recognized video from the hotel surveillance cameras on How's monitor.

"The hotel's cameras caught two men leaving the back of the building around the time of the murders. But they kept their heads down, so we don't even have partial faces. They were alone. We haven't seen Darlene leaving through any of the hotel exits," Lucky said, brushing back a lock of her dark hair from her face. "No contact with any of her friends. She has no family and hasn't shown up at the gym for her daily practice. They say she's always there by early afternoon."

"The video from the northwest staircase was looped. The perps may have gotten in and out that way. The hallway leading to that is very close to the back entrance of the hotel. Maybe they killed her and hid her somewhere in the building before leaving. If so, we haven't found a body yet," How said.

"But why hide her body when they left two dead detectives in the room?" Gabriel asked.

The other two detectives shook their heads and shrugged.

"Can you show me the video of those two suspects?" Gabriel asked.

"Of course." How brought up the video from the relevant time frame.

The men came in through the back door at 11:16 a.m. and exited the same way at 11:41 a.m. They used their hands to shield their averted faces. Both of the men seemed very familiar—too familiar—but he didn't want to jump to conclusions. He called Irene to come look at the video.

"Bolton, doesn't that one walk like the man in the hospital video? It's the same military gait, and he has his head down," he said, pointing.

"Yeah, could be but without the red hair and lab coat." Then Irene's face turned ashen. She said, "Go back. Look at the other man's right hand. Focus on his pinky."

How reversed and zoomed in, but the picture was pixelated. "Looks like a ring but not a wedding ring. A class ring? It looks dark."

"Hmmm. Maybe. Is that a white stripe in it or something?" Gabriel asked. "Can you zoom in even more?"

How used the digital enhancer, but the grainy image deteriorated. He shook his head. "The resolution of the hotel camera's shit. This is the best we can get."

Gabriel looked at his partner, who was silent. She avoided his gaze.

"Anything else you wanted to see?" he asked Irene, who shook her head. Something suddenly struck him. "Hey, what gym does Darlene go to?"

"Her neighbor said she goes to the one on Cerise in Hawthorne," replied Lucky.

"The one with gymnastics?"

Nodding, Lucky said, "She's apparently a star gymnast and will probably make the Olympic team next year."

For the first time in two days, Gabriel grinned. "That's it. She's alive." The others looked at him. "She must've heard the commotion in the outer room and ran."

"Ran where?" Irene asked.

"Out the only way she could go—the balcony. The door was bolted. That gave her enough time to get out while they were trying to break through. She climbed to the balcony above—knowing most people will look down first. They can't see much of that balcony from below. All she had to do was stay back from the edge. They'd made enough noise that they expected security any moment. So they had to leave before they could check the room above."

"But what happened to her? Where is she? We don't see her leaving the hotel," Lucky asked.

"These cameras just cover the entrances. She could've climbed down the balconies. Do they have cameras covering the grounds?"

How nodded. "But we didn't see anyone leave the premises on those views. But there are gaps in the coverage."

"Thanks. Keep us informed if there are any new developments."

"Of course," Lucky replied.

Back at their office, Gabriel scrutinized his partner, who was still pale with a grim expression on her face. "You recognized that ring, didn't you?

It's Weston's," he guessed.

His partner swallowed and tucked a stray blonde lock behind an ear. After a moment, she looked up at Gabriel and slowly nodded. "He has one that's similar—a class ring—on his right pinky. It's black onyx with a white streak through it."

They were both quiet.

"When do you see him again?"

"He said he'd be out of town until tomorrow." Her voice wavered.

He could tell she was trying not to cry. Gabriel said, "It's getting pretty late. Let's call it a day."

She shook her head. "I'll keep going through these videos," she said, her voice tight.

"Do you want any help?"

With a weak smile, Irene said, "I can get through them a lot faster by myself. You worked late the last few days. It's my turn."

"As you wish."

Gabriel received a message from the Medical Examiner's Office. He headed over to escort the bodies of the Haddad family to the mosque for preparation and burial.

"I'm going to nail these guys' asses, *akhi*," he said out loud to the transport stretcher containing the remains of Ahmed as it was loaded onto the van the mosque provided to transport the family. "I'll get justice for you and all the others they murdered." They finally made a mistake that could ID them. He smiled to himself. Probably nothing that would hold up in court, but maybe it wouldn't have to . . .

CHAPTER 22

Sunday Night

Gabriel arrived home just after ten p.m. The brief service and then burial for the Haddad family was over. Tears still welled up at the memory of his shroud-wrapped friends being lowered into their cold graves, especially Adeline's small body. At least he buried them according to their faith, even if it cost him a month's salary.

After removing his police uniform and equipment, he pulled on a pair of sweatpants. Gabriel listened to his messages while forcing himself to swallow a dinner he couldn't taste. There was one from Katherine asking to get together that evening. He called to let her know that he just arrived home. She sounded sleepy and said she would get back to him the following day. As Gabriel was finishing, his comms indicated an incoming call from a fast-food burger joint.

"Hello?"

"Hello, is this Detective Furst?" whispered a familiar, nervous voice.

Gabriel recognized it. "Darlene! You're all right!"

"I left my comms at the hotel, so I haven't been able to call, and I have no money."

"Stay right there. I'll come to you. Don't talk to anyone."

Gabriel didn't know whether his comms was being monitored. He had to get to her quickly before someone else could intercept her. He hastily donned a T-shirt and had Robert pack the leftovers and fill a thermos with water. He locked his comms in a shielded bag and turned off the GPS on the Raptor to avoid being tracked. These were the most common tracking methods, but he couldn't turn off his RFID chip. On the way out the door, he picked up his Glock.

Gabriel raced to the restaurant in a cold sweat, fervently hoping no one would beat him to Darlene. He parked in front and quickly surveyed the surrounding area. His pulse finally slowed when he saw her, safe and unharmed at a table in the rear. She saw him and ran into his arms.

"Where have you been? We've been so worried about you!"

"I was hiding. I knew they might be watching anyone I know," she whispered, her voice shaking.

After checking the surroundings again, he hustled her into his vehicle and took off in a fast U-turn. He kept scanning the traffic behind them looking for a tail. After several evasive maneuvers, Gabriel finally let out a cautious sigh but remained vigilant. He had an idea of how to keep her safe, but it would not go over well with the Captain or the brass. But better to ask forgiveness than permission.

He offered her the leftovers and water, which she downed voraciously.

"How did you get away at the hotel?" Gabriel asked.

"I heard the noises, gunshots and people falling in the outside room. I knew they were coming for me. I'd locked and bolted the door, just like you told me. That gave me time to get to the balcony."

"You climbed up?" he asked.

She nodded. "I hid on the balcony above. I knew they couldn't follow me, and they couldn't shoot through the concrete. Then I went up again and again after I heard them go back inside."

He smiled. "Smart girl. That gymnastics saved your life."

"Yeah. The Reverend always thought I'd go to the Olympics someday, but now he'll never see me there," she said, her voice shaking.

Gabriel gave her a moment to recover, then asked gently but firmly, "Darlene, what didn't you tell us? Why do these guys want you bad enough to kill two cops?"

"I don't know," she said in a small voice.

He could tell she was holding back. "They know you know something. What is it?"

She was silent.

"You need to tell me. Otherwise Patton, the Reverend, his bodyguards, Chuck Coffer, the two detectives all died for nothing."

"Chuck's dead, too?" Fear and shock crept in her voice.

"Yes."

Darlene sniffled and swallowed hard. After a minute, she said, "Then they'll get me, too."

"No, I can protect you."

"How? Those two detectives died protecting me."

"I know some place else. It'll be a little—unconventional, but you'll be absolutely safe." He hoped.

She was quiet for a few moments. "You're sure?"

"Yes, I promise. Tell me everything. You said Patton was working on Project Atropos. Was that a kill switch for robots?"

Shaking her head, Darlene said, "No, it's not for the robots. It's for the chips inside *us*."

Gabriel froze, his worst fears confirmed.

"That's why Dr. Patton needed the Reverend's guidance. They forced him to do it."

"How?"

"He told the Reverend they killed his wife. And they threatened his daughter and her family if he didn't finish the project."

"Did he say how it worked?"

Darlene shrugged. "He did, but I didn't understand all the tech talk. He said they could push a button and make someone just drop dead. It'd look like they had a heart attack or stroke or something."

"Was this project for the DNS?"

"He never really said—just that Carmichael was forcing him to do it."

Gabriel's gut wrenched as he considered the infinite ways the DNS could abuse such technology. It all made sense now.

"Where are we going?"

"You'll see."

In the dim light of the crescent moon, he flew to the northwest side of the city toward one of the No Man's Lands. He turned off the headlights and activated the Raptor's defense protocols as he approached and flew over the wall. Machine gun fire or rocket-propelled grenades or other flammable, explosive projectiles were the most popular greeting to any vehicle at night—especially police vehicles. At least he was in an unmarked car. He hovered over an unlit area looking for the best place to land in the near total blackness. The geo-radar displayed a contour map of the immediate area—buildings still in ruins and debris strewn around. He placed his gun in the center console before landing.

He turned to Darlene, who looked at him with a terrified expression.

"Stay inside until I say it's OK. If something happens to me, hit this button, and it'll automatically take you to Beck Tower. Then press this button to call my partner, Irene—you met her. The vehicle is completely bulletproof. You understand?" He decided not to mention it was not RPG-proof.

She nodded, wide-eyed, looking at him as if she were seriously questioning the wisdom of having come to him for help. He smiled reassuringly and patted her white knuckles clenching the thermos. He hoped she wouldn't have to experience yet another traumatic event in her young life by watching him die in a hail of bullets. And he really preferred not dying just yet.

Gabriel landed in a patch of dirt that was barely clear of debris. Several tough-looking, tattooed men in camouflage immediately surrounded them, blinding him with bright floodlights. All were armed with automatic weapons pointed at him. He took a deep breath, opened the door just wide enough to ease himself outside. He quickly shut the door, which locked behind him. The pungent, ripe odor of unwashed bodies enveloped him, almost making him gag. He forced down his nausea. No need to offend the trigger-happy natives.

Hopefully, Foley remembered his debt after all this time.

"What d'ya want, pig?" A muzzle pressed against Gabriel's chest over the heart. How do these gangs always recognize cops? I'm in a T-shirt and jeans and not the camo uniform, and I was in an unmarked car.

"I'm here to see Foley."

"He's sleeping."

"Well, wake him up."

"What makes you think he wants to see you?"

"He knows me. Just tell him Furst is here calling in his marker."

The young man eyed him with a sneer but spoke into his comms. His eyes widened when he got the reply. He motioned for the others to lower their weapons, which they did so—slowly.

Gabriel motioned to Darlene to get out of the car. She looked around, bit her lip, and hesitantly got out of the Raptor.

NMLs were very dangerous at night, especially for law enforcement. Surrounded by the gang and blinded by the flashlights pointed at him, Gabriel could barely make out the gang graffiti marking their territory. He and Darlene followed their guide across the rubble-strewn street into a half-standing ruin of what used to be an apartment building. A reddish-brown "6-4" was painted in what looked suspiciously like dried blood on the wall next to the broken glass door. Only their escorts' hand-held lights illuminated the stairway down. They were patted down for weapons. Gabriel left his in the Raptor. Two of their guides unceremoniously put hoods put over their heads.

Darlene cried out in surprise.

"It'll be OK," Gabriel said, his voice muffled by the black hood.

Rough hands pulled them down the steps and pushed them around confusing turns through an underground maze. Finally, they stopped, their hoods removed. They stood outside a locked, heavy, metal door.

One man rapped on the armored steel door with the butt of his weapon and looked up at the nearly invisible mini-camera embedded in the wall over the entry. Two muscular, tattooed, armed men opened the door, their weapons pointed at Gabriel and Darlene as the uninvited guests stepped inside. The heavy door clanged shut behind them.

The spartan, dimly lit room contained two scarred, metal tables; some unpadded, metal chairs; and an ancient refrigerator with a bad compressor motor. In jarring contrast, the opposite wall was covered with state-of-the-art monitors showing not only the hallway entrance they just came through but also views of nearly their entire territory. They must have a portable generator since electrical service didn't exist in the NMLs. Are we even still inside the NML?

Gabriel suspected the dark stains on the hard-packed dirt floor might be dried blood but decided now was not the best time to ask. He looked toward the back of the room, where a large man sat in the shadows. For a few moments, there was complete silence.

"Leave—all of you," the shadowed man ordered in a deep, rumbling voice.

"You sure, boss?" one man asked.

"I . . . said . . . go . . . now," he said slowly, without raising his voice. His men turned and quickly left the room. The door locked behind them.

Stepping out of the shadow, the pale, bald, muscular man was average height. A long scar that ran above his left eyebrow and down his cheek made him appear menacing. He wore tactical camos and twirled a gleaming tantō blade in his right hand. "Your marker expired a long time ago, pig."

Chapter 22

"A marker for saving your sorry ass never expires," Gabriel said evenly, sounding more confident than he felt.

The other man moved with surprising speed and thrust the point of the tantō against Gabriel's neck.

Darlene stepped back and gasped.

Appearing outwardly calm, Gabriel stood his ground. "Oh, put that toy knife down, Ryan. You're not going to kill me—yet."

After a moment, Foley grinned and sheathed the blade. "Furst, you're a fucking whack job. No other LAPD cop comes into my turf without at least a small— eh, maybe a medium-sized—army, especially at night."

Gabriel rubbed his neck where the blade had been. He was surprised— and relieved—at the lack of blood. It sure felt awfully sharp. "Yeah, well, no one else in the LAPD has saved your ugly butt—twice."

"True."

Both laughed, hugged and slapped each other on the back.

Ryan Foley's gaze moved to the teenaged girl. Gabriel saw Darlene's eyes widen as she probably realized this was the legendary, ruthless leader of the notorious 6-4 gang, known for its vicious feuds with other gangs as well as law enforcement. They got the name "6-4" from hanging their enemies upside down before disemboweling and quartering them— preferably in public.

"What do we have here?" Foley asked.

"Foley, this is Darlene, a friend. I need you to keep her safe—very safe. Some very nasty people are after her. They've already killed several people."

"You pigs can't protect her?"

"They killed two cops that were protecting her."

Foley raised an eyebrow. "The hotel job? She must be very important if you're using up your marker. Who's after her?"

"DNS, probably. Think your men can handle this?"

The older man's smile turned feral, his blue eyes even icier. "It would be my pleasure. They set us up and took out a couple of my men a few months ago before we could get to them, so I owe them big time. My little army can handle them." LAPD estimated his "little army" had over two hundred of the fiercest, best-armed and experienced fighters. Some were Special Ops veterans, who knew a hundred ways to kill people. Others were better trained and more ferocious and efficient than any Spec Ops force since they weren't restrained by any rules of engagement. All were utterly loyal, willing to fight to the death for their gang and their leader. No 6-4 member had ever been captured alive by their enemies, including the LAPD.

"I'll have Maya look after her."

Maya, Foley's wife, used to be an active member of his gang and was as deadly as any of the men. She was also mother to their four children.

"Good," Gabriel said.

"Of course. Would you like to go say hi? I think she's still up with the baby."

"I'd like to, but it's getting late. Next time?"

"Well, she'll be sorry she missed you." Indicating Darlene, Foley asked, "So, how long can we expect to have the pleasure of this young lady's company?"

"A few days at most until this all blows over."

"We'll be square after this."

"You owe me two."

"The first one was just a little first aid."

"Which saved your life."

"Yeah. But this is a big ask. Especially if the DNS comes in."

"OK, so if they come, you can count this as two favors, and we'll be square."

Foley nodded. They clasped hands in their old gang handshake.

The gang leader smiled and sent orders through his comms. He opened the door, and the other gang members re-entered. Foley told one of the guards to take Darlene to his wife and that she was under their protection, a solemn vow binding the whole gang to protect her—to the death, if necessary.

Darlene started to object, but Gabriel quietly reassured her. She looked at him for a long moment and then gave him a tight hug. He gave her a comforting squeeze and murmured, "You'll be safe here. Trust me."

She finally released him and obediently followed her guide.

Gabriel nodded to his friend. "Give Maya my best." The hood was placed back over his head—maybe slightly less roughly—for his journey to the surface.

A few years older, Ryan Foley had once been a close friend early in Gabriel's high school years. They hung out together with their crew, committing petty crimes. Ryan became a surrogate older brother when

Chapter 22   **167**

Gabriel's brother Wes left for college, and Gabriel trusted him with his life. Although classified a hopeless delinquent, Foley had old school values—honor and loyalty above all else—which he pounded into his protégé's head.

As the cops closed in on their last job together, Gabriel volunteered to stay, distract the police and take the rap. He was the youngest and would probably get probation. But Ryan had to escape. If he were caught, he'd have to do serious time in prison, where there was a contract out on him.

That decision changed Gabriel's life. It was how he met his defense attorney and mentor, Jon Frieze. He went on to college and then the LAPD while Ryan joined the Marines and then the 6-4 gang. The last time they saw each other was ten years ago at a party, before The Big One and just after Foley married Maya. Despite Gabriel's LAPD status, his old friend greeted him warmly and introduced his new bride, a petite, muscular Hispanic woman with 6-4 tattoos peeking out from under the sleeve of her blouse. Apparently, Foley told her about Gabriel's sacrifice since she hugged him tightly and thanked him for saving her new husband's life all those years ago.

Gabriel climbed back into the Raptor and flew out of the NML in the dark. He turned on the headlights to merge onto the airlanes on his way home and let out a heavy sigh of relief. With a shaky hand, he brushed back his sweat-dampened hair. *God, I hope no one finds out where I stashed Darlene. Already got enough enemies—some very powerful enemies—out for my head—or worse.*

CHAPTER 23

Monday Morning

Gabriel walked into his office whistling. It was best for Irene and her career not to know about Darlene's whereabouts.

His partner looked up from her desk. "You're in a good mood."

"I've got enough to go talk to Carmichael again," he said, smiling.

"Yeah, well, we might need a séance for that. Gerry Carmichael was found dead this morning in his bathtub."

Gabriel froze. "What?" His good mood evaporated.

"Johnsen and Fitzsimmons are already there."

Gabriel updated Irene on Darlene's new information on the way to the Carmichael estate.

"It's a kill switch for people? How do they do that?"

"I don't know, but we can ask Paul."

"Well, that explains why they're trying to wipe out witnesses. Do you honestly think the DNS had something like that made?"

"Absolutely." Gabriel looked down at the streets below, orienting himself.

"You really don't like them."

"For good reason. Did you hear from Phil about the DNA results?"

"Yeah, he called this morning."

"And—?"

Irene said in a quiet voice, "You were right. It matched."

He reached over to briefly squeeze her hand. "I'm sorry." He paused. "Can you take him down when the time comes?"

Her jaw set. "Absolutely. He and Harmon killed two of ours and all those other innocent people." After a few moments, she asked, "Where's

Darlene?"

"You don't want to know." He avoided looking at her.

"Furst, how can we be partners if you don't trust me?"

"It's not about trust. I trusted you at the meeting with the Zimburgs. Remember?"

She nodded.

"It's better if you don't know. The brass would nail my ass—and yours—if they knew where I stashed her."

He sensed Irene's intense scrutiny. "How can you be sure she's safe?" she asked.

"She's in one of the safest places in the world—from the DNS anyway."

Irene started to speak, but he shot her a warning glance. She quieted.

After a moment, he asked, "So, you think Carmichael's really a suicide, or did our friends get to him?"

"Why would they go after him? He's their guy at Titan."

"Maybe he's also the weak link. They know that we believe he bombed the café. And if they finished Project Atropos, they don't need him anymore. But," he added, wrinkling his brow, "something feels off."

Several news drones circled the sky just outside the police cordon around Carmichael's Bel Air estate, not far from Patton's mansion. Multiple police, Forensic Science Division and coroner vehicles already packed the driveway. Gabriel had to park just inside the ornate front gate. He eyed the vast expanse of well-manicured lawn as he and Irene walked up the long driveway. A good-sized subdivision could easily fit just in the front lawn—and use a lot less water. They finally arrived at the front steps of the white, two-story mansion, a colonnade of Ionic pillars lining the front portico.

They donned the white crime scene coveralls in the portable dressing booth set up in front of the porch. Climbing the white marble steps, Gabriel noticed the elaborate moldings and relief on the front double doors, all covered in gold leaf. Inside, FSD techs systematically collected their samples. One FSD tech motioned for them to go up one of the two wide, plush-carpeted circular staircases on either side of the grand foyer. More gold gleamed from the elaborate crystal chandelier hung high in the domed ceiling, lined and sectioned by gold crown moldings. Even the window casings and wainscoting were gold.

As they walked up the curving stairs, Gabriel furtively pressed a fingernail into the bannister. Yep, pure gold—not just gold-plated. Between Titan HQ and the private mansion, the Carmichaels must've used up half the world's supply of gold.

The palatial master suite was located at the top of the staircase. The gold-trimmed double doors opened into a room centered on the king-sized bed, guarded by four golden pillars and an ornate gold headboard. Mirrors covered the entire bedroom ceiling.

Standing just outside the adjoining master bath, Phil was telling Fitz that the 3-D laser digital reconstruction of the bathroom was complete. His crew was nearly done gathering the preliminary evidence.

Seeing Gabriel and Irene, Fitz said, "The maid found the body this morning at 6:20 a.m. He usually ate breakfast at six. But when he didn't appear, she came upstairs and found this."

The unmistakable rusty smell of blood greeted Irene and Gabriel as they entered the master bath. The spacious room had thick, white wool Berber carpet and Italian marble counters encasing the separate his and hers gold sinks on adjacent walls. They passed a large, solid granite walk-in shower to the over-sized Jacuzzi tub, also with gold faucet and handles. The whole room was a temple to conspicuous water consumption. Most people lived within their monthly water ration allowance, unable to afford the exorbitant excessive water use rates that came with Jacuzzis or pools—obviously something Carmichael did not worry about.

"There are whole houses smaller than that shower, much less this bathroom." Fitz whistled, shaking his head, looking around, still wide-eyed.

The oversized, pure gold tub was filled with bloody water. The naked, pallid body of Gerry Carmichael lay supine with his head tilted left toward the detectives and the left side of his face partially submerged, the water covering his chest. He looked incongruously peaceful amid the crimson sea. Various lotions and scented bath oils on the ledge above the head of the bathtub were all perfectly lined up two inches from each other except the slightly askew bottles of shampoo and conditioner in the middle.

Gabriel leaned over to smell Carmichael's head. From the corner of his eye, he saw Irene watching him and then looking over at Fitz, who shrugged.

Two burly coroner techs, dressed in their white bunny suits and wearing waterproof nitrilon gloves, lifted the stiff, nude corpse out of the

Chapter 23   **169**

bloody bathwater. A sharp boning knife appeared, lying on Carmichael's belly with the handle pointing toward the detectives.

"Hold on," Fitz said and called a FSD tech back to take more pictures. Fitz then bagged the knife. The coroner techs hefted the corpse onto the plastic-lined bed of the hovering gurney, which was raised to waist level.

Dr. Cranston, the Medical Examiner on the scene, examined the body quickly while Fitz and Gabriel looked over his shoulder. Carmichael's skin was like alabaster except for the purplish red discoloration along the buttocks and lower back and the back of his legs. Now that he was out of the water, they could see that his left wrist had been slashed deeply along the length of the radial artery, from the wrist and halfway up the forearm.

"Interesting," Gabriel said.

"What's that?" his partner asked.

"Most people slash their wrists across the wrist, not along the arm." No coming back from that. "No hesitation marks, too. He probably had help." Gabriel glanced at the M.E., who glared at him.

"That's for me to decide, Detective. I don't do your job for you."

Fitz elbowed him before Gabriel could retort, "Well, you barely even do your job." He was already in deep political hot water with the brass and didn't need another complaint from the well-connected Cranston to be the final excuse to fire him. So, he bit back his frustration and added, "And the handle of the knife was on our side, his left side. If a rightie did this, you'd think it'd be on his right side. Carmichael was right-handed."

The M.E. scowled at him. "It could have turned around when he dropped it into the water." Cranston opened one of Carmichael's eyelids. Gabriel could see the cornea had clouded over before the M.E. jabbed a probe into the eye to measure the potassium level, which helped determine the time of death. Cranston skewered the liver with another probe, measured the water and air temperatures, and entered the data into his comms. "TOD between eight to ten p.m. last night."

The techs pressed a button, raising the gurney's transparent sides to curve over the body and lock with an audible click. The refrigeration unit activated, and the gurney lifted with only the quiet hum of the antigrav rotors audible. The techs guided it over the gold handrail and lowered it into the foyer, accompanied by the surly M.E.

After Cranston left, Gabriel asked Fitz. "Was there an open wine bottle or used wineglasses in the house?"

"No wine bottle, but there are some glasses in the rack in the kitchen."

"How many?"

"Don't know. I'll have Smiley check." He called Johnsen, who was downstairs.

Gabriel examined the polished, white granite ledge at the head of the tub from a shallow angle toward the light streaming in through the frosted glass windows.

"What are you thinking?" Irene asked.

"My guess—he had company, and it probably wasn't his wife. He didn't have time to wash his hair yet. Look here. These are water spots, possibly from condensation, and then someone wiped it—maybe with a hand—after he or she removed the wine bottle and glasses and then replaced the bottles of shampoo and conditioner." He indicated the barely visible marks. "Do we have the whereabouts for the wife for last night?" he asked.

"According to the maid, she left yesterday afternoon for a resort in La Jolla. She's on her way back," Fitz said. His comms beeped. "Yeah."

Johnsen's voice said, "We got twenty-two wine glasses. The maid says there were twenty-four wine glasses hanging on that rack yesterday afternoon when she left."

Gabriel nodded. "So, the wine was probably drugged, which is why she—assuming Carmichael's company was a woman—had to take the bottle and the glasses."

"How long for a tox screen and DNA?" Fitz asked Phil.

"I'll put a rush on them. Maybe two to three days at best."

"Have Johnsen ask the maid when she last cleaned this bathtub ledge," Gabriel said to Fitz, who was back on his comms to his partner.

"The master bathroom counters are cleaned every day. Last time was early yesterday afternoon."

Gabriel nodded, stroking his chin.

"Mrs. Carmichael just arrived," Fitz said after closing communications with his partner. "She's in the guest house in the back. Our guys cleared it already."

At the top of the staircase, Gabriel glimpsed a set of elevator doors at the end the hallway. Fitz and Irene followed him into the elaborate, golden elevator, reminiscent of the one at Titan. Wide-eyed, Fitz looked around and whistled in awe. Gabriel smiled.

The team went to the guesthouse located in the rear of the estate.

Standing just outside the entrance with a police officer was a handsome, young man in a chauffeur's uniform who appeared to be in his late teens to early twenties. He fidgeted, shuffling his feet. Fitz asked the patrolman to move the chauffeur away from the bungalow so they could interview the widow in private. The young man shot a worried look toward the guesthouse before following the officer to the pool while the RHD team went inside.

In the living room, the grieving widow sat on the gold-trimmed, overstuffed couch. She sobbed on the stoic Johnsen's shoulder, her flowing, blonde hair splayed over his bunny suit. Looking uncomfortable, he sent a desperate "rescue me" look to his fellow detectives as they entered.

Seven years ago, nineteen year-old supermodel Cynthia Taylor married the middle-aged multibillionaire. It was her first marriage and his fourth. Even with a tear-streaked face and red-rimmed eyes, she was still breathtakingly stunning in a low-cut, green silk mini-dress, which hugged her million-dollar swimsuit model body, barely covering her generous assets. Her five-inch heels made her already long, shapely legs appear to go on forever.

"Mrs. Carmichael, these are the other detectives I work with—Detectives Fitzsimmons, Bolton and Furst," Johnsen said, followed by a fresh burst of sobs from the widow, who briefly glanced up at the new arrivals.

Irene tried to disentangle the weeping widow's arms from Johnsen, but she clung on even tighter.

"I'm sorry for your loss, Mrs. Carmichael, but we need to ask you some questions." Gabriel sat on her other side. She finally released a clearly relieved Johnsen and clung onto Gabriel instead. He could see down her low-cut sundress that she had no underwear. He averted his eyes.

Fitz asked in a gentle voice, "Mrs. Carmichael, when did you last see your husband?"

"Yesterday morning before he left for work," she replied between sobs.

"When did you leave here for the resort?"

"I—I think it was around 2:30."

"Was anyone with you?"

"No, just my driver, who stayed last night—in a separate room, of course."

Fitz nodded. "Did anyone see you? Did you have dinner at the restaurant there?"

"Why are you asking these questions? Do you think I could have done this?" she asked with a wondrous tone.

"We need to account for everyone's whereabouts and activities. That way, we can rule you out as a suspect," he explained.

"Oh. I was in the spa for most of the afternoon, and then we—I had room service."

"What time was that?"

"I think it arrived around 6:30."

"When did you decide to go to the resort?" Gabriel asked.

"Yesterday morning. Gerry and I had a huge fight, and I wanted to get away," she replied, resuming her sobbing.

Fitz asked, "What did you argue about?"

She faced Fitz. "What we usually argue about—his women!"

"You think he was having an affair?"

"After the last time, he promised there'd be no more affairs, but I think he was seeing someone—even though he said he had to work late for some important project."

"Mrs. Carmichael, your husband died between eight and ten last night. Can anyone vouch for you at that time?"

She hesitated and then shook her head. "I went to bed early."

"Who were you with last night, Mrs. Carmichael? " Gabriel asked directly.

"What makes you think I was with someone?" she asked, looking up at him, indignant and flushed. She abruptly pulled away him, smoothed back her lustrous, honey-blonde hair back with her hand, and straightened her dress to emphasize her voluptuous figure.

"You had a fight with your husband about another woman. You left for La Jolla at 2:30 and stayed overnight. I'm sure when we check with the hotel, we'll find you had room service for two. And we can check the entry times for your room and your chauffeur's room," Gabriel said.

She stared at him wide-eyed, as if in disbelief he could be immune to her charms. Little did she know he already had extensive experience with very beautiful, very manipulative women.

Gabriel continued, "You were with him all night."

"How dare you!" She seemed flustered. Then, appealing to Fitz and Johnsen, she exclaimed, "You can't believe that I'd sleep with the—the

Chapter 23   **169**

hired help!"

"Did you?" Fitz asked.

"Well, I never!" She rose up from the couch and turned around, hands on her hips in all her supermodel glory.

Fitz told his partner, "Go talk to the chauffeur."

Johnsen started toward the door.

"No," the widow quickly interrupted. "You don't need to do that. You're right. He was with me all night."

"From about what time?" asked Fitz.

"From when we left here until this morning," she admitted, her tears miraculously ceased. She glared at Gabriel. "We arrived after three, had sex, went to the spa, then went back to my room and had sex. We ordered room service and had sex all night."

"When did you last bathe or shower in the master bath here?" Fitz asked.

"Yesterday morning. I like to shower at night and in the morning—and before and after sex."

Gabriel regarded her with a cynical eye. She must be the cleanest person on the planet.

CHAPTER 24

Monday Morning

They found Edward, the chauffeur, puffing by the pool. He was flustered and protective of Mrs. Carmichael and denied everything at first. However, confronted with her confession, he confirmed the details of the spa tryst.

Irene contacted the La Jolla resort. They corroborated Cindy Carmichael's timeline, confirming both alibis for the entire night. Unsurprised, Gabriel grunted. The suddenly dry-eyed widow and her boy toy are completely cleared—of murder, anyway.

Once allowed into the guesthouse, Edward sat with his arms around his mistress as she clung onto him. His eyes frequently wandered down her plunging cleavage.

"Man, who can blame the kid?" Fitz muttered under his breath to Gabriel as they shed their bunny suits at the front portico.

Gabriel snorted. "Anybody find Carmichael's comms yet?"

Fitz shook his head. "Forensics is still looking for it in the house."

"We get a GPS read on it yet?"

"Electronics is working on that. It must be completely powered off." Usually, a wrist computer was trackable unless the battery was removed or completely dead.

"Strange for a suicide, eh?"

Shrugging, Fitz said, "Lots of strange things about this 'suicide.' We're going to need a warrant for the cloud backup."

"Yeah, right." The cloud storage companies always contested search warrants, citing privacy rights. It was often weeks, or even months, before that data would be available.

Since Fitz and Johnsen were lead on the case, Fitz took off to attend the autopsy for Gerry Carmichael, which the mayor himself elevated to the highest priority, while Johnsen stayed to finish working the scene. Gabriel and Irene headed back to Beck Tower.

In the Raptor, Irene asked, "How'd you figure that those bottles by the bathtub had been moved?"

Gabriel directed the car away from the estate, deftly avoiding the multiple news mobiles hovering overhead. "All the bottles were precisely placed, labels facing forward except those two bottles—the shampoo and conditioner. While it's possible they were used and placed back there, he hadn't washed his hair yet. And there were no bubbles in the bath water, even after all that dripping and splashing while they moved his body out. So those two bottles must've been pushed out of the way for something else, most likely a wine bottle or wineglasses. The killer moved them back but not as perfectly positioned as before. I also saw dried drip marks just below the ledge, like someone wiped the counter above with a hand to remove the condensation from the wine bottle. Luckily, those counters are kept spotless."

"Ah."

"I bet the woman didn't get in the bathtub yet, so we probably won't find her DNA in the water samples. But we might get touch DNA from the counter where she wiped her hand or from his lips."

"Well, I guess we can't blame this one on the DNS," Irene said.

"Not so fast. This woman could be DNS or maybe just bait to get him in that position. We'll see what's on the tox screen, and maybe the aerial or touch samples'll show something."

"It could still be a suicide."

Gabriel shook his head. "It's too convenient—just when we're closing in on him."

"Maybe that's what sent him over the edge."

"Yeah, maybe, but I don't think he's the type to off himself—too much ego. And I'm sure he's got rich lawyers who could've gotten him off."

"Then, who's running the show if Carmichael wasn't the brains?"

"I think there's another player here that we haven't quite considered, but I'm not sure who yet. In the Titan records, do they have a system that tracks where people go after they enter the building?" Gabriel asked.

"Yes, in certain high-security locations, they record who and when they entered and exited."

"How far back do those records go?"

"They gave us the last month or so."

"Did Carmichael have a sensor in his office?"

Irene paused, projecting the screen from her comms onto the Raptor's on-board display. She quickly scrolled through several screens at a dizzying rate for Gabriel, who decided it was best to focus on driving. "Let's see— the Chip Design Lab, the Chip Manufacturing Facility, Research Labs I to XIV. I don't see anything about his office."

"Don't you think that's strange? Wouldn't his office be a highly secure area?"

She rapidly swiped backwards through several pages. "Oh, wait, there's info on his office a month ago for a couple of days but nothing since that. Let me see." Studying the screens, she was quiet for a few moments. "Hmmm . . . this is interesting. Most of his meetings involve several people, but he met alone with only one staff member on both days— Andrea Lisle—for over an hour starting at three p.m."

"Patton's assistant?"

"Yeah."

Gabriel stroked his chin. "See if you can trace Lisle's movements for the days prior to Patton's death."

Irene quietly studied several pages. "OK. It looks like she and Patton used to leave together around 10:45 and get back to the lab at 2:30."

"When you say 'leave together,' do you mean they left Titan?"

"Let me check the garage log." Irene said after a moment, "Yes, it looks like they take Patton's vehicle."

"So, they're going to and from K-Tech, like his GPS told us."

"When they return to Titan, Patton stays until around six p.m. Lisle leaves the lab before three p.m., comes back at four-ish and then goes home at six," Irene said.

"For all we know, she continued her visits to Carmichael's office at three every day." Gabriel paused. "How about on the day of the bombing?"

Irene checked the records. "Yes, she left the lab just before three and came back after four."

"Her usual time with Carmichael? But he was meeting Patton at the café."

"Yeah, but records show Gerry Carmichael left Titan at 2:49 that day."

"But she still goes to his office—maybe. Does Harold Carmichael show up in any of the monitored areas?"

Irene scanned through the Titan logs with her HDI. "Nothing other than Gerry's office a few weeks ago and occasional short visits through many of the research labs, including Patton's lab."

"So, whichever office he works in is not monitored," Gabriel said, disappointed.

Irene nodded.

"That's strange. You'd think he'd be in a secure office."

"Yeah, especially since he's the Executive Director of Research and Development," Irene agreed. She scrolled through some more screens. "Interesting."

"What?"

"The garage logs have him checking in every day at one p.m. and leaving at seven or so."

"He doesn't get to Titan until the afternoon every day?"

"Yeah."

"Either he gets to sleep in late every day, or he's somewhere else in the mornings," Gabriel speculated. His brows knitted together in deep thought. "We'll need to speak with Andrea again about what she's doing with Gerry Carmichael every day at three. What's her background?"

After searching the OmniNet, Irene read aloud, "Andrea Michelle Lisle. Born in 2034. Parents were in the Army. Attended MIT and graduated with a couple of doctorates—neuroscience and robotic engineering—at age twenty-four. Worked at Titan since obtaining her doctorates two years ago. Unmarried."

"Wow. Brilliant woman. What did her parents do in the Army?"

"Let's see. Father was in Military Intelligence, then retired to run a travel agency. Mom was also MI and retired to run the travel agency with her husband." Military Intelligence was now part of the DNS. The DNS only acknowledged service for retired or deceased MI agents—if at all.

Gabriel was thoughtful. "Want to bet those are both covers? MI officers don't retire to run travel agencies."

"You think they're still DNS agents?"

"I'd bet my life on it. Does it say where they were stationed?"

Irene shook her head. That kind of detail was usually redacted, even for law enforcement. They would have to submit a request to the DNS for that. "Do you think their daughter is also DNS?"

"Probably. Find out if her parents have any connection to our two DNS friends."

Irene quickly searched through a few more screens. "Well, there's no overlap with either Harmon or Weston that I can tell. Neither was in Intelligence. Harmon was a Marine and Weston Navy."

Gabriel was quiet and then remembered the photo on Andrea's desk. "How about Harold Carmichael? He was MI also. Was he ever in Kosovo?"

His partner was quiet for a moment. "Let's see—Harold Carmichael—he was Military Intelligence, but no details about where he served. I'll look through his social media." She was silent for a few moments, scrolling through the scant pictures and posts.

Gabriel glanced back and forth between the screen and the airlanes. "Stop. Go back."

Irene mentally swiped to the previous photo. Harold Carmichael was standing with his arms crossed, leaning against a familiar, Greek *pi*-shaped structure.

"That's it! That's in Kosovo. There's a picture on Andrea's desk of her as a teenager with her family in Kosovo in front of that very monument. Even the clouds look exactly the same, so they must have gone to this memorial at the same time, if not together."

"So they knew each other before he left MI."

"Yeah." Gabriel landed the Raptor on the parking deck at Beck Tower.

They stopped in Corwin's office to update him on the latest developments.

Gabriel leaned on the Lieutenant's desk. "We need Titan's records for entries and exits yesterday."

Corwin nodded, connected his videocomms to Titan Robotics Security Office. The on-duty guard took a few moments to reply. His request for the log of the entries and exits for the previous day was denied by the CEO's office. "I'm sending my detectives over there, and it had better be available when they arrive!" the normally convivial lieutenant growled and then pointed to the door, wordlessly ordering them to go.

Roberta, the executive assistant, greeted Gabriel and Irene when they arrived at Titan. She escorted them to the reception area of the CEO's office. They waited in the large and lavish antechamber with all the amenities—baked goods and drinks, including a bar. The Stepford gynoid gracefully motioned with both hands for them to sit down on the plush sofas surrounding a large, circular glass coffee table.

"We apologize for the wait. As you might expect, the company is in an upheaval at present. The Board is meeting now and will conclude shortly," she said in a lilting voice. "May I serve you a beverage while you are waiting?"

Both detectives declined. Roberta sat down at her desk.

"Roberta, you're the executive assistant for the CEO, right?" Gabriel asked.

"Yes, you may consider me that."

"So, you see who goes in and out of the office?"

"Of course."

"You must have Gerry Carmichael's appointment calendar in your memory. In the past month, did Andrea Lisle meet with him every day at three?"

"I am very sorry, but I am not at liberty to discuss company meetings and attendees without a warrant. You will need to discuss that with our new CEO." She sounded so sincere that Gabriel was impressed by the advancement in technology over his Automated Home System. He again noticed that she, like late her employer, never used contractions.

"Who's the new CEO?" Irene asked.

"They board is selecting one right now. That is why we could not give clearance for your superior's request for information. It must be approved by the CEO."

"I see," Irene replied.

A few minutes passed.

"The meeting has concluded, and your request for the entry logs from yesterday has been approved. Here it is," Roberta announced and transferred the information to their comms.

The inner office elevator door opened, and several people stepped out, most of them men, grim-faced and solemn, along with two women with eyes still red from crying. They ignored the detectives and crossed the anteroom to the main elevators, which promptly opened, and disappeared from view as the doors slid closed.

"He will see you now." Roberta rose and led them to the door into the CEO's office.

The door opened, and Gabriel saw Harold Carmichael gazing out the gold-tinted windows overlooking the city. His profile looked exactly like his twin brother Gerry, especially without the suddenly absent mustache. Putting his glasses back on, he turned around to greet them, his expression somber. He shook their hands, his comms visible just under the frayed right cuff of his well-worn, gray sweater.

"Detectives, sorry to make you wait. It has been a stressful day around here as you can imagine."

"Of course," replied Irene.

"You received the logs from yesterday?" Carmichael asked.

Gabriel nodded.

"Is there anything else I can help you with?"

"Yes. Can you think of anyone who may have wanted your brother dead?" Gabriel asked.

Harold looked at them and then nodded with a sigh. "This business is very competitive. My brother secured many contracts, beating out many rivals. I am sure there is a long list of people he alienated."

"Do you know if he was having an affair?" Gabriel asked.

"He frequently had other women. I have no knowledge who his latest conquest was."

"Could it be Andrea Lisle?"

There was a slight, almost imperceptible hesitation before he replied, "Andrea? Jim's assistant? Why would you think that?"

"She had an appointment with him almost every afternoon."

"And they both came in yesterday on a Sunday and left around the same time," added Irene, who must have been quickly reviewing the updated logs.

"I am sure that was mere coincidence. I left around that time as well yesterday."

"Where were you yesterday evening?"

"I happened to be with Miss Lisle—all evening until this morning."

"Where?"

"At my house."

"Were there any other witnesses?"

"No, but surely you do not really think I would have anything to do with my own brother's death?" Harold protested calmly, his left hand splayed on his chest.

"Can you prove you were with Miss Lisle all evening?" Gabriel asked, not at all convinced.

"Well, you can look at the security logs for my house if you would like. I have a sensor at my residence."

"We'd like that."

"Then, I will have it delivered to you, Detective. Now, is there anything else? I have many matters that require my immediate attention. I am sure you understand."

"Of course. One other thing—why is there no log of the visitors to this office the past month?"

"What?" Harold appeared startled. "Maybe my brother had the sensor turned off."

"He can do that?"

"He was the CEO. He could have requested the monitor to be temporarily deactivated. I will have to make sure that gets turned back on."

"We need to see your brother's appointment calendar for the past month."

"Is that not on his comms?"

Gabriel shook his head. "We haven't been able to find it."

"Really? He always wore it. I will have Roberta send that information to you as well."

"And we will need to speak with Miss Lisle."

Carmichael nodded. "Of course. Roberta can take you to her lab." He reached his hand to shake theirs as his other hand brushed back the unruly lock of blond hair that fell onto his forehead.

Gabriel froze for a moment and stared at Harold Carmichael, but he quickly recovered. Fortunately, neither Irene nor Carmichael seemed to notice anything amiss.

CHAPTER 25

Monday Afternoon

Roberta was waiting for them in the anteroom and transferred the entry logs for Harold Carmichael's residence to their comms. The life-like gynoid then guided them to the Robotic Chip Design Lab where Andrea Lisle was wrapping up the daily staff meeting. Everyone quietly returned to his or her work area, a few with covert glances at their new director and the LAPD detectives. Andrea approached them as Roberta turned and left.

"Detectives, how may I help you?" she asked them in a solemn tone.

"May we speak somewhere private?" Irene asked.

Andrea gestured to her office in the back, and they followed her inside. The door silently slid shut behind them.

"Miss Lisle, all this must be quite upsetting for you," Irene said.

Andrea's eyes watered. "Well, to have lost Jim and Chuck and now Gerry in just a few days—" her voice broke.

Gabriel picked up the digital picture frame from her desk. "Well, I'm sure with Harold Carmichael is CEO, everything will carry on as before."

"Harold has been elected CEO?" Her face brightened as she gave a small smile.

"Yes, haven't you heard?"

"He hasn't contacted me since this morning."

"So you haven't heard from him in the last hour?"

"No. You saw I was in a meeting."

The picture of Andrea with her parents at the Kosovo monument appeared on the digital frame. Gabriel angled it to show his partner. "Where did you go after work yesterday?"

Noticing Irene's glance at the picture, Andrea's eyes darted back and forth between the detectives. She hesitated before replying, "I was with Harold at his place all evening."

"For the entire night?"

"Yes."

"How long have you been seeing each other?" Gabriel asked.

Her fingers twirled a lock of red hair. "Oh, for about six months but we wanted to keep it quiet because—you know—the company."

"Of course." Irene paused before asking, "Why were you going to Gerry Carmichael's office every afternoon in the past month?"

"We meet—I mean—we met so I could update him on the lab's progress since Jim was too busy to do it himself."

"This would take an hour every day?"

Andrea nodded. "R & D is one of the most critical divisions at Titan. Most people thought Gerry was just the figurehead of Titan. But he was quite involved in all aspects of the projects. He had a lot of ideas that he wanted implemented. We spent part of the time discussing those ideas."

"Why did these meetings just start in the past month?" Irene asked.

"Well, I think Gerry always wanted daily meetings, but Jim was too busy to have them more than once a week. Jim finally gave in and sent me instead."

"So, what do you think of Harold Carmichael as CEO?"

"Well, I'm glad for him—but under such terrible circumstances— his twin brother—" her voice broke. "Harold is brilliant, so I'm sure the company will continue to grow. Of course, I may be a little biased." She blushed.

Gabriel moved to stand in front of her desk. "Where were you on the day of the bombing at three p.m.? We know Gerry was meeting Patton at that time."

She stopped twirling her hair. "I was with Harold."

"In Gerry's office?"

She looked at him, her eyes widened. "How did you guess?"

He didn't buy her surprised expression. "Have you ever been in Gerry Carmichael's house?"

"Only for company parties."

"Never in his bedroom or the master bathroom?"

"No, of course not."

"So we won't find your DNA in our aerial or touch sample from his bathroom?"

Gabriel noticed an almost imperceptible hesitation before she replied, "Come to think of it, I might have used the master bathroom during one of their dinner parties recently."

Gabriel leaned over the desk closer to her. "Why did you lie about Patton not working at K-Tech?"

"I'm sorry?"

"You were his main research assistant. You knew he worked there. In fact, you went with him every day."

"He was working on a secret company critical project. You have not been cleared for that information."

"This is a murder investigation!" Gabriel growled in her face. "I have whatever clearance I need!"

"I thought Jim and Gerry committed suicide," Andrea replied, seemingly unfazed.

"It's looking more like murder with so many people hiding all the facts!"

"We have not been hiding anything relevant," she insisted without raising her voice.

"I think you have, Miss Lisle, and you're in the middle of all of this!"

"I have cooperated fully with the police and will continue to do so despite your rudeness. But your supervisor will be receiving a complaint from me."

"Go ahead. Add it to the pile!" Gabriel slammed down the digital photo frame and stalked out of the lab. Waiting for them outside the entrance of the lab was a security bot that guided them to the garage. They didn't speak until the doors of the Raptor closed and locked and they were heading away from Titan.

"What was all that about?" Irene asked.

Gabriel smiled and calmly said, "That is one cool lady. I think her parents and the DNS trained her well—not even the slightest twitch or sweat when I was yelling at her. She's one of the best liars I've ever seen—and those crocodile tears . . ."

"Yeah, but are you sure that's the best approach?"

"Just want to stir things up a bit—rattle them. They have to make a mistake soon."

Chapter 25

Gabriel deftly weaved the Raptor through L.A. traffic while Irene quickly scanned the security log from Harold Carmichael's house. Lines flowed in a blur across the car's screen.

"It confirms that Carmichael and Lisle were at his house from about 7:15 p.m. until this morning."

"Can this log and those from Titan be altered?"

"Possibly."

"Would Carmichael be able to do this?" Gabriel asked.

"I'm pretty sure Harold Carmichael has an HDI."

"Yeah, I noticed he communicated with Roberta without using his comms."

"He was head of R&D. So he has the tools and know-how to interact secretly with digital devices. Or he could've had Roberta do it. Since she's the executive assistant, she probably has high-level access and could've used it to alter Titan's records. She could do it very quickly and not leave a trace."

Gabriel grunted. "So, basically, we can't trust the logs they gave us."

Irene's lips thinned as she gave a quick nod.

"Shit." He slammed his hand against the steering wheel, blew out a breath and thought silently for a few moments. He decided to share a nagging suspicion. "Do you think it's possible for someone to change their RFID temporarily to someone else's?"

"No. The ID section is write-once and the unique code programmed at the factory. It's burned into the chip, so you can't reprogram that part. What're you thinking?"

Gabriel drew a deep breath. "I'm wondering whether Patton actually met with Gerry Carmichael or Harold Carmichael at the café. Harold could have reprogrammed his chip to pretend to be Gerry—if that were possible."

"Why do you think it might've been Harold?"

"Gerry's forelock was on the right, and Harold's the left. Gerry is right-handed and Harold a leftie. On the bank surveillance video across the street from the café, Carmichael's forelock was on the right side, but he brushed it back with his left hand—the one that Harold used just now. Also, Gerry drank lattes with extra cream, but Harold drinks espressos—black. Remember, that's what Laila told us the Carmichael in the café ordered."

His partner looked at him with a raised brow. "That's hardly going to hold up in court. What about his mustache when we first saw him?"

"A fake one. And suddenly today there's no mustache."

"Patton knew them since they were kids. Do you really think he could've mixed them up?"

"Yeah. They may not look exactly alike now, but if you look closely enough, I'm sure they're identical twins. Many people can't tell identical twins apart, especially if one's trying to be the other. And their voices are very similar."

"If Harold reprogrammed his chip and pretended to be Gerry, what happened to the real Gerry's signal?"

"Maybe he kept his usual three p.m. appointment with Andrea Lisle in the CEO's office with the broken sensor—like he said."

"How about Titan's facial rec and retinal scans? How did Harold get through them?"

"Without his mustache, he could get through facial rec since they're identical twins. There're contact lenses on the black market that can duplicate retinas, but they have to be perfectly placed to fool the scanners. But I'm sure Harold would have access to the biometric data files at Titan."

"We don't have any concrete proof that either Carmichael met with Patton. Harmon and Weston have the original recordings, and all our files got wiped. If they're really behind this, they're not going return those recordings. And we can't use ours in court since they're unofficial copies."

"No. I bet they already destroyed the original recordings," Gabriel agreed, his mind racing. "How about Regional? They archive the street camera recordings for years, don't they? They'll have the video feed—if Weston and Harmon haven't gotten to them yet." The Regional Holo-Recording Authority stored all the recordings from the street cameras.

"Do you want me to call and tell them we're on our way?"

Gabriel shook his head. "No, we don't want to give the DNS any advance warning."

Turning the Raptor east to San Bernardino, they passed over some walled No Man's Lands. Gabriel looked down. Some inhabitants scrounged around in the rubble-strewn streets under the relative safety of daylight. He knew finding anything to use or trade might improve their meager existence. He flew on in grim silence.

They arrived at a six-story, drab gray, concrete building, its rooftop

Chapter 25

packed with satellite receivers. Visitors parked in the front on the ground floor—with no shade. A blast furnace greeted them as they climbed out of the cool Raptor.

"Welcome to the Inland Empire, otherwise known as Hell. No, Hell is probably cooler," Gabriel muttered.

The parking lot shimmered in the intense and unrelenting sunlight. Every year it seemed to get a lot hotter out here—especially in the black tactical uniforms they had to wear.

Irene sighed, unbuttoned the top button of her black camo shirt, and rolled up her sleeves. They crossed the parking lot to the sliding duraglass door marked "Visitor's Entrance." Thankfully, it was cool inside though Gabriel could feel sweat still dripping down his back.

A blonde receptionist looked up from her screen as the glass doors slid silently closed behind them. She gestured them to the bioscanner on her desk to verify their identities.

Irene requested access to all of the street-level holorecords from the day of the café bombing.

The receptionist was silent for a few moments and then said, "Special Agent Albert will see you now." She gave them directions to the office of the SAC, located on the top floor.

Traveling up the semitransparent elevator shaft, Gabriel saw the endless cubicles on each floor. Reaching the sixth floor, they walked to the office labeled "L. Albert, Special Agent-in-Charge HR Data Storage." Another biometric scan again confirmed their identities. Approved, they stepped through the frosted duraglass sliding door.

A neatly-coifed, blond-haired man in his early thirties in a gray suit rose from his desk and greeted them. "Welcome, Detectives Furst and Bolton. I understand you need to look at some records?"

"Yes," Gabriel explained. "We need the recordings from eight days ago, any cameras within four blocks of Spring and First in downtown L.A. from two to four p.m."

"The café bombing? That's near the old PAB and City Hall, isn't it?" SAC Albert asked in a cheerful voice.

"Yeah, where my old office used to be." The old Police Administration Building had housed Robbery-Homicide until the move to Beck Tower.

Albert sat down in front of his monitor. The screens whizzed by.

He must be using an HDI to control his computer but maybe not as adeptly as Irene. She's probably faster, so he probably didn't get his HDI implanted as a young child like her.

"Well, let's see here . . ." he began and then trailed off, looking puzzled.

"What's the matter?" Irene asked.

"I—I can't find them. It should be here in last week's records since they don't get transferred to long-term storage until after two weeks. But I'm missing the recordings from the entire downtown area for that day between 13:42 and 18:05. There must have been a glitch in the system or something."

"Or something," Gabriel muttered under his breath. "How often does that happen? Could someone have taken or erased those records?"

"I'll look in the logs of the techs that day and see if they noted anything. Someone in the Viewing Room can watch the live feed. But erasing the feed from there without the tech knowing? No way." He paused and studied his screen for a few moments. "The tech covering that area noted a total blackout of the incoming feed from all downtown cameras. They later found it was due to a problem in the receiver covering those cameras and fixed it a few hours later. But the backup system should have kicked in. I don't understand why that didn't happen," he said in a bewildered tone.

"Could the system have been sabotaged?" Gabriel asked.

"Well—yeah, it's possible, but they'd have to access it here. It's a closed, one-way system, and our security is pretty tight. Everyone crossing that front desk has to be cleared, and there's a log. Let's see . . ."

"May I look?" Irene asked.

Albert nodded, motioning for her to stand by his side as he perused the entry logs on his screen. She leaned over beside him, and Gabriel stood behind them. The screens flashed by so fast it made him dizzy, but Irene and Albert seemed to analyze the data quite easily.

"Can someone who doesn't work here get in?" Gabriel asked.

"No, only authorized people are allowed to go above the Visitor's level. All our parking entrances are locked, and only our personnel who work here can enter."

"Would other DNS agents be able to get in?"

"Well, it depends—some, yes, but the system would still record their entry and exit times."

"Check for the past two weeks," Gabriel suggested.

Albert nodded. "I'm flagging anybody who doesn't work here."

"Do you have security video of the receiver array from the past two weeks?"

Albert retrieved the records and scanned and processed them at lightning speed. "There's nothing here, but . . ." He looked perplexed.

"What's the matter?" Irene asked.

"It didn't record the blown fuse for the receiver, which should have caused a small explosion. What the . . .?" he broke off, confusion evident on his face.

"Can we get a copy of the logs and the security video for the last two weeks?" Gabriel requested.

"Sure. And I'll go over this and see if I can figure out what happened and get back to you," Albert offered. He copied that information onto a data drive and handed it to them. They thanked him for his help and shook hands. The SAC still wore a puzzled expression as the door closed behind them.

When they got back into the Raptor after passing through the furnace again, Irene said, "Inside job?"

"Yeah." Gabriel took a deep breath and sighed. These DNS guys are too damned thorough!

CHAPTER 26

Monday Evening

Back at Beck Tower, Irene went to the office while Gabriel stopped by the Electronics Unit to look for Paul Zimburg, but he was out in the field. He then headed to the Forensic Science Division to find Phil, a brilliant hacker in his own right and almost as good as his brother.

"We need to talk in private," Gabriel said to Phil under his breath.

Phil nodded. They went to his small office in the back of FSD and shut the door. The criminalist activated an electronic jammer, the green light indicating it was on.

"Do you know if the identification portion of RFID chips can be reprogrammed?" Gabriel asked.

"Why do you ask?" Phil stroked his blond mustache.

"I think James Patton really met with Harold Carmichael, pretending to be his brother, at the Rialto."

Phil's eyes widened. "I've never heard of that capability, but I know someone I can ask. He was one of the original designers of the human RFID system. You really think Harold Carmichael reprogrammed his chip and bombed the café?"

"Yeah and back again."

"And he fooled the other bioscans." Phil blew out a breath. "Cool—and diabolical. He set up his own twin brother. Wow."

"Yeah."

"I'll ask my source and get back to you."

"ASAP."

Phil nodded and switched off the jammer.

At the case summary meeting that afternoon, Gabriel updated the squad on his and Irene's findings. But his theory about the Carmichaels twins' switch was met with general skepticism for the same reason Irene doubted it: the RFID chip's identification component was simply not reprogrammable. Also, while most commercial and consumer eye scanners may be fallible, reproducing retinal patterns in the exact orientation and physiology to fool the highly advanced scanners at Titan would be very difficult.

"But it is possible," Gabriel insisted. "And if anybody has the resources, Harold Carmichael would."

Captain Yokino conceded that point. "Then bring me proof we can use in court."

Katherine was working a late shift, so Gabriel headed home. After another simple but delicious dinner by his dom-bot, Robert, he collapsed onto his favorite recliner to watch an old rerun of *Sherlock*, the classic series from earlier in the century with Benedict Cumberbatch playing the famous detective. He was drifting off when the high-rise's security office called.

"You have a visitor, Philip Zimburg. Shall we let him in?"

"Yes." He walked over to the door and poked his head out looking at the parking area in the center of the complex. He saw Phil set his vehicle down in the visitor's area and then approach Gabriel's unit. Phil looked back and around before entering the residence. The door shut automatically.

"Don't think I was followed," Phil said. "We're taking a ride."

"Where?"

"To see that friend about the chip. He thought it'd be better to talk in person." Phil took out a device that looked like a Star Trek tricorder and pointed it at Gabriel, who raised a brow. "It's OK. It simulates your RFID so they'll think you're still here while we're away."

Gabriel nodded.

"I've got another jammer that camouflages our RFIDs and my car's ID while we're running around so they can't track us," Phil explained as he activated the RFID simulator. "OK, they should now think we're still here—unless they got actual eyes on us, of course."

"Should? Haven't you used this before?" Gabriel asked.

"Well, only in the workshop with Paul; this is the first time out in the field. We're the guinea pigs," Phil said in a cheerful voice, apparently oblivious to Gabriel's obvious apprehension as he motioned him to follow.

"Great. Hopefully, no one is watching us right now." He grabbed his gun and holster out of habit.

"Let's go." Phil led the way to his car. After buckling himself in, he took out another device and activated it. "We're clear—and digitally invisible to the DNS, but you might want to get down just in case they're watching for you."

Gabriel scooted down so that the top of his head was below the windshield. Phil pulled a blanket over him.

Phil programmed a destination into the GPS. Gabriel peeked and saw it was coordinates rather than an address. The vehicle lifted off and joined the heavy flow of traffic heading east, avoiding the walled-off No Man's Lands. They were both quiet, but it was the comfortable silence between old friends.

Phil looked behind and around them several times. "Looks clear. No obvious tail."

Traffic thinned out the further east they went. Gabriel sat up and looked around. He recognized the street signs in the Coachella Valley. They left the main airlanes and turned south. Traffic dwindled. Phil turned off the headlights as the auto-drive continued its course. "Just in case anyone's following us," he said.

They rode in the dark for several minutes, then circled over a fenced-in area, which appeared to be a junkyard. Gabriel could not discern much in the dark, moonless night. Using the geo-radar, Phil found a clear landing area on the south side, just outside of the enclosure.

"Your friend lives here?"

"Yeah."

Phil turned off the interior door lights before they both got out of the vehicle into the near total blackness.

"Wait a minute for your eyes to adjust," Phil suggested.

At first, Gabriel could see nothing, but gradually he could make out some faint, green, glow-in-the-dark markers beyond the closed gate of the chain-linked fence. They walked up to the gate, but it was locked.

"You're sure he's expecting us?" Gabriel asked.

"Yeah, but he's a little security-conscious."

Chapter 26

A narrow, horizontal ray of red light with billowing clouds appeared, getting bigger and brighter. Gabriel could barely make out the profile of a hunchbacked old man, pointing what looked suspiciously like the silhouette of a shotgun at them.

"Zimburg, is that you, boy?" he asked in a gruff voice with a slow, melodious, Southern drawl.

"Yeah, Arnie, it's me. I brought that friend I told you about."

The old man shuffled to the gate, unlocked the padlocked chain to let the visitors in and then relocked it behind them. He ushered them into what turned out to be the trunk of an antique, black Oldsmobile 88 with stairs leading down into an underground bunker. "Hurry, hurry!"

They descended the steps past the dry ice machine responsible for the profuse fog, presumably intended as countermeasures against any infrared scanners from above. The trunk door shut behind them, and the overhead lights came on. The old man switched off the dry ice. Gabriel could now see their host better. The wizened old man had wrinkles upon wrinkles, a grizzled gray beard matching his closely cropped hair, and bright, blue eyes behind thick, horn-rimmed glasses. With his shotgun, he motioned for them to go down the tunnel while he followed with the double barrels still pointed at their backs. Phil led the way, so Gabriel wasn't sure whether his friend noticed the weapon still aimed in their direction.

All the LED lights were motion-activated, turning on and off with their progress down the narrow passage. They walked by dirt-packed walls lined on either side with storage shelves filled with containers of fuel, water, dried food and supplies. Reaching the bunker's operations room, Gabriel saw eight-foot tall shelves along both sides of the large room packed with neatly stacked grenades, guns, sniper rifles, assault weapons and several thousands—possibly several hundreds of thousands—of rounds of ammunition. There were also rocket launchers with their respective projectiles close by. On the far wall, screens from security cameras set up all around the junkyard displayed infrared images of the surrounding areas.

Gabriel swallowed. *What kind of crazy survivalist shit has Phil gotten me into?*

The old geezer in ratty jeans and a frayed white T-shirt, wearing a bullet-proof vest, saw Gabriel eying the outdated arsenal. "More dependable than those modern electronic zappy things," he said.

Gabriel nodded, his index finger cautiously indicating the gun in his holster without touching it, lest the crazy old man view that as a threat. "I hear you." He was one of the few policemen in the LAPD who had not "upgraded" to a blaster. He preferred his 9 mil Glock over the new-fangled blasters any day. Blasters required less than a quarter of a second to fully re-energize in between discharges. In that amount of time, Gabriel could get off at least a few rounds with deadly accuracy.

The old man nodded back at Gabriel but still eyed him, squinting through his thick glasses.

Phil introduced them, seemingly oblivious of the shotgun still directed at Gabriel. "Arnie here was one of the developers of the RFID system for the government before the DNS took it over. He used to work with my father. If anybody knows about them, it's this guy."

"Yeah, that's why I don't have one," Arnie said.

"You don't have an implant?" Gabriel asked in amazement.

"That's right. As far as the DNS is concerned, I'm dead—invisible."

"They could shoot you on sight."

"Yeah, let them try. I'd take a hell lot of them out with me before I go," he drawled, indicating the multiple shelves of weapons.

Smiling, but eyeing the shotgun warily, Gabriel was starting to like this guy and probably would like him even better had he not been on the business end of the double-barreled shotgun.

Arnie followed his gaze. "Oh, sorry, I forgot." He lowered the shotgun and placed it down on the conference table in the middle of the room. "I stay off the grid, too. This," he said, waving his hand, "is all run by a mini liquid metal cooled nuclear reactor. Should last another sixty to seventy years without refueling."

Gabriel raised his eyebrow, looking around, impressed. "You got one of those?"

"Yeah, before they made them illegal cause they'd put the big power companies out of business, of course."

Nodding, Gabriel asked, "What do you do out here?"

"As you might've seen in the yard, I collect old junk and parts and repair old things."

"What kinds of things?"

"Oh, anything. Cars, computers, robots, old tech—you name it—I probably got some parts for it and can fix it."

"Uh, I'll keep that in mind."

Chapter 26

"So, what do you want to know about RFIDs?" Arnie asked. Gabriel guessed that some might underestimate the old man with his Southern drawl, but the keen intelligence in his eyes clearly shone through.

"Can the chips be reprogrammed with someone else's ID code and then programmed back?"

"Well, of course, they can, son."

"But I thought they were a write-once chip," Phil said in a surprised tone.

"Yeah, the chips they use now are hybrids. As you probably know, the part that carries the personal identifier is write-once and programmed at the factory and assigned at birth or wherever you get the chip at. The other part that carries your other info—like what school you went to and how much you have in your bank account and company access codes and all that—is rewritable. But the initial chips were completely rewritable. Of course, they outlawed and destroyed those when they began implanting them into the general public. But it's old tech. I'm sure someone could still make them in secret or have a stash somewhere."

"Is there any way to distinguish the original from a copy?"

"What do you mean?"

"Can someone reprogram their chip to simulate someone else's ID without getting caught?"

Arnie stroked his chin. "Well, yeah, but he'd still have to be able to pass the other bioscans if those are around."

"I think that an identical twin may have pulled this off."

"And you think he might've got hold of a reprogrammable chip?"

"He helps run the company that makes RFID chips."

Nodding, Arnie said, "Ah, certainly then, he'd have the resources. But every chip's different on the atomic level—even if one were reprogrammed. The hand-held scanners used by the feds can detect the differences between the same data on two different chips—almost like a fingerprint— if set to the highest sensitivity. But that takes time to scan, so I doubt that most agents have them set that high."

"What if he didn't need to fool the feds? He just needed to do this for a few hours and then go back to being himself."

"Then, yeah, of course."

"But he'd have to go through the security at Titan, which I assume would have a sophisticated, highly-sensitive system like that available to the DNS," Gabriel said.

"He'd be detected—unless, of course, there's a manual override of the security system."

"An override?"

"Sure, a system admin with high enough clearance could change the sensitivity of the company's detectors for any bioscans—chip scanners, facial rec, or retinal scanners."

"Would anyone notice?"

"Not unless they're looking for it."

Stroking his chin, Gabriel said slowly, "So someone could compromise the bioscanner system and get through without a perfect retinal scan or RFID."

"Yeah."

Gabriel nodded, taking in all the new information and pondering the potential ramifications. After a moment, he asked, "Can these implantable chips be made to kill someone?"

The older man scratched his brow slowly and after a moment said, "Well, back in the early part of the century, someone made a chip that had cyanide in it, but it was never patented or mass-produced. The creator, as well as the creation, was destroyed in the MEH. So, yeah, probably—it's been done."

"Could it be made to look like a heart attack or stroke or something not as obvious as cyanide?"

"Well, sure, either one. If you have an active chip—that is, a battery-powered chip—instead of a passive chip like the ones you all have, then you can make it zap the nervous system or release toxic nanomolecules or nanobots or something like that. But, of course, the one that's in use nowadays can't do that since they're passive chips. But, knowing the DNS, I'm sure they're developing active chips as we speak if they don't already have them."

"So it could be used to target a specific person?"

Arnie peered at him through his thick glasses. "Sure. The most difficult part would be to not get caught. It has to look exactly like the old one, so on autopsy, no one would know the difference. Usually, with an active chip, it needs to be bigger because of the battery, which has to last a lifetime. That'd be the biggest challenge."

Gabriel nodded, deep in thought.

"It may eventually be possible to power a chip through the body's own electrical charge. Then that chip could look like any old chip unless you look at it microscopically."

"Which most medical examiners won't do unless they know to look for it."

"Exactly."

"Well, thanks, Arnie. I really appreciate your help." Gabriel reached out and shook hands with the older man.

"Well, if you got any more questions, send them through Zimburg here. He knows how to get in touch with me without being tracked. Or come back sometime. Just let me know ahead of time so I don't shoot you since I don't see so good."

CHAPTER 27

Monday Night

After arriving back at Gabriel's, Phil removed the RFID simulator and left. Gabriel ordered the AHS to lock the doors and heard the loud clicks of multiple bolts engaging.

"Will you be needing anything else tonight, sir?" Robert asked.

"No, that's all. You can shut down."

"Thank you, sir."

The robot powered down to sleep, with only a red light slowly blinking from one eye indicating its "resting status." This was somewhat misleading since he was always on guard, processing any audio or visual input for suspicious activity, and could power up in a fraction of a second should the need arise.

On transparent mode, the large duraglass window in Gabriel's unit overlooked the nighttime skyline of Los Angeles—a breathtaking view with the lights of the city in the foreground and the blackness of the ocean behind it. This luxury unit had been way beyond his budget. Luckily, on one of his first cases with Robbery-Homicide, he helped solve the murder of the son of a billionaire real estate magnate when everyone else considered it impossible. As a result, the very grateful developer had practically given him this unit. The condo was on the fifteenth floor and had a state-of-the-art security system with the AHS, reinforced doors, floors, ceilings and windows in addition to the magnificent ocean view. His secured, private parking ramp was usually prohibitively expensive to all but the upper class.

Regulations regarding accepting favors from victims and their families had been relaxed after The Big One as long as these were appropriately reported and recorded, and the officer recused himself from any cases which might present a conflict of interest. Gabriel usually didn't accept favors, but he had gotten close to the family during the investigation—and the grateful billionaire had insisted.

He tapped the wall by the refrigerator. The wine refrigerator appeared. He asked for the available malbec selections, prompting the relevant bottles to be rotated to the front. Gabriel tapped the glass over an Argentinian selection. The wine dispenser aspirated the wine and transferred it into the wineglass. Then the air was replaced with argon gas and the bottle resealed. The glass door slid open. He reached for the wineglass, swirling it and inhaling the aroma. He sipped the vibrant, dark purple-colored liquid. Mmmmm! Smoky with hints of blueberries.

Although much simpler now, he missed the old days of opening corks from the bottles of wine, but that had been a very long time ago. These days, wine was a luxury. Although grape vines themselves don't need bees for pollination, the companion plants that help keep vineyards healthy do, and with the scarcity of bees, most vineyards were much less productive. So wine was very expensive, but it was really the only indulgence Gabriel allowed himself.

He would never admit to the other guys at RHD that he enjoyed wine much more than he ever did beer, probably a consequence of spending his delinquent, impressionable teen years under the wing of his mentor, the murdered defense attorney, Jon Frieze. The lawyer had loved all the finer things in life, and he had introduced Gabriel to expensive wine and classical music, among other things.

Gabriel settled down in his favorite recliner and propped his feet up on the coffee table. His eyes were tired, so he decided on audio entertainment instead of resuming the *Sherlock* episode. "Play Beethoven's *Pathetique*, Barenboim," he ordered the AHS. Beethoven was his favorite composer, and Daniel Barenboim one of the finest pianists of the last century.

The familiar strains of the first movement started. Sipping his wine, he sighed and closed his eyes, following the descending chromatic arpeggio to the next section, where he began tapping his toes to the faster tempo. He placed the wineglass on a side table without opening his eyes. He was vaguely aware of the start of the beautiful, melodic second movement before drifting off.

Project A

Something startled him awake. It took a few milliseconds to get his bearings. The music had stopped. He looked around the living room, not noticing anything of concern except that Robert had activated himself, the soft click followed by a hum, which probably woke Gabriel up. Looking out the window, Gabriel saw a faint shadow against the dark night sky hovering as if it were looking into his apartment.

"Activate window block," he ordered the AHS, expecting the window to become opaque. Nothing happened. He repeated the order with the same lack of effect. The lights of a bot suddenly turned on, allowing him to see the gun muzzles protruding from it.

Gabriel was tackled to the floor by Robert as the attackbot's two muzzles unleashed a fierce barrage of blaster fire onto the windows. The reinforced smartglass absorbed several rounds of blasts but shattered after a few seconds under the constant bombardment. Burn marks covered the walls and the chair where Gabriel had been sitting.

"Stay down, sir," Robert said over the din.

"I need to get my shotgun," Gabriel told him quickly. "It's going to come inside."

The android rolled off of him, grabbed the coffee table to use as a shield and rose to place himself and the heavy, stone table between the attackbot and Gabriel. The bot, entering the unit through the broken smartglass, paused its assault to visually assess the damage as the smoke began to clear. Gabriel rolled away, sprang up and sprinted around the corner toward the bedroom. He looked back briefly and saw the attackbot trying to go around Robert, but the loyal dom-bot dropped the stone table and grabbed the intruder on either side from behind.

Gabriel heard the attackbot's high-pitched whine as it repeatedly tried to propel itself forward. He grabbed his shotgun and shells from the gun locker he kept under his bed. He heard two blasts followed by a loud thump from the hallway as he racked the shotgun.

The attackbot's eye and muzzles turned around in the hallway and headed toward the bedroom as Gabriel fired two heavy armor-piercing, high explosive shells. The attackbot exploded, splintered into several pieces, and collapsed in a heap of singed metal and melted silicon.

Reloading and cocking the double-barrel shotgun, Gabriel cautiously walked into the hallway over the destroyed attackbot, Robert's prostrate body, the broken stone coffee table, and then into the living room. The couch and the chair he was reclining on only moments before were vigorously smoldering with multiple scorch marks from the blaster fire. Remarkably, his wineglass stood intact on the side table.

Looking out the window on either side and up and down, Gabriel didn't detect any more attackbots in the night sky. He backed up toward Robert, stepping over him so that he still faced the window in case more attacks came from that direction.

He bent down by the android's body and turned him over. Robert had two huge black holes in the upper torso from the point-blank blaster fire. The lights in Robert's eyes were still on, but he was unable to move his arms or legs.

"Are you all right, sir?" Robert asked.

"Yes, thank you, my friend." His eyes watered as he bent down and touched the body around one of the holes. It was still searing hot from the blaster fire. "You saved my life. I promise I'll get you fixed. I won't let you get trashed."

"Yes, sir," he seemed to answer gratefully.

As the security guards arrived, Gabriel called 911 using his comms since the AHS was still not responding.

It turned out to be a very long night. The officers from the night shift responded to the call. He sent a message to his partner as well, warning her.

"Reinforced smartglass," one of the uniformed officers said, wide-eyed. "Lucky you had that. It probably gave you a few more seconds before giving out under all that blaster fire."

Regular duraglass, fives times stronger than regular glass, would have disintegrated after a few blasts in the same spot. Gabriel's reinforced smartglass was ten times stronger that that.

Minutes later, Irene rushed in and asked breathlessly, "Are you all right?"

"Yeah, just needed a little ventilation in the place." He indicated the broken window.

She did not look amused and walked over to the attackbot. "What'd you hit it with?"

"A couple of high-explosive, armor-piercing shotgun rounds."

She smiled. "And you just happen to keep those around?"

"Yeah, in case the robots become self-aware and rise up against us." He didn't add the real reason, which was in case the DNS decided to officially take over the country. She already thought him too paranoid.

Lieutenant Corwin arrived, looking grim and angry. "I heard. You all right?"

"Yeah, but I think someone hacked my AHS." He explained what happened just before the attack.

"Let me see." Irene was silent for a minute as she communicated with the AHS. "Yes, it's working now, but someone deactivated it a couple of minutes before the attack. And the hacker removed his digital footprint and IP address."

"That's supposed to be a top-of-the-line, ultra-secure system," Corwin commented. "How can they access that?"

"Through the company," Irene stated after finishing her analysis. She and Gabriel looked at each other grimly. The DNS can do that.

It took hours for FSD to process the scene. Lieutenant Corwin left in the early hours of the morning. When the uniformed officers and forensic techs were finally done, Gabriel was allowed to keep Robert after they downloaded his memory chip rather than having him boxed up with the remainder of the evidentiary material. Only Irene remained behind.

"You got a place to stay?" she asked. "If not, I've got a couch."

Gabriel preferred to go to Katherine's but didn't want to wake her up in the middle of the night or put her in danger. "It might be very hazardous to be around me right now," he warned.

Irene patted her blaster. "I'm a big girl, and you're my partner."

"All right. Thanks." He grabbed his service weapon and Robert, who had been manually deactivated. Damn! Forgot that androids were so heavy.!

"What are you going to do with that?" she asked, indicating the android.

"Get him repaired."

"Why don't you just get a new one? It'll probably cost you an arm and a leg to get it fixed."

"Yeah, well, he just saved my life, and we've been through a lot together."

Irene smiled, shaking her head. She was probably thinking he was being silly for being so attached to a robot. But in addition to being the best wedding present, Robert was truly like an old friend, one he could

Chapter 27

always count on for his loyalty, as he more than proved tonight.

"The modern dom-bots—they're part of the AHS, so whoever did what they did tonight could've used the bot to kill me or totally inactivated it. But luckily they can't control this model externally." Gabriel patted Robert.

Tilting her head, Irene nodded, as if conceding his point.

As they headed out, they activated the crime scene perimeter shield to prevent access to his apartment. She gave him her address, and he instructed the AHS to secure the parking area after their departure.

CHAPTER 28

Tuesday Morning

It seemed like only a couple of minutes since Gabriel laid down on the couch before his comms' alarm woke him. He groaned and looked around at the unfamiliar surroundings before remembering the events of last night. In contrast to Katherine's place, Irene's apartment was spartan—no family pictures or artwork on the walls and no decorations or knick-knacks anywhere. The living room consisted of a couch, two chairs, a coffee table and the large media screen.

Irene was already up, showered and ready to go when he groggily stumbed from the couch. He ran his fingers through his gray-streaked, brown hair as a makeshift comb.

She was drinking an orange liquid from a glass. "Want some orange juice?"

"Oh, yeah! I haven't had OJ since I was a kid—before the bees were wiped out. Where'd you get this stuff?" Robotic bees were still not as efficient pollinators as real bees.

"You got to have connections." She smiled, poured his drink and then placed the pitcher back into the wall-mounted refrigeration unit, which disappeared into with the wall after the door slid shut.

"Aaaaaah," he sighed after gulping it all down. "This is heaven!"

"It should be—at ten credits an ounce."

"Shit! That was eighty credits I chugged in three seconds?"

She nodded.

He shook his head in disbelief, staring at the empty glass in his hand. "Way beyond my pay grade."

"Yeah, would be for me, too, but my dad is a deputy chief. He's got connections."

"So, what are you going to tell your dad when he finds out we spent the night together?" He smiled mischievously.

"The whole two hours—with you on the couch?" She shrugged. "He'll probably have a heart attack."

"What'd he do when he found out you got me as a partner?"

"Yes, he was rather upset about that."

"Why didn't he get your assignment changed?"

She looked at him levelly. "I asked to be assigned your partner."

Gabriel was dumbfounded. "Why?"

"Because you have the highest clearance rate in the department, and I wanted to learn from the best."

"I don't think your dad shares that opinion."

"He thinks you're a smart cop, but he doesn't like your methods—not to mention he thinks you lied about that shooting of the two teens."

He shrugged. "And here I thought your dad might've sent you to spy on me."

She glared at him. "We're partners."

"So you're not going to rat me out?"

"A lot of guys don't want to work with me because of my dad's position. It would prove all of them right if I ratted on my partner. So, no way am I going to give them that satisfaction." She looked at him square in the eye. "The other day at the Beck cantina you trusted me. I won't betray that trust—as long as you don't do anything *too* illegal or unethical."

Gabriel digested what she said. His instincts about her were right.

He surveyed the kitchen—also minimal with only necessary appliances. There were no clocks anywhere. "You don't have any pictures?"

She tapped the side of her head. "I have it all in my head and comms. Why do I need to put up things to remind me of things I already know and can see anytime I want to access them?"

He nodded. "True, but what happens if something compromises that implant, or it malfunctions or something."

"It's never happened."

"Anything electronic is bound to malfunction."

"True, but then I'll be just like you." She grinned. "Get in the shower. We should get going soon."

"Uh, yeah, but before we go, can I have another glass of OJ?"

She chuckled, shaking her head, and opened the refrigerator. "This is the last time I'm having you over. You're going to bankrupt me!"

Gabriel received the expected sympathetic condolences on the events of the previous night from his team at the office.

"Hey, Mav, heard your place was getting a little too stuffy anyway."

"Way to go—hiding behind that poor rusty old robot. You know the newer models are actually armed and would've taken out that attackbot."

"Heard you got luxe digs, Mav! Party at your place—after it gets cleaned up a bit—and you get new furniture—and you get the holes in the wall fixed!"

Since Gabriel didn't actually get hurt, everyone laughed good-naturedly except Captain Yokino, who stood at the front of the conference room with his arms crossed and a furious expression on his face. Lt. Corwin sat on the corner of the conference table, also with a grim expression.

"Everyone has heard about Detective Furst's adventure last night. We must be getting close, so you need to update everybody on everything you know. Do I make myself absolutely clear?" Yokino looked directly at Gabriel.

Gabriel cleared his throat, swallowed, and rose to his feet. "Yeah, uh, well, I know this is going to sound crazy. As I said before, Patton was working on a top-secret project, which we believe was developing a chip for K-Tech to kill people."

That was met with skeptical looks and a few snorts of disbelief.

"Do you have any evidence for this?" Yokino demanded.

Gabriel tilted his head. "Sort of. Our witness, Darlene, overheard Patton telling the Reverend about his project to create a chip that kills people. But that's hearsay and may not hold up in court."

Yokino stared hard at Gabriel, "When did she tell you this? And where is she?"

"She's very safe, but I—uh—I'm sorry, but I can't tell you where she is."

"What do you mean you can't tell me?" The captain flushed even redder and glared at Gabriel, who remained silent. "Bolton, you know where she is?"

"No, sir. I'm sorry, sir."

Gabriel saw the jaw muscles of the Captain working hard to restrain himself in front of the squad.

Fitz said, "Well, Mav must be on to something since they tried to kill him last night."

Yokino glared at Fitz, who looked away and tried to appear nonchalant.

Gabriel continued. "Also, as I hypothesized before, Harold Carmichael could've impersonated his brother at the café by altering his chip. He may have wanted to kill Patton because he wouldn't work on the project any more. Last night, I found out from one of the original developers that the old RFID chips were completely rewritable, so anyone getting one of those chips or making their own, could have switched IDs."

"But how did he defeat the biometric systems at Titan? Aren't they supposed to be the best in the business?" Fitz asked.

"He could've changed the sensitivity of the bioscanners and wore a lens with a duplicate retina."

"Can we prove it?" Yokino asked.

"If we can get access to their security system, we may be able to trace any modifications made to it," Irene replied.

"And are they going to give us access since Harold is now the CEO?" Yokino asked.

Gabriel and Irene were silent for a moment.

"Even if he did, he would've already covered his tracks," Irene said.

Gabriel walked up to the front of the room. "There are differences between the twins that indicate Harold took Gerry's place at the café. Gerry drinks lattes with cream, but Harold takes espressos black. The Carmichael at the café drank a double shot espresso—straight with no cream. Gerry is right-handed and Harold left-handed. The one that went to the café used his left hand to brush his hair back and to hold the pen containing the explosive."

Some of his fellow detectives still looked skeptical.

"Why would they blow him up in a café instead of killing him quietly?" Smiley asked.

Gabriel said, "They had to discredit him. If he'd already told anyone about the project, but he was a terrorist who blew up a café, then nobody would believe anything he'd said."

A few of his fellow detectives wore less skeptical expressions.

"Do you have any proof?" asked Yokino.

Sighing, Gabriel said. "Everybody except Darlene has been killed, and the DNS took all our evidence from the bombing."

Yokino turned to Irene. "Bolton, what do you think?"

Irene looked at her partner and then back at their boss. "If Harold is guilty of what Furst just said, he's covered his tracks well. We do have DNA at Patton's place of two unknowns—one matched to Sam Weston, one of the DNS agents who came here. We also believe he and his partner have the same size shoes as those found at Patton's, so if we can find them, we can get do microbial and particulate analyses on their shoes."

The team regarded her quietly.

She rose to stand beside Gabriel. "Furthermore, the surveillance video from the hotel shows two men coming and leaving the back around the time of Darlene's disappearance. From his class ring, one of them appears to be Weston."

There was silence as the team digested the information.

"What was the real Gerry Carmichael doing when his brother was presumably meeting Patton?" Corwin asked.

Gabriel nodded. "We suspect that Patton's assistant, Andrea Lisle, was having an affair with Gerry and was probably with him at that time of the bombing. She admitted to meeting with him every afternoon at three but claims she was with Harold in Gerry's office at the time of the bombing. His office security system has been off-line for the past month, so we can't confirm who was in the office at that time. We suspect she also may have been the one who was with Gerry when he was killed although Harold's home security system says that she was with Harold at the time."

"She's banging both brothers?" Fitz asked, his eyes wide.

"She was probably using Gerry to help Harold get rid of his brother so he could take over Titan."

Fitz shook his balding head in wonder. "That's pretty cold."

Yokino asked, "How difficult is it to alter those home security records?"

"It's quite difficult, but we believe Harold is very tech-savvy since he probably has an HDI. He could've cloned Andrea's RFID to place her at his house during the time of the murder," Gabriel replied. He looked at his partner. "Bolton, you have Harold's home security log from the day of Gerry's death?"

"Of course."

"See if she left the house and then came back inside during that time."

Chapter 28

Irene was silent for a few moments as she accessed the records and scanned them. She nodded. "At 20:27, she left the house for a couple of minutes—"

"With Harold?"

She nodded. "—And then came back in."

"What does that mean?" asked Smiley.

"It means that if he had a chip cloner, he could pretend she was there with him and then take it outside when the real Andrea arrived, so she could be logged in for real."

"And that's within the window of the time of death," added Irene.

"So she had time to kill him, clean up and get to his brother's house." Gabriel let that sink in. "In Gerry's home security log, what time did he get home?"

She mentally scanned it. "The security system logged that Gerry came home at 19:12, but no one was with him. Maybe she activated a personal chip jammer."

"Do those even exist?" Fitz asked.

Gabriel really didn't want to answer that question. Since they were illegal, he didn't want to explain how he absolutely knew of their existence and get his friend, Phil Zimburg, into trouble.

Fortunately, Irene answered, "I'm sure someone has made one by now, and with Carmichael's resources, he could get one easily—if his company didn't invent it in the first place."

Yokino stroked his chin in thought. "Do we have the DNA back from Gerry Carmichael's bathroom?"

Looking at the report on his comms, Fitz said, "Yeah, there was Carmichael's, his wife's and the housekeeper's DNA."

"No one else?"

Fitz shook his head.

"Who ran the tests?" Gabriel asked.

Fitz looked at the bottom of the report. "Booker."

"Not Zimburg?"

"No. Why?"

"The aerial DNA analysis from Patton's study initially showed five samples, but two were omitted from the final report. Zimburg looked at the preliminary result before the computer automatically deleted the other two. If Booker didn't look at the results until the computer made its final report, he might've missed someone else's DNA who was there."

"You said we know whose DNA were removed at the Patton scene?" Yokino asked.

Irene hesitated. "One of them, yes. We matched that DNA to Sam Weston, one of the DNS agents who took our files on the bombing."

"How did we get his DNA?"

Gabriel and Irene looked at each other. "Um, I—" Irene began uncomfortably.

"Weston used a tissue when he was here, so we got it off that," Gabriel interrupted to prevent his partner from admitting her intimate involvement with one of their prime suspects and thereby destroy her promising future with LAPD. "We assume that the other was probably his partner, but we don't have a sample of his DNA."

Yokino nodded. "If the FSD computer automatically removes the DNS agents' DNA results, how do you know it was Weston's?"

"Zimburg ran it at home. He's got an old machine attached to an air-gapped computer, which doesn't automatically delete DNS samples."

Yokino blew out a breath. "So, we can't use the results in court."

"No, sir."

His face once again flushed, Yokino asked, "Do we have any evidence at all we can use in court that isn't going to get thrown out by the D.A., much less the defense?"

Everybody was silent.

"All right. Get out there and give me something solid! Furst, stay here!" the Captain bellowed.

Corwin and a few of Gabriel's fellow detectives looked at him with a sympathetic expression as they filed out. The door closed behind them.

Captain Yokino scowled at him. "What. Do. You. Mean. You. Can't. Tell. Me. Where. Our. Only. Witness. Is?"

"They would not approve of it upstairs. It's better for you not to know since I could get fired for putting her there, and this way, you have plausible deniability, sir."

"I would look like a fool for not knowing what's going on in my department!"

"But you'd still have a job," Gabriel replied. "And she's absolutely safe."

Breathing heavily, his irate captain glared at him for a long time in silence, his face red and his eyes narrowed. Then he sat down on the conference room table and sighed. "You're sure she's safe?"

Gabriel nodded. "They can't get to her."

Yokino swallowed several times. "You're suspended without pay for a week after this case is resolved. Don't ever put me in this position again, do you hear? I'll have your badge faster than you can blink!"

"Yes, sir."

"Get out of my conference room!" Yokino yelled, one hand rubbing his stomach and the other digging a bottle of antacids out of his pocket.

Gabriel left the conference room with a silent sigh of relief. Irene and Fitz were waiting for him in the hallway.

Fitz asked in an anxious tone, "Mav, you still on the job?"

"Yeah, but I'll be on a week's vacation without pay after all this is over."

Fitz sighed. "Well, that's not too bad. But could you try—just for one day—not to piss off the boss or some other VIP, OK?"

Before Gabriel could reply, his comms vibrated, notifying him there was a call on his videocomms. The wrist comms system was still not taking calls from outside the department due to the surveillance countermeasures in the office. He stepped into his office and tapped the videocomms. "Furst here."

"Go to privacy mode," an electronically altered voice said. "Someone's life depends on it."

"Who is this?"

"Just do it."

Gabriel slipped on his visor while Irene and Fitz were still chatting in the hallway. "What do you want?"

"We have your girlfriend. If you want to see her alive again, you'll follow our instructions to the letter."

A chill went down Gabriel's spine. "How do I know you're telling the truth?"

The screen panned around to show Katherine, blindfolded, gagged and bound, lying on a concrete floor.

"How do I know she's still alive?"

A foot kicked her in the stomach, and she cried out in pain.

Cold fury welled up inside of him.

"Go to the Diamond Café and sit at booth three. Come alone. Turn your comms off, and turn off your GPS. We'll be listening in and watching you. If you tell anyone or anyone comes with you or follows you, she dies."

Project A

The caller disconnected.

Irene poked her head inside the office. "What is it? How do you know who's alive?"

He looked around, uncertain whether all the surveillance devices were deactivated. "Uh, nothing—just my cat. I've got to do an errand. Cover for me, okay, guys?" he asked, his voice tight, as he walked away quickly.

"Of course," she said after him. As he walked out of earshot, he heard her ask Fitz faintly, "Cat?"

At the Diamond Café, he found a message instructing him where to go next. Gabriel raced through the gray, cloud-covered skies to the remnants of Bamboo Plaza, long-time home of what was one of L.A.'s finest dim-sum restaurants before The Big One. Most of Chinatown was still littered with rubble since it was not high on the city's list of priorities. A gray car sat in the middle of a clearing inside the plaza, but there was not enough open space to land his Raptor. Gabriel marked the front of the gray car with his comms and then parked just outside on a fairly level area of what used to be Hill Street.

He covertly programmed his comms, opened the trunk and stuffed extra ammo into his tactical suit. He left the trunk slightly ajar though it would appear closed from a distance. He knew they would take away his weapons, so the extra ammo would probably be superfluous, but he needed an excuse to get into the trunk. He then proceeded cautiously toward the inside of the complex, making his way through the debris-strewn obstacle course to the center of the plaza.

The sky started to drizzle.

As he approached the gray car, he was not surprised to find DNS Special Agent Harmon standing beside the trunk, which faced Gabriel. He pointed a blaster straight at him.

"Take out your weapon, and drop it on the ground," Harmon ordered.

Gabriel complied.

"Kick it over here."

Gabriel kicked it so that it twirled around on the ground, not going very far. "Sorry—I was always bad at soccer."

Harmon did not look amused. "And your other piece. Kick it over here."

Sighing, Gabriel removed the small pistol from his ankle holster and threw it down, kicking it halfway to Harmon.

He said to Gabriel, "Now throw me your comms."

Gabriel slipped off his comms and tossed it to the older agent, who caught it, dropped it on the ground, crushed it under his foot, and blasted it.

"Where is she?"

Harmon smiled, his blue eyes ice cold. He wordlessly popped the trunk of his car, reached in, and pulled up a woman by her long, brown hair. She was still blindfolded, bound and gagged, and she struggled when her head was unceremoniously yanked up. It was Katherine. Harmon released her head abruptly and slammed the trunk lid down.

"As you can see, she's still alive."

Gabriel was furious that the Special Agent had treated Katherine so roughly—which meant he was probably not going to let her live. Gabriel quickly forced himself to calm down so he could think more clearly. "Let her go. You have what you want. You have me."

"That might be a little premature." Harmon gazed past Gabriel.

Special Agent Sam Weston walked towards them with his blaster pointed at Gabriel.

CHAPTER 29

Tuesday Late Morning

"He's alone." Weston approached the center of the plaza, stopping about ten feet away to Gabriel's left, with a broken, turquoise column lying on its side between them.

Harmon nodded. "Good."

He looked at Gabriel with cold eyes. "This was all supposed to have been simple."

"You mean setting up Patton as a patsy for the bombing? Or thinking the case would be kicked to you? The Deputy Chief hates the DNS after his team got burned for your mistakes last year."

"We'll remember that for next time," Harmon said.

"You also killed anyone who might have known about your secret little project."

"Which we wouldn't have had to do if you hadn't been snooping around."

Bile came up his throat at the thought he may have been partially responsible for the other murders following the bombing.

Harmon continued, "Well, I guess since you have it all figured out, we can't just let you walk out of here."

"You weren't going to let me live anyway. But you can let the doc go since she hasn't seen your faces, and she doesn't know anything."

"Only if you give us what we want."

"And what is that?"

"The girl—Darlene. You can have your girl when we get our girl."

"So you can silence her as well?"

"What we do with her is not your concern. Your girlfriend's life should be your only concern."

He couldn't hand Darlene over to be killed. "Release Dr. Miller, and I'll take you to Darlene."

Harmon looked amused. "We'll release the good doctor when you give us the girl—no sooner."

"How can I be sure you won't harm Dr. Miller even if I give you Darlene?"

"I give you my word."

"That doesn't mean a lot coming from a man who has killed what—at least eight people—in the last week?"

"When it comes to national security, collateral damage is an unfortunate necessity."

"Why did you kill Laila Harvey in the hospital?"

"Well, we preferred to have no witnesses or evidence that could place Carmichael in the café."

"We had him on video."

"We destroyed all the video from the street cameras."

"You forgot about the bank camera."

"It was broken."

"It got repaired that morning."

"Damn, it wasn't supposed to be repaired until the following day. I must find out which company they used. It's so hard to find good tech support these days," the older agent remarked with a cold smile.

"Why did you kill Gerry Carmichael?"

"Well, you were getting too close, and we couldn't have him figure out that his brother had taken his place at the café, could we?"

Gabriel shook his head in disbelief.

"Enough of this small talk! Take us to the girl," Harmon ordered in an icy tone.

"No one is going anywhere!" Fitz yelled as he approached them from the other side of the plaza. He pointed his blaster at Harmon. Gabriel smiled to himself in relief. His friend figured it out. "Drop your weapons, and put your hands up. You're under arrest."

Harmon pointed his blaster at Fitz. "You're outnumbered."

"No, he's not," Irene stated, stepping out from behind a large broken column, close to Fitz. She pointed her blaster at Weston.

Harmon smiled, the smile not reaching his eyes. "Then it looks like we are at an impasse. Two of you against two of us."

They all looked at each other for several moments. Suddenly, gunfire erupted behind Harmon. He turned and blasted at the flashes from an unseen turret. The invisible drone crashed.

As soon as Harmon had turned toward the drone, Gabriel lunged right toward his gun. Turning back after dispatching the drone, Harmon fired at him, missed, and moved to the other side of the car. Gabriel rolled up, blindly firing at where Harmon had been standing. Missed, dammit!

After the drone fired, Irene hesitated for a brief moment, giving Weston time to fire a lethal blast aimed at her chest. She ducked just in time and rolled behind a pile of broken flooring. She looked at where she had been standing and the scorch mark on the wall behind it.

Weston dashed behind another pile of debris. He and Irene exchanged several rounds of blaster fire.

Fitz moved behind a collapsed ceiling. Harmon blasted the broken concrete overhanging Fitz's last position. The latter cried out in pain as large pieces of the ceiling fell on him.

Harmon crouched behind his car. Gabriel tried to move to get a better view of him, but the latter's cover blaster fire pinned him in place. He couldn't blindly shoot back for fear of hitting Katherine in the crossfire. Irene and Weston continued exchanging blaster fire.

The trunk opened. Katherine tried to sit up. The DNS agent yanked her by the hair and roughly pulled her up and out to stand in front of him, his blaster aimed at her head. The blindfold slipped off in the scuffle. Blinded by the sudden light, she squinted and blinked rapidly.

"Furst, put down your weapon, or I'm going to fry her pretty, little head! Now!"

Oh, shit! After a few seconds, he called out, "OK, OK. I'm here. Don't hurt her." He held his weapon up as he slowly came out from behind his cover. He could see Irene out of the corner of his eye. She nodded her head at him and surreptitiously pointed toward Weston and herself and then at Gabriel and Harmon. He acknowledged her by blinking twice at her. She would have a better angle on Weston. Gabriel could only see a small part of the younger agent's leg past the large broken column between them.

"Put down that gun!" Harmon ordered.

Gabriel slowly acquiesced, laying his Glock on the ground in front of him.

"Bolton, show yourself, and put down your weapon! Your backup, too! Kick them away from you!"

Irene came out into the open, her weapon pointed upward. Weston emerged from behind his barrier, his blaster trained on her. She looked at him, put both weapons down slowly and booted them away from her.

As Harmon drew Katherine closer to him, Gabriel saw her slam the back of her head into his face, smashing his nose with an audible crunch. The Special Agent cried out in agonizing pain, blood pouring from his nose, blinding him for a moment and causing the hand holding the blaster to instinctively reach for his face. Katherine twisted her head and body down and away as he briefly loosened his grip from the pain just enough so that Gabriel, quickly recovering his gun, shot him in the head. The hollow-point penetrated Harmon's forehead and slammed his head backwards onto the open trunk door with a sickening thud. He fell, pulling Katherine down with him. Still bound, she wriggled away from his corpse toward the side of the car away from Weston.

Weston fired at Irene before she could reach her weapons on the ground, and she had to dart for cover behind another large piece of concrete block close to where Fitz was buried. Weston quickly pocketed her weapons.

Gabriel took cover behind some large pieces of debris as Weston ran around the column between them and blasted furiously at him. Gabriel couldn't get a good shot in due to the constant barrage of blaster fire. He blindly fired at the Special Agent, but one of Weston's blasts finally caught him on the leg. Burning pain seared his left thigh, and Gabriel collapsed, dropping his gun.

Weston walked over to where Gabriel was lying on the ground, clutching his burned leg, his gun out of reach. The Special Agent pointed his blaster at Gabriel, kicked the Glock away and smiled grimly.

"You've been a real pain in the ass, Furst, and now you killed my partner. You just don't know when to quit, do you?" He surveyed Gabriel's leg dispassionately and paused. "Well, this time, my blaster's fully charged, so it'll cause more than a little burn. This is for Harmon," he said, aiming at Gabriel's chest, his finger tightening on the trigger.

The boom of a blaster rang out. Weston stood still and then collapsed with a look of shock mixed with pain, the left side of his chest a smoking barbecue. Irene walked towards him as he lay there in agony, moaning and taking his last gasps, his left lung and ribs blackened. She kicked his blaster away.

"Didn't think you'd do it," he barely wheezed out with one of his final breaths.

"You overestimate your charms," she replied. She aimed Fitz's blaster at her ex-lover's head.

Gabriel held up a hand. "Don't," he gasped out in pain. "He's not worth it. It'll end your career."

"My career is already ruined."

"IAD doesn't need to know about you and Weston," he whispered so no one could overhear. "I won't tell, and the only other ones that know are here, dead or dying."

"What if they told their boss?" she asked in a low voice.

"Then he'd have to admit he knew what these guys were doing. They can't bring you down without bringing themselves down." He paused. "Don't throw your career away."

She hesitated for a few moments, then nodded. Walking away from the dying DNS agent, she went to her partner's side.

Gabriel looked down at the burn on his leg. "See, this is why I don't use blasters."

"Yeah, you're lucky you didn't get hit with a full charge."

"Yeah, lucky." He grimaced. "We got to get to Fitz."

"Let's check out your leg first." She knelt down, examining his left thigh. "Nice move with the invisible drone."

Gabriel tried to smile. "A little modification from standard police issue. Thought it might come in handy someday." The drones used by police officers usually did not include stealth mode or time delay, both modifications that Gabriel had Paul Zimburg install a few months ago in a less-than-official capacity.

"I see you got the invite for the party," he said.

"You should've told us what was going down." Irene's brow furrowed.

"You're right," he admitted. "But I wasn't sure if the office was safe, and they said they were going to kill Katherine if I did." He paused. "I mentioned the cat and figured you'd know something was up."

She frowned at him. "You turned off your GPS." Irene got up and was looking around the debris for something.

Chapter 29

"I turned it back on after I got to the Diamond Café, so you guys would be able to figure out where I was. I figured they'd be watching me until I got here."

"Yeah, we followed your GPS signal as soon as it was turned back on."

"Let's call for help and get Fitz out of there," Gabriel said to Irene, indicating the pile of debris that had fallen on his friend.

Having finally managed to remove her bindings, Katherine ran over to him, her face teary-eyed. Hugging him, she took a deep breath and then evaluated his burned leg. "You'll be OK. It's a second-degree burn, and it'll hurt like hell."

He winced. "Yeah, I sorta figured that part out."

"Let's get you up," she said, helping him get to his feet as Irene handed him a loose piece of rebar to use as a cane before she headed over to where Fitz had fallen. Using her HDI, Irene called Dispatch, walking past Weston's dead body without a glance.

"That was a very dangerous thing you did. He could've shot you," Gabriel admonished.

"But he didn't, and you got him—just as I expected," she replied. "And he was probably going to kill me anyway." He shook his head at her in wonder. Most hostages would have been panicking or frozen with fear but not her.

"I told you before—my dad had us go through self-defense and hostage training."

"We gotta go help Fitz."

"You're hurt," Katherine objected.

"Yeah, but not as bad as he is. Fitz!" he called out, limping over to the pile where his good friend was buried, wincing with each step from the excruciating pain. He could see Fitz's right arm sticking out from under the rubble.

They began helping Irene carefully remove the broken concrete pieces and repeatedly yelled out Fitz's name. A weak moan came from under the pile, and the exposed hand moved slightly.

The rain stopped, and the clouds parted. Sirens approached.

Katherine shooed away the nurses and ER techs and insisted on personally dressing Gabriel's leg wound even though she wasn't working that shift. She commandeered a private exam room at the University

Hospital ER, insulating them from the surrounding chaos and cacophony. He lay on a stretcher as she applied a special, herbal oil that was not on the formulary. Gabriel felt the pain go away almost immediately.

"Wow, what is that stuff?" he asked.

"It's my secret stash. I keep it in my locker and only use it only on very, very special patients." She smiled at him, her hair disheveled, some blood and dirt streaking her cheeks and some of her clothing torn.

She never looked more beautiful.

"My mom used this on us when we were kids, but they're no longer allowed to make it—legally, anyways." Only medicines made by Big Pharma were legal. "It'll tide you over until you can get into the Regeneration Chamber. You'll need an hour today and for the next three to four days to help your skin heal."

"Yes, Doc."

A black, female doctor poked her head into the room. "Kath, it looks like the other detective will be OK. He's still in OR, but they're closing him up now."

Gabriel smiled in relief.

"Thanks for the update," Katherine said as her friend stepped out.

A few minutes later, Captain Yokino stalked into the room, his face red, his jaw tight and his eyes narrowed. Acknowledging Gabriel with a nod, he was yelling into his comms. "What do you mean they went rogue? . . . How could you not know what they were doing for the past week? . . . They almost killed my detectives! . . . Yeah, I *bet* you knew nothing about this!" He disconnected, stabbing his finger forcefully into his comms. He told Gabriel, "We found two .45's in their trunk. We're running ballistics against the bullets used to kill the preacher at the church and our guys. FSD is running their shoes and DNA."

"So, we got Harmon and Weston?"

"Probably. But the DA says even with Darlene's testimony, we don't have enough to charge Harold Carmichael or Andrea Lisle."

Gabriel frowned in frustration, thinking of Ahmed and his family and all the other innocent victims from the café. "We'll get them both," he vowed. "At least we got the men who killed our guys and all the witnesses."

"Yeah."

"And we'll stop this Project Atropos."

Yokino raised a brow. "How do you plan on doing that?"

"These black projects need to stay secret. We'll blow their cover and make it public. Then they'll never be able to use it."

"The DNS'll never let them announce it on the News."

"No, but there are other ways to get it out to the public."

Yokino cocked a half smile. Maybe he knew the Onion News Network was going to break the story. He didn't ask. He did ask, "Will you bring Darlene back now?"

Gabriel nodded. "Yeah, I can go get her and bring her back to the station after I get out of here. Since the DA won't use her testimony, she should be safe."

"Remember, you're suspended for a week after you finish the case report. And FID is waiting to see you." Force Investigation Division investigated all police-involved shootings.

"Later," Katherine stated firmly. "Right now, he needs to get into Regen." She opened the door and ordered the transport bots to take him to one of the Regeneration Chambers.

As Gabriel's stretcher headed out of the ER, he saw Yokino shake his head and sigh. The Captain popped an antacid tablet into his mouth as he stalked out of the ER.

CHAPTER 30

Wednesday Late Afternoon

"What are you doing here, Dad?" Jonathan asked with apparent lack of enthusiasm as he answered the door at the Monroe mansion.

Gabriel held up two tickets. "We're going to the Dodger game."

"When?"

"Now."

"Now? I can't."

"What are you doing?"

"Uh—homework," Jonathan replied, his right hand holding a Virtual Reality headgear.

Gabriel looked down at the gaming gear. "Seriously?" he said as Jonathan tried to hide the gear behind his back. "Where's Gabby?"

"With her boyfriend, of course. What happened to your leg?" Jonathan stared down at the bandage on Gabriel's leg, showing from under his shorts.

"It got in the way of a blaster yesterday."

"Are you OK?" Jonathan looked worried and sounded genuinely concerned.

Shrugging, Gabriel said, "No big deal. Hey, I want to take you to the game, OK? Don't you want to see us kick the Giants' butt?"

Jonathan looked ready to object but then nodded. Maybe he was inwardly pleased for the rare opportunity to spend alone time with his father but trying to act oh-so-cool about it.

"You want to take my car?" the tall, lanky teen asked, indicating the cherry red sports car sitting on the driveway.

Gabriel looked at his own aged Raptor and then at his son's brand new

Ferrari.

"Hell, yeah! You're not on anything right now, right?"

His son shook his head. "I'd never drive on stuff, Dad."

"Uh huh."

Jonathan put the VR gear on the bench in the foyer, shut the front door and walked down the long pathway to the large circular driveway as his father limped along beside him.

"So, can I get a beer?"

"Are you twenty-one?"

"No."

They got into the car. "How about a hot dog?"

"OK."

"Nachos?"

"Sure."

"Cracker Jacks?"

Gabriel nodded. "Whatever you want, except for anything with alcohol."

"Great! But can I at least have just one sip of your beer?"

Laughing, Gabriel tousled his son's shaggy blond hair as they lifted off and headed toward Titan Stadium.

EPILOGUE

Wednesday Late Afternoon

The afternoon sun streamed in through the large golden windows in the penthouse office at Titan Robotics. DNS Assistant Director-in-Charge of the Los Angeles Field Office Jack Thurston sat with his arms crossed and a deep frown on his face. Across the large, mahogany desk from him, Harold Carmichael sat in his plush, brown leather executive chair. Both grimly watched the continuously looping Onion News report that somehow hijacked (again!) the official News broadcast a few minutes ago. It revealed a secret joint project from K-Tech and the DNS aimed at using the RFID chips to selectively kill people.

"This is an unmitigated disaster—and I lost two of my best agents," Thurston growled as he rose from his chair and started pacing.

"This will all blow over. No one believes that idiotic news outlet anyway," Harold stated, composed, masking his cold anger over the latest developments. "Speaking of which—when are you going to find and quash that worthless, annoying Onion News Network?"

"We've been working on it, sir, but they keep moving their center of operations and broadcasting from a different place every day. They stream through multiple international servers that are very difficult to trace in time to stop them."

"Well, you need to control that situation—and soon. We cannot keep having them contradict our News reports. The public and stupid conspiracy theorists are going to start believing them instead of the official News we feed them."

"I know, I know. We've got a lot of guys working on it." He stopped pacing and faced Harold. "But I'm more concerned about Atropos; we've lost the project. It can't ever be used. Two years and billions of dollars down the drain—not to mention the several dozens of test subjects—wasted!"

"We will find some other means to achieve our goals," Harold stated.

"How?"

"Do not worry, Jack, just deny everything. People will forget all about this very soon, and then we can resume that project." Harold tilted his head. "Maybe you could arrange for another—incident—to take their minds off of all this . . ."

"Yeah, I'll see what we can come up with." Thurston paused, debating to himself which false flag event he could use. "What about the girl?"

"Unfortunately, now that this has gone public, we cannot just eliminate the girl outright—too many eyes on her. But no one will believe her story anyway—after all, she is just a young girl who misunderstood what she overheard. When Titan becomes her sponsor and makes sure she becomes an Olympian, I am sure we will come to a mutually beneficial arrangement. When she achieves her life's goal of winning the all-around gold, that will be great publicity for us—coming to the aid of a poor, little orphan after her family all died in The Big One, and her guardian was brutally murdered." Harold smiled, his eyes cold.

"By us."

"By your men. They were never cleared to do that."

"They took the initiative; they thought the Reverend knew too much."

"It was too messy—too many people killed. It raised suspicions that there was something to hide."

"There *was* something to hide."

"Well, we might have gotten away with it all if your men had not—taken the initiative, as you call it. It just made the LAPD more suspicious. And killing those two detectives was a very bad move; LAPD was never going to rest until the cop killers were found."

"My guys did what they thought they had to do to get to the last witness," Thurston said heatedly, leaning forward with his hands on the desk.

"And they paid for it," Carmichael stated, unruffled. He sat back in his chair, his hands relaxed on the armrests. "I find that most people can be very reasonable with a little monetary incentive."

"Yeah, but the problem is they're still alive and able to talk."

"Well, then they need to understand the more permanent alternative. But next time, Thurston, keep a tighter leash on your thugs."

Thurston pounded his fist on the desk. "It's all because of that nosy LAPD detective! He's the cause of all this! What's his name?"

"Gabriel Furst. Do not worry, my friend—I will take care of him." Harold Carmichael stood up and reached out to shake Thurston's hand, in effect ending the meeting. Together, they walked toward the private elevator.

"All right. He's too persistent for his own good. I don't want him finding out about our other—uh—joint ventures." With that, Thurston stepped into the elevator and left.

Andrea, who had been sitting quietly in the corner, got up from the couch and approached Harold, who smiled and settled himself back down on his leather executive chair. She hiked up her dress to straddle him, kissing his forehead. "He seems a little upset."

Harold shrugged. "Well, his men created all the problems. They deserved what they got. But we do need to take care of that detective. He knows too much and suspects us."

She started undoing his shirt. "He can't prove anything."

"No, but if he gets in the way again, we'll have to take care of him permanently. I don't think he'll be receptive to monetary incentives."

"He has a family. We can use them as leverage."

"Yes, maybe."

Andrea tossed her lustrous red hair back and caressed his cheek with her thumb. "I thought you'd be a little exhausted from our—activities last night—and this morning." She removed his glasses, which she placed on the desk, and kissed his lips. She sighed. "I'm so glad I don't have to do this with Gerry anymore in this office. I had to imagine that idiot was you every time. I had to pretend to enjoy having his hands all over me and having him inside of me when I really just wanted to choke him."

"Yes, you were quite the little actress. However, at least you got the privilege of eliminating him in the end."

She smiled. "You should have seen his face when he realized he was going to die—after I paralyzed him and just before I sliced into his arm. The light in one's eyes really does fade as he's dying."

"That wasn't your first kill."

"No, but I never got to stay and watch."

He sighed. "Oh, the sacrifices we both had to make to get where we are—I, to lose my beloved twin brother—a little earlier than we originally planned—and you, to pretend to be in love with him all that time."

"I had to endure a lot worse than you." She shuddered. "It was a shame about James, though. He was such a brilliant man."

Harold mentally notified Roberta not to disturb them. "Yes, Uncle Jim—but he was about to blow the whistle on the whole project, which we could not allow to happen."

"No, but we lost it anyway."

He lifted the dress over her head and tore at her flimsy underwear. "We can't use it for now, but people will forget."

She smiled, laughing throatily.

The End

ACKNOWLEDGEMENTS

The author would like to thank all of her beta readers and the St. Philips' Writers Workshop for their support and helpful critique. Thanks also to the officers, both past and present, of the Oro Valley Police Department, the Tucson Police Department and the Pima County Bomb Squad for their assistance in providing education on law enforcement practice and procedures, some of which were adapted for the very different, future world of 2060 Los Angeles.

Lastly but definitely not least, very special and profuse thanks to my wonderful sister for her help in developing details of this future world as well as her dedicated and invaluable technical assistance.

ABOUT THE AUTHOR

H.S. Thompson is a retired physician and mother of two young adults. Now that her children are out of the house, she has time to spend on her dream job—being a writer. She loves reading, doing yoga, and learning about a wide variety of topics.

Find out more about Gabriel Furst's world at hsthomp.com.

EXCERPT FROM THE NEXT BOOK IN THE GABRIEL

FURST SERIES

THE TIP OF THE SPEAR

PREVIEW

PROLOGUE

May 8, 2058

In the moonless night, dressed in all black and equipped with night-vision goggles, two operatives crouched in the woods at the back of the estate just outside of Aix-en-Provence, France. Their target's family car rose up and flew away with the wife and two children on board—on their way to the children's school choir practice, according to the conversations caught on the surveillance devices placed in the house two weeks ago. The target was finally alone.

We'll be done long before they get back, Aleph thought. He motioned to Bet, indicating it was time to go in.

Bet nodded and screwed on the suppressor for her handgun. Aleph did the same. Although the houses here were spread out, and it was unlikely someone would hear a gunshot, it's always safer to make as little noise as possible.

Silently, they crossed the vast expanse of unlit lawn to the back of the mansion and removed their goggles. The electronic lock of the rear French doors clicked open as his comms transmitted the correct code. He smiled. His team always came through.

Arabic music blared from the hidden speakers throughout the mansion as they quietly searched the first floor. No one downstairs. The target must be upstairs.

They found him in the master bedroom, undressing, with his back turned to them.

"Hands up. Don't move," Aleph ordered.

The paunchy man's hands went up. "Who are you?" he asked, his voice shaking.

"*Naqam*," Aleph replied in Hebrew. Vengeance.

Nadav knew what it meant. He grew up in Israel.

The assassin could smell his fear. "Sit down," Aleph continued.

Nadav complied and sat at the edge of his king-sized bed. He looked up at the two covert operatives. Aleph was almost six feet, lean, with dark hair and cold, dark eyes and an unremarkable face that was easily forgettable, an advantage in his line of work. Bet was five-six, of Ethiopian descent, muscular, with luminous black skin and hair and brown eyes fuming with hatred.

Bet pushed the man flat onto the bed.

"What are you doing?" Nadav protested.

Without a word, she turned him around face down and zip tied his hands and feet. She then flipped him over onto his back.

Aleph noticed the zip ties cutting into the other man's hands and ankles, his hands already turning purple. The assassin remained unmoved and indicated to Bet with a nod to start her lookout duties. She left the room.

"Why are you here? I don't know anything. I haven't done anything," the man said in desperation, a bead of sweat trickling down his balding pate, onto the bedcover. "I'm just a retired software engineer."

"Who programmed my family—my country—out of existence."

"What are you talking about? I did nothing of the sort. My name is Nadav Cohen. I'm an Israeli Jew, just like you!"

Aleph regarded him with expressionless eyes. "Your real name is Nabil Mahmoud. You're a Syrian IS orphan. After the Islamic State collapsed, you were abandoned in the camps by your British mother until you were adopted by the Cohens when you were five. They scrubbed your identity so they could take you back to Israel."

"That's not true," Nabil said in a wavering voice.

"You repaid their kindness by destroying them. We tracked your real identity, Nabil, before the records were all destroyed."

Nabil lay silent, trembling on the bed.

"Who hired you? Who paid you?"

"I don't know what you're talking about." His sweat dampened the lace bedcover.

Aleph's hand pressed down firmly on the Nabil's chest while holding the pistol to his forehead.

"I know it was you. We followed you from Tel Aviv to Paris. Just before the bombs blew."

Nabil's eyes widened. "I didn't do that!"

"Did you think this day would never come? It's been six years, but we found you again."

"It wasn't me!" His voice quivered.

The assassin caressed Nabil's cheek with the tip of the gun. "Do you still want to be playing this game when your family gets back? Perhaps you would like me to put a bullet through your wife's head? Or your daughter's? Or better yet your son's?"

All color drained from Nabil's face.

"Tell me who hired you."

"I don't know anything!"

Aleph fired a round into Nabil's femur, avoiding the femoral artery. He didn't want Nabil bleeding out before he gave up his sponsor. The IS orphan screamed in agony.

"Let's try that again, shall we?"

In less than an hour, Aleph and Bet were done—long before the Cohen family returned to find their father and husband dead on his bed, shot in both legs and twice in the abdomen. He'd finally bled out from the carefully placed second shot to the gut, which lacerated a major vessel.

For Aleph, it was disheartening to learn that the hatred instilled in Nabil in the first five years of his life had outweighed the many years of love and kindness the Cohens had shown him afterward. Aleph regretted the relatively quick death, but unfortunately he didn't have time to prolong the software engineer's well-deserved suffering. Without the resources they used to have, they couldn't just kidnap the target and take him to a soundproofed safe house to be more thoroughly—and leisurely—interrogated. This was so much better than the traitor deserved—and better than what our families and the hundreds of millions of Israelis and Arabs got six years ago. There was nothing noble about Nadav/Nabil, despite his name—either in Hebrew or Arabic.

"You got the info," Bet stated.

Aleph had never failed in any of the several dozens of missions they had undertaken together—except the one to take out the present target six years ago. But that tragically had been scheduled for too late, and then all hell broke loose, and they lost track of Nabil.

Aleph nodded. "We have our next targets."

The assassins melted away into the night, leaving no traces of their presence except the bloodied corpse.